A SEASON AT WAR

JERRY AUTIERI

1

Though Varro stalked the woods, he knew something stalked him in turn. The others of his contubernium spread out behind, each placing cautious steps atop the orange and brown carpet of debris. He glanced to Falco at his right. His scutum shield, freshly painted black, hid all but his head and sandaled feet. His bronze helmet glinted with yellow light that fell through the canopy above. He stared ahead, eyes wide and alert. The tip of his pilum pointed the path forward.

Varro's forearm throbbed where it had been broken. He and Falco had barely been out of the hospital when placed back in line. Only dismemberment disqualified a soldier for duty, and even then, if he could make do with one arm, the officers found him work. Varro shrugged off the throb and focused on the tightening rows of trees ahead.

Moss clung to the rugged oak trunks. They seemed to form a natural tunnel, with brilliant yellows and oranges forming an archway that invited him into the shadows. Varro reviled the woodland stench of wet leaves and damp earth. He had never spent time among trees as a boy for fear of wandering spirits. As a soldier, he hated forests all the more for the living enemies they hid.

Like these trees. He was certain. The sensation of eyes following him never left.

Every snapping twig behind him sounded like a cracking beam. His heart raced and his face radiated heat. His hand tightened around his pilum and he pulled his scutum close. He wanted to turn around now, report back that they had found nothing and the suspicion of an enemy presence was invalid. But he had a duty to probe deeper, lest he overlook a hidden foe that would visit death upon him and his countrymen. He swallowed hard and continued forward.

"There's nothing here," Gallio muttered from behind Varro's left shoulder. "How far out do we have to go?"

"Far enough to be sure," Varro said.

"And how far is that?" Gallio followed his question with a long sigh.

"Shut up," Falco said. "Can't hear the enemy with your complaining."

Varro searched ahead, feeling like a fool for not encountering an enemy. The strange conflict bounced around his thoughts: hoping to return to camp in peace but also hoping for an enemy to validate his hunch. He had warned of movement in the deeper trees. Falco had backed him on that claim. Though maybe he had done so as a supportive friend. In any case, Varro had broken a key rule of army life, which was to say nothing more than necessary in front of an officer. Now he had drawn the unfortunate duty of leading the effort to prove himself wrong.

Since the troubles with Optio Latro and all the ensuing stays in the hospital, he was more aware of danger. Or so he believed. No matter, he recognized the difference between a stray fear and a real hunch. This sense was a skill the others lacked.

And now he was paying for it.

They proceeded farther into the natural archway of trees. Again, Varro felt as if he were being watched. Yet whenever he paused and his seven other companions dropped into fighting crouches, he found nothing. The faint objects behind bushes revealed themselves as old stumps or gray rocks.

Not enemies.

"I guess I was wrong," he said at last. He reached the end of the natural path, where the trees grew thicker together and the late day sun failed to enter. He set his pilum down, along with his shield which weighed on his arm. "If there was anyone here, they're gone now."

He turned to face the contubernium. Falco and Gallio were closest, their dark faces gleamed with sweat even though the cool air beneath the trees presaged winter. Curio stood behind Gallio, and Panthera followed Falco. The arrangement, though coincidental, gave Varro cause to smirk. Panthera and Curio seemed each to have adopted Falco and Gallio as their respective wards. Both Falco and Gallio were prone to argue and fight, and generally create mischief that could bring trouble to the entire contubernium. The remaining three soldiers trailed behind, all replacements for three casualties.

"If the cavalry can't find Philip's troops, then why did you think you could?" Gallio butted his pilum to the ground.

"Aren't you glad no enemy showed?" Falco rubbed the sweat from his face. His bronze pectoral square flashed as he turned to Gallio. "Did you want to discover a thousand Macedonians out here?"

"I'm glad enough. But we could've been on the road back to camp if we didn't have to chase shadows. Besides, if the Macedonians were this close, the cavalry scouts would've found them before us. This is a waste of time."

Panthera waved Gallio to silence. He ran his finger along the leather strap of his helmet as he spoke. "If you think we'd have a rest at camp, then you and I haven't been serving in the same army. Varro had a hunch and we checked it out. That's lighter duty than anything waiting us back at camp."

Gallio scowled but grunted agreement.

The heat on Varro's face throbbed and he looked aside from Gallio. His imagination had run away, and he had convinced everyone to follow him. He had seven men in his contubernium to look after, and all seven had chosen him for that role. Now he had led them off to share in his foolishness. He dreaded the teasing the rest of the century would inflict upon them after standing-by for imaginary enemies.

"Let's report back," Varro said, shrugging. "We've been gone long enough."

The rough line of soldiers turned on their heels to return the way they had come. The ground sloped gently down toward thinning trees and brighter daylight. Varro would be glad to escape the shadowy enclosure and its damp odors. With the reversal of the line, he now walked in the rear. He kept his head down, accepting only a glance from Falco, who rolled his eyes.

"You too? Why is everyone eager to fight the Macedonians? We'll find each other sooner or later. I'm all for finding them later, preferably never. I like having two eyes and two arms and a head safely attached to my neck."

"It's not that," Varro said, allowing Gallio and the others to peel ahead while Falco dropped to his pace. "I feel stupid for getting everyone behind me on this. It was a waste of time."

"I saw something too. It was fast, and human. So not wolves or dogs. And more than one. I guess they were just locals that probably just didn't want to get too close."

"I'm imagining things," Varro said. "That's not good. You've seen those Punic Wars vets? They jump at every falling log. You hear them screaming battle curses when they should be sleeping.

But they've been at war for years. I've not even been enlisted for a campaign season and I'm already losing my mind."

Falco clucked his tongue. "You're too hard on yourself. I'm sure you saw something, just not Macedonian soldiers."

Varro shrugged and followed the others. Each tree he passed felt like an officer judging him for his anxiousness. His sandals crunched branches and dried leaves as he studied his feet.

Then something fell into his path.

It flashed iron gray. Something hard and circular that disturbed the carpet of debris. He stopped short at it, then bent to pick it up. It was a small iron loop, with a needle-point opening.

"A slave's earring?" Varro held it up. Falco stopped and stared wide-eyed at it.

Varro blinked, then looked into the high oak trees.

A man stared down at him. Swathed in shadows and clad in gray rags, he clung to a heavy overhanging branch. A bronze edge shimmered in his thin hand.

"They're in the trees!"

Gallio turned, a frown on his face and a complaint forming.

But the man in the tree leapt down on Varro.

He screamed and Varro twisted aside, avoiding the worst of the hit but still knocked off balance. The man slammed into the ground in a pile.

Short javelins rained down from above. At least a dozen, though while prone Varro thought the entire sky had opened up with pale shafts. Gallio cursed as a javelin struck his exposed arm. Falco ducked behind his shield to deflect another aside.

Varro had lost his pilum when knocked over, but held fast to his scutum. The man who had dropped on him now rose groggily. Dead leaves clung to his wild beard and spit hung down from his mouth.

The rest of the contubernium turned with shields overhead. The final patter of javelins on the ground and thumping over shields ended and were answered with a throaty call from the deeper woods.

"Get in formation," Varro shouted as he clambered to his feet. "Line up!"

The ragged man who had desperately thrown himself at Varro now staggered up. But Varro did not allow him time to recover. He slammed his shield across the man's back, flattening him and driving the wind from his lungs. He screamed with the pain of the iron rim driving into his back. Another soldier would have killed him without a thought. But Varro still held fast to his swiftly eroding vow to not kill another man if he could avoid it. This one was no longer a threat. He did not need to die.

The underbrush shuddered and scores of cries rose up from the shadow.

Varro backed next to Falco, who had joined with the others to form a tiny testudo, the turtle formation. He and Falco held their shields to the front, while two men formed each side and two others held their shields aloft. Only the rear remained exposed, but Varro expected no danger from that direction.

"This is fucking crazy!" Gallio shouted. "It's just us against how many?"

Varro recalled he held the whistle. He fumbled with the cord necklace and pulled the wooden whistle out of his tunic. He had a moment for three shrill blasts.

Then the enemy emerged from the woods.

No more javelins followed. The men in the trees swung down from their positions to join their companions emerging from all around.

"Gallio is right," Falco muttered. "Eight to eighty is bad odds."

Scores of wild men burst out at them. They gripped spears and some carried small plate-like shields. Others wielded only long knives. All were dirty and wide-eyed, dressed in little more than rags. Were it not for their numbers, Varro guessed he and his fellows could wipe away this scum.

No one gave a retreat order. Yet the testudo formation broke, with the three newest recruits first to flee. Varro and Falco faced the initial wave, two fools against three times their number.

Varro's shield shuddered as the clumsy, unskilled blows struck at him. It was as if these vagabonds aimed for the iron boss of his shield rather than his exposed flesh. Varro and Falco both expertly drew their short swords and began the brutal work of dispatching the first six men to face them.

Hot blood shot along Varro's arm. The gladius was a weapon unlike anything else in the world, and he was proud of his own. It delivered a deep stab to an exposed stomach, unspooling foul guts into the dirt. He then punched with his shield, knocking away the second attacker, then stabbed again to slice off the hand of the next man. When the third had recovered, Varro had cut across to open the attacker's belly.

It was butchery, and even though only he and Falco stood shoulder to shoulder, the horrific sight of six disemboweled men heaped at their feet caused the next wave of attackers to pause.

"That should've bought the others time," Varro said. "Let's run."

"A wise order, sir."

He and Falco fled through what seemed a receiving line of enemies. They had emerged to either side screaming for blood. Some hurled their spears, but inexpert casts landed harmlessly in the dirt. They danced among the spent javelins to flee down the slope in the tracks of the others who had already gone ahead.

As he ran, Varro blasted the whistle three more times.

Falco glanced over his shoulder. "I don't think they're following."

"They know where we're going. They've seen our full numbers, remember?"

Through the trees ahead, he saw the flickering colors of the century. Huge scutum shields of every color danced as their bearers clambered up the shallow slope. Throaty commands echoed around the trees, driving the soldiers on.

Centurion Drusus, who had taken Varro and his contubernium for his own command after Centurion Protus died in his sleep, now led the charge. His stern and creased face glared up at them.

"More soldiers running away? What is your fucking problem?"

But Drusus's rage ebbed when his eyes fell to the blood-sprayed faces of his two soldiers. Varro stopped on the spot, and pointed with his gladius back up the slope.

"More than fifty, not soldiers, or at least not professionals any more, sir. Ambushed us from the trees."

"Not professionals?" Centurion Drusus pounded up the slope to Varro. His sneer returned. "Then get in line and kill more of them."

Finding Gallio, Panthera, and the others, he and Falco fell in. Gallio bled heavily from his shoulder, turning his sword arm red.

"Is it serious?" Varro asked. But Gallio simply shook his head and grunted. They had time for nothing more. They followed Centurion Drusus up the slope, shields forward and swords readied.

The enemy leapt back into the trees at the Roman approach. They had made a warning of their ambush, Varro guessed, but did not want to face a Roman century on their own.

An engagement among trees posed significant challenges to the conventional way of fighting. No proper army would venture into woodlands for battle. But in the end, Varro guessed he had uncovered a den of bandits, and such dishonorable men would never meet on the battlefield. Like rats, they had to be killed in their holes.

They swept past the ambush point, where Drusus led his men around the corpses like a river flowing around a plug of land.

"No one get too far ahead," he shouted. "Stay behind me. No springing another trap."

Their charge slowed. The trees naturally broke up any formation, but men stuck close together. The shouting and crashing amid the woods echoed all around. Varro felt a chill on his skin. Even knowing these were mere men, their howls still reminded him of restless spirits lost in the dark woods. Brown, dead leaves eddied in the wake of the Roman push.

They proceeded with more care, but still swiftly enough to keep their target in sight. The enemy continued to shrink away and reappear the moment it seemed the Romans had lost them.

"Sir, this doesn't feel right." Varro caught up to Drusus, leaving Falco and the others.

"I said stay behind me!" But Drusus did not look back or pause. The longer these enemies evaded him the angrier he became, and the faster his pace.

"Yes, sir. But I think they're leading us into a trap."

"You think so? Well, so do I. Now keep your fucking eyes open. We're Rome's finest soldiers and these ass-droppings are going to know it soon enough."

Admission that they were running into a trap caused a visible ripple along the row of men keeping pace with Drusus. Falco joined Varro, who let himself fade back from the fore.

"He thinks this is a trap?"

"It feels like it," Varro said. "Whenever they get too far ahead, they reappear to keep us following."

"They're working with the Macedonians?"

"Who else? We're in their country, after all. Gods, Falco, just keep your wits."

"Hey, listen to me, lily. If we're running into a trap, then all our work was for nothing."

Varro gave him a sympathetic look, but Drusus's orders were absolute. They plodded on, the trees slowing their pace to little better than a slow march.

Trees. Of course.

Varro looked up again.

"Sir, I see something in the branches!"

It was long and gray and carefully hid amid the branches and the multihued leaves that had yet to fall. Drusus did not even look up before he called a halt.

But he was still beneath the trap.

A wide net fell atop the lead Romans, Drusus included. The heavy ropes flopped down on them, entangling on their pila and sword points.

Their cries were met with a mad counterstrike by the ragged bandits.

"Get in front of them!" Varro roared. He raised his shield and without another thought, rushed to stunt the enemy charge.

The second and third lines flowed around their struggling comrades. But the enemy were prepared and they charged in with lowered spears in hopes of killing their trapped prey.

"Kill the fucking bastards!" Drusus's roaring curses cut above the wild cries of the enemy and the rage of the trapped soldiers.

Varro leapt the end of the net trap and was among the first to plant himself before Drusus. Falco, Curio, Gallio, and the others followed, forming a line with their body-length scutum shields. The heavy wall of wood and iron smashed the enemy back from the netted Romans. Yet they still jabbed into the rope-laden victims.

"To the center," Varro shouted. "Push them into that clearing."

Drusus hollered the same command from within his net.

"Keep them off us. Break their center!"

Varro and his line joined with another line forming on the left. Even with trees to break up the tight ranks, they became a wall of shields and swords. The enemy had barely a chance to close on their trapped victims. Varro's feet shifted on loose netting. They had sprung the trap far too early and wasted the size of their net.

Inexorably the bandits fell back into the clearing. They fought with the ferocity of cornered wolves. A spear blade scored across Varro's bronze pectoral. A swipe from another spear cut all the black feathers from Falco's helmet. Yet neither endured any injury. They shoved and stabbed the enemy away.

And then they broke.

"Halt! Don't pursue." Centurion Drusus had hacked away the net, as had most of the others. He sneered at the fleeing enemies. "They're finished."

Varro watched the gray-garbed, thin men fleeing into the woods. Their fallen remained dead or dying on the blanket of leaves. The stench of blood and entrails rose in the air. Combined with the woodlands dank Varro already detested, he had to put a finger to his nose.

"Get in formation," Drusus shouted. Then he looked to Varro and nodded before moving off. "You too. Good eyes, boy."

"A compliment," Falco whispered from behind. "More precious than gold, don't you think?"

"Don't worry," Gallio said. "I'm sure he'll make you pay for that compliment."

Varro smiled. He did not doubt it.

2

Varro stood at attention with his contubernium before the command tent of Tribune Primanus. Centurion Drusus stood with them, also at attention before the tribune. The night breeze was cold over Varro's exposed arms. He wished for his cloak, but he and the others had been summoned to the tribune shortly after returning. He had barely time to wash the gore from his hands and face. The sweet scent of cooking fires filled the air and his stomach growled.

Primanus was a lean man with graying temples. He had small eyes with heavy black lashes that emphasized his look of constant suspicion. Yet he smiled easily and the men generally liked him.

Except when he was upset, which seemed his mood after hearing Varro's report.

"And so these were simple bandits?" Primanus asked, waving his hand in an airy twirl. He sat in a chair outside the entrance to his tent, while all else stood. A slave hovered behind him with a cup and jug he had not yet been called to produce. Two guards stood on either side of the entrance, but neither gave any expression of hearing despite being close enough to touch the tribune.

Varro looked sideways to Drusus, assuming the question was for him. His centurion cleared his throat.

"Bandits, sir, yes. But there were hundreds camped there. They had set traps to protect the approaches, sir. We uncovered pits and deadfalls, sir, as well as another net trap. There were no walls around them, but the traps were deterrent enough."

"And you, Varro, claim they were following your patrol?"

"I saw men watching us, sir. That's when I informed my officer, sir."

Drusus again cleared his throat. "He's a sharp boy, sir. I trusted his eyes and was not wrong. We killed as many as we could lay hands on, and scattered the rest. Burned their tents and captured a fair number. Most were escaped slaves or other scum. No real threat unless the enemy decided to arm and train them. But there are Macedonian deserters among them, sir."

Despite the overall victory and the possibility of enemy intelligence, Varro felt he had just participated in a disaster. Tribune Primanus's eyes skimmed over the men before him, and rested on some point behind them. He seemed unwilling to look at anyone.

"While it is possible we could wring something useful from those wretches, I doubt they are from Philip's main army. More likely they're left over from the cities Apustius just sacked."

Drusus stood straighter and Varro saw his jaw muscles clench. But Drusus was a senior centurion and knew how to behave around a tribune. Varro, who had only been this close to a tribune during his dilectus, feared to open his mouth even when directly addressed. So he followed his officer's lead and stared straight ahead.

"Very well, Centurion Drusus. What did this cost me and what was the gain?" Primanus shifted on his chair, his heavy lashes drooping as he looked to the officer.

"Sir, we took no casualties. Just the cuts and bruises of battle."

Varro could feel Gallio's heat standing behind him. His

shoulder wound was still seeping and needed attention. Falco stood to his left and the feathers in his helmet were mere stumps from an enemy spear. No one had died, but many had come close to it. Drusus continued in a brighter voice.

"One hundred twenty casualties to the bandits, two for every one of us. And about thirty captives. We completely routed them, sir."

"Yet about as many escaped as were killed. Isn't that true, Centurion?"

Drusus's smile dropped and his face darkened. Varro wondered what the tribune expected of them. They had faced more than two hundred desperate men and defeated them. With more discipline and intelligence on the enemy's part, their numbers could have proved overwhelming. Words piled up behind his teeth, but he said nothing just like Drusus.

"I don't suppose they had much of value in that camp. Still, you were wise to carry off what you did. Every bit of scrap helps in the field."

Varro and all the others carried off cooking pots and trestles, grain sacks, spearheads, grindstones, and anything else they could carry. It was all junk to his eyes, but the army was amazing in its frugality. Someone would turn the garbage into profit for the Roman war-machine.

"I expect better against common bandits," Primanus said. "But given your resources and situation, this was satisfactory. Good job, Centurion Drusus. And same to you, Varro, for spotting the trouble. Rabble like those you faced today can only cause us trouble and compete for resources. Better to eradicate them. You are all dismissed."

The tribune rose, and his slave tucked the cup under arm and carried the chair off with his free hand. Varro and the others all stood at attention until Primanus had vanished back into his spacious command tent. The two guards closed the flaps and stared ahead. They had drawn guard duty for the night, and probably had enjoyed the most interesting post of anyone in the camp. Whenever Varro had this duty, no one interesting visited the tribune's tent.

They followed Drusus through the main road and away from the command center where the consul, tribunes, and their staff managed the affairs of the camp. The sky had darkened early with the coming of winter and the lights of cooking fires outside of barracks dotted the edges of the walled camp. Varro's stomach growled and he expected a curse from Drusus. But he marched on in stolid silence. They followed the narrower roads to their own barracks, passing other men of the century who stood as Drusus passed them. But he did not look at anyone in return.

Once they were before their own tiny barracks, he turned to study them. His face was dark and angry.

"You cowards disgust me," he said through gritted teeth. "You ran from a bunch of flea-infested, half-starved mongrels."

Varro stepped back in astonishment. He knew Drusus was upset with the tribune's lukewarm compliments. But he did not expect anger, especially at his own.

"Sir?" Varro hated the quivering in his voice. "We held them off long enough for you to bring —"

"Are you soldiers of Rome or little boys playing with toy swords?"

Drusus roared out his question, drawing stares from the other soldiers squatting around their cooking fires.

"Sir, with respect, we were out—"

"Are you going to instruct me on your orders, Varro?" Drusus's face had turned red. "All of you should be flogged for cowardice. You fucking useless pieces of shit! You do not run from the enemy. Ever! You are my soldiers. My soldiers either fight or die. They never run. Never."

Drusus grabbed his round head with both hands as if trying to keep it from blowing off his shoulders. In the low light of surrounding cooking fires, his eyes gleamed orange.

"Sir —"

Falco elbowed Varro in the ribs, doubling him over. Drusus did not seem to notice any of it.

"I would flog all of you myself. To death! You're lucky the tribune didn't order it. I will not have my honor stained again. Are you hungry, Varro? Your stomach gave a better report to the tribune than your mouth. All of you are on barley rations for a week. I've a mind to make it for the rest of your fucking lives, which better not be too long."

Varro straightened from Falco's elbow. He and the others stood at rigid attention and said nothing. Smoothing out his tunic, Varro did the same.

Drusus looked them over from sandal to crown. The creases of his forehead filled with black shadow. At last he dropped his hands from his head and balled fists at his sides.

"Get in your barracks and don't let me see you until tomorrow. I've got to go wash off the shit stink of you. Jupiter preserve me."

The urge to speak out made Varro shake. But Falco gave a warning look and imperceptibly shook his head. So he bit his lip as Centurion Drusus stomped off muttering to himself.

The soldiers from the other barracks attended their cooking fires with manic intensity, and many found reason to duck back into their barracks.

"We better get inside before we're flogged for insubordination." Panthera offered them a weak smile. "Come on, it won't be the first time you boys went hungry, right?"

"It's not fair," Curio said. "I'm starving."

Varro did not disagree, but remained silent as he piled into the cramped barracks with the others. In the front room, they set down their gear in their designated spots. Each man carefully arranged his pieces. Varro ran his fingers over the stubs of Falco's shorn helmet feathers.

"No doubt you can buy replacements for about five times what they're worth. But don't rush. I like looking taller than you."

"If you had kept your mouth flapping with Drusus, you'd be a good deal shorter than me. He could've cut you in half."

"I could've done the same to him," Varro said. But conviction failed his voice and Falco snorted in disbelief.

"Remember your great-grandfather. No killing except in self-defense. Or for revenge. Or when I tell you to kill because you're too stubborn to do what's needed."

"Stop it, Falco. I don't feel like joking."

"Not a joke, friend. But I get it."

Varro batted at his tunic as if he could chase off the mossy smells still clinging to it. As he and Falco fell to silence, the room filled with the thump and clack of their stowing gear. Panthera bent over and bumped into Varro, who in turn bumped Curio. Their tiny room heated with their bodies and smelled of oiled metal and leather, sour sweat, and old blood. Falco sniffed at his underarms and turned his head aside with a gasp.

"At least Drusus didn't forbid us from bathing."

With their gear stowed, they filed into the bunk room. Gallio sat on a bottom bunk. He had switched with Curio since he claimed it hurt to climb after he had taken a spear to his gut. His tunic dropped to his lap and his torso shined in the low lamplight. Dark blood seeped out of a cut on his shoulder. A flap of pale skin stuck up from it, translucent in the light.

"I need to see the doctor," Gallio said while using a cloth to wipe his shoulder. "This is going to bleed all over my mattress."

"We've been confined to our barracks tonight," Varro said.

Gallio paused wiping and tilted his head at Varro.

"Don't I know it? I was there when Drusus lost his fucking

mind. All his hot air didn't help my shoulder, though. And it burns."

"Let me have a look at it," Varro said.

"You? You've got no more training in field aid than I do. And that's only good if you cut your finger sharpening a sword. This is a bit deeper than that."

"Let me look. Out of all of us, I've been to the hospital the most," Varro said, while the others climbed into their bunks. Only Curio joined him in examining the wound.

In truth, Varro did not know how to help Gallio. Being a patient and treating an injury were unrelated. But he thought if he could make Gallio feel as if he were doing something useful, then it might help him.

The wound was deep but not deadly. The cut ran atop his shoulder in a neat line. The javelin's owner had kept a sharp edge on it. Varro did not see any cloth or dirt in the trench of bloody flesh. Though Gallio had cleaned it at a stream before the return to camp. The old bandage was useless now. So Varro took the bandage cloth from Gallio and wrapped his shoulder.

"Well that's something, at least," Gallio said. When Varro stepped back, Curio tightened the bandage and slapped Gallio on the other shoulder.

"At least it's not your right arm, eh?"

"What's that supposed to mean?"

Curio laughed and deftly vaulted into his bunk above. Varro wiped his hands off then threw the old cloth into the corner. He would clean up in the morning. His stomach growled and Falco laughed at it. Everyone had climbed into their bunks, and sleep had already overtaken one of the new recruits.

"It's going to leak through," Gallio said. "I need a real doctor."

"Gods, Gallio," Curio said. "Does anything make you happy anymore?"

"What's to be happy about in this place? I gave up my whole

life to be here, to serve Rome. And look at me. I can't even get permission to have my wounds treated by someone who knows what they're doing. Sorry, Varro, I know you tried."

"Don't worry for it." But Varro himself worried. He rested in his top bunk, and the dull brown ceiling pressed on him. But he turned to his side to look down at Gallio, who had yet to extinguish the lamp. Someone snored from a corner.

"That javelin could've went through my eye instead of my shoulder. And for what? So that the rest of you could be called cowards? I'd die fighting some shit-eating thief off in some woods in a place no one ever heard of, just so you'd all be put on barley rations and threatened with death by flogging. Really? Are any of you happy with that?"

"Gallio, it has been a long fucking day," Falco said. His voice was deep and tired beneath Varro's bunk. He heard his friend shifting on his mattress. "You didn't die. We didn't get flogged to death. Don't think of shit that hasn't happened. Drusus has a temper. You know that."

"Don't make excuses for him. He tore us up in front of the others. He cut our rations, the bastard. We don't even have the slaves to help us that the others have. When he picked us for his century, I thought we'd see something good from it. But it has all been shit."

"And it has hardly been a month since Protus died," Panthera said from across the room. "Gallio, really, just get some rest and you'll feel better tomorrow."

"Rest? While my shoulder is on fire and bleeding all over my mattress? How can I?"

"Should we get you some wine?" Panthera offered. "Maybe that'll numb it a bit."

"We're on barley rations, you fool. How weak is your memory?"

Varro sat up. "All right, that's enough. We're all in the same shit, Gallio. None of us want to be reminded of it and would like to sleep. Sorry about your shoulder. It could've been any of us. But it was you. So just grit your teeth and let the rest of us sleep. Get through seven days of barley porridge and things will be back to normal."

Gallio folded his arms and turned over to put his back to Varro. Falco thumped the bottom of his bunk in thanks.

"And someone snuff the lamp," Varro said. "I'm too tired to jump down there myself."

Though the bronze lamp was within arm's reach of Gallio, one of the new recruits extinguished it. The room fell into blackness as thick and heavy as a woolen cloak.

Varro again lay back, closing his eyes and listening to the animated talk outside his barracks of men cleaning up after their meals. He might be hungry, but at least he was getting extra sleep. He considered this a boon from the centurion, and maybe his bluster had all been a show to grant them extra rest.

And maybe Venus herself might carry him off in the night for a romantic adventure.

Varro chuckled at the thought, then turned over to sleep.

After a moment, his stomach growled again.

And Gallio muttered in response.

"I hate this fucking army."

3

Three days after eating only barley porridge, Varro no longer anticipated breakfast. He crouched around the campfire and drew his wool cloak over his shoulders. Panthera handed him a bowl, and he accepted it with a grateful nod. Ignoring the delicious scents wafting across from the other campfires was not as easy as ignoring the happy talk of the soldiers. Still he tried by turning to face the barracks as he squatted in the grass to eat his meal.

They had just completed a dawn march around the camp with Drusus leading them. Varro felt it more of a run than a march, and Drusus selected every craggy incline along the route. It could not be true, Varro knew, but it seemed they had marched uphill all morning. His legs ached.

Falco crouched beside him. His heavy brows caused his eye sockets to fill with shadow in the morning sun.

"Our families grow this stuff." He swirled his bowl and studied it. "You'd think it'd make me feel grateful for barley."

"Grateful?" Gallio sat opposite them, frowning into his bowl.

"Barley is animal feed. That's why it's a punishment. Get your head straight."

"My head's straight, but if you want to talk to me like that, I'd be happy to tilt your little round head."

"Falco," Varro said in his sternest voice. "Let it go. Gallio is just being himself."

"Gallio needs a new attitude," he said, staring across the top of his bowl. "Three days of complaining is enough for anyone."

"So we've got sword drills this afternoon," Panthera said, sitting beside Falco and nudging him with his knee. "You owe me a match today. Let's see who's better, eh?"

"I'm better," Falco said. "I'll be certain to remind you."

He continued to glare over his bowl at Gallio, but soon gulped down his porridge. Panthera prattled on about drills while Gallio finished his meal. He stood up, leaving the rest of them to return to the barracks.

The conversation died, and as slaves delivered water for washing their bowls, they all stood. Varro glanced at the barrack door, hoping Gallio would appear. But when he did not, Curio went to fetch him. He emerged just as the slaves set the basin down. Without a word, Gallio knelt to clean his wood bowl. The others set their own bowls beside his.

"I'll never eat barley again," he muttered. "I'm not an animal."

Falco stepped forward as if he planned to inflame Gallio's volatile mood. Yet he was cut short when Optio Tertius rounded the barracks. Everyone stood to attention, except for Gallio who polished his bowl as if it were a golden crown.

"Enjoy your breakfast?

As Centurion Drusus's second, Tertius ruled the soldiers' lives with his vine cane. He carried it now in his gnarled hands, gently swishing it like a cat about to pounce. As far as officers went, Tertius was not as bad as Latro had been. But he was not much better.

"Yes, sir," they answered in unison. Gallio remained squatting over the basin while rinsing bowls.

Tertius was nearly as short as Curio, but had corded muscles that quivered with power. What he lacked in height he compensated for in raw power. In this way, he was much like Drusus. Tertius looked like a man who knew how to get anything done, no matter what it might be. He could build a granary, forge a sword, sew a tunic, design a bridge, milk a goat, whatever needed to be done, Tertius always appeared the most competent man for the task. Varro wondered if there was anything beyond his ability. The one thing Tertius seemed incapable of was a genuine smile.

"Gallio, get on your feet when an officer is addressing you."

Gallio flung a bowl into the water with a splash, then stood to attention with the others. He offered a long sigh that might as well have been a kick to Tertius's mouth.

Varro had been wrong, he discovered. Tertius could smile, as he did now standing before Gallio.

"Such an economy of words. You've managed to say so much without a sound."

"Sir," Gallio said, frowning into the distance.

Tertius narrowed his eyes at Gallio, and leaned in closer as he spoke.

"Really, if you've something to say, why not say it clearly? Come now, we're all in this together. You can tell me what's bothering you."

Varro bit his lip, staring ahead and hoping Gallio could keep his mouth shut. Whatever good sense he formerly possessed seemed to have vanished. When Gallio grunted, Varro closed his eyes.

"Sir, this punishment is not fair. We did nothing wrong and shouldn't be humiliated before the rest of the century."

Varro pressed his eyes together hard enough to stain the blackness behind his lids with white sparks. Yet he imagined the predatory smile forming on Tertius's face.

"Not fair, you say? Well, that's just terrible. Brings a tear to my eye thinking my men have been dealt with unfairly. Maybe you can enlighten me on the facts as you know them."

"Sir," Gallio said, now more enthusiastic. "We were only sent to locate a possible enemy, not engage an entire army of bandits. There were only eight of us, sir. We would've died confronting that many."

"Died! Oh my, Gallio. I had no idea things were so dire. You could have been killed."

"Sir? We're not here to die for bandits. We're here to save Greece and defeat Philip. It makes no sense to throw our lives away on bandits."

Tertius clicked his tongue. "What a profound sense to duty you have. I really had no idea, Gallio. You have clearly envisioned the aims of this entire campaign. I am pleased that you can explain them to me, with my narrow and foolish views of military operations, the entire conception of what you know to be the will of the Senate and the plans of our consul and tribunes. To think, we could've lost your vast wisdom in a bandit ambush."

Varro opened his eyes now. Falco fought laughter beside him, but Varro knew this was no joke. Gallio, whose common sense seemed to have been a casualty of that bandit ambush, stepped right into Tertius's clumsy trap.

"I'm not sure of the Senate, sir. But honestly, we had to retreat. And if we hadn't uncovered those bandits, the enemy might use them against us. We should be thanked for our efforts and not punished. It's not fair."

"Yes, you mentioned that." Tertius had both arms folded at his back, and his vine can swished violently behind him.

"Sir, Gallio hasn't been well since he was cut." Curio stepped in, also against common sense. Varro winced, wishing he could shout everyone to silence.

"Wounded in battle," Tertius said, smiling at Gallio. "A price enough to pay, isn't it?"

"Yes, sir."

"Well, this has been the most enlightening conversation of my life. Gallio, I'll just remind you that while all your points are valid, they matter for nothing."

Varro closed his eyes again. The trap now folded over Gallio and he could not bear to watch.

"In fact," Tertius continued. "None of what we think matters. We are soldiers. Our tools are swords and shields to execute the will of Rome and its people as represented by the Senate. Our thoughts are best left at home. If a good idea comes to you, I suggest you root it up and destroy it like you would a diseased rat. Because that is what it is, a diseased rat eating through your thoughts. You've no use for thoughts. Your officers will tell you what to think."

Varro heard Gallio grunt again.

"Sir, I'm sorry."

"There are a hundred different ways I can make you feel even sorrier," Tertius said. "But here's what I'll do. Anger takes energy, Gallio. You have too much energy. So get in full gear and pack, and you will march around the camp perimeter until I tell you to stop. And as I have such a busy day ahead, I probably won't get back to you until your feet are stubs."

"Sir!" Gallio shouted, snapping to attention.

"That's better. And Curio, you are going to ensure your friend does not slow his pace. You are to position yourself to watch Gallio at all times and keep him moving by any means needed. Again, keep at it until I relieve you of this duty. If I find either of you have slackened a moment, then we'll get to the real punishments for the entire contubernium."

Varro shook his head, feeling pity for Gallio.

"Varro, open your eyes!" Tertius shouted. "Do I bore you? Need to take a nap while I'm speaking?

"Sir, no sir. I apologize, sir."

Tertius now appeared before him, his sneer drawing deep lines in his face. "Well, it was you I came to find anyway. You and Falco, both of you are excused from sword drills today. I've volunteered you for a construction crew. The war elephants will be arriving any day, and there's a lot to be done yet. You'll join us for morning marches and as needed, but otherwise you're on that team until the work is done."

With his orders issued, Tertius released his hands to fall by his side. He tilted his head back at all of them.

"Retreat is never an option. You fight until your centurion ends your shift. You're just hastati, so you can be excused once for your inexperience. Don't expect that a second time, boys. You'll die either way. So make it fighting an enemy and not being beaten to death by your fellow soldiers."

Varro and the rest stood at attention while Tertius stalked off. Everyone turned to Gallio, whose face had shaded to purple. Curio hung his head and pointed at the barracks in a silent order for Gallio to gear up. He turned, kicking the water basin before he entered the barracks.

"That put a spot of heat in a cold morning," Falco whispered.

"We better get to our assignment," Varro said. "There's nothing more for us to do today."

Panthera wavered between following Curio and Gallio and joining the others, who sullenly resumed cleaning the remaining bowls. He looked to Varro as if pleading for help.

"Just keep the recruits busy and make sure Curio does his job."

"This is a mess," Panthera said. "What has got into Gallio?"

"It'll pass," Varro said. But he wondered. The words sounded patronizing even to himself. Yet Panthera seemed eager to believe it, nodding vigorously and joining the recruits at the wash basin.

Once Varro left the barracks behind, he turned to Falco.

"You're lucky Tertius didn't see you laughing. Are you crazy?"

"Yet you're the one called out for taking a nap. I should ask you the same thing."

Continuing along the road, they passed teams of workers, slaves, and messengers. Varro found it remarkable how the army could construct a fort within a week that seemed as if it had been standing for decades. Despite the scent of fresh-cut wood and the glaring brightness of new paint, this camp was much like the one back in Apollonia. If Consul Galba ordered another relocation, this one would break down and set up as swiftly. Shouts from workers echoed along the walled perimeter. Hammers banged out rhythms in the distance. It was another morning in the camp, marred only by Gallio's foolishness.

"Tertius is more imaginative than Latro was," Falco said. "He's better with words, too."

"But just as dangerous," Varro said. "He loves to torment us."

"You feel that way about all officers. I think it's because you think you could do better."

Varro stopped again, turning slack-jawed to his friend.

"What? I've never said anything of the sort."

"Yeah, well, you've assumed leadership for the contubernium. That just didn't happen. You basically made it clear we're doing things your way."

"Stop accusing me of things I never did."

"Oh, come on, Tribune Varro!" He shoved Varro with a laugh. The two continued in companionable silence until arriving at their new post.

Their construction team lead barely looked at them as he escorted them to their worksite.

"You boys look young," he said. "Ever seen a war elephant before?"

"I saw them in Rome once," Varro said. "But I was just a child and they were far off."

"Yeah? Well, you'll see one good and close now." The team leader was an older man with dark skin like leather. His thin arms were still strong. His hook nose was sunburned and peeling, sticking far out from his bronze helmet. "You two will be building the mounting stations for their riders."

Varro shielded his eyes from the morning sun and scanned the worksite. A score of men were bent over piles of wood planking. Three dragged suitable planks out of the pile and handed these to the others.

"Sir, how long will we be working?" Falco asked. He too held his hand over his heavy brow against the sun.

"A few days. But don't think it'll free you from other duties. You'll work twice as hard as everyone else, and I'll be sure of it. You recruits need to earn your place."

"Are we still recruits?" Falco asked with a chuckle. But their team leader did not find the humor. His face pinched with anger.

"Children, that's what you are. You've had a fight or two? Think you've seen it all?"

Varro put up his hands. "No, sir. That's not—"

"Well, you've not seen anything." The veteran soldier leaned into Falco, jabbing his finger into his chest. "Look at me, boy. I've been fighting and fighting and fighting. First Hannibal now Philip. How many other battles do I have to go? No rest for me. My friends are dead. My farm is dust. I've no money left. But here I am, fighting. And do I get an easy assignment?"

"Sir, I meant no offense," Falco said. "It was a poor jest. I am sorry."

The apology seemed to mollify the veteran, who frowned but gave a curt nod.

"Well, you're not funny. I'll agree to that. Now, elephants are coming. Fucking monsters. Each one of them could drink the Tiber dry in a day. They eat and shit like you wouldn't believe. They've got a temper. So watch out around them. I don't see the use for these things. But we captured them from Hannibal, so now we're going to use them, which is stupid. If they didn't work for him, why do we want them?"

"It's a good question, sir," Falco said.

"Of course it's a good question. And it's not like elephants are hard to deal with in battle. Just stick them with javelins until they go mad. Then they'll run amok over anyone, even our own men. Just stay away from them if you can. And if you can't, keep an eye on them or else I'll have to scrape you off their feet later."

The two were then introduced to the work team and immediately set to the most arduous labors the veterans could find for them. Varro and Falco traversed the camp on errands, fetching everything from buckets of water from the cisterns to lumber and tools. They never sat down.

By the end of the day, Varro's feet ached from the constant pounding. Yet he joined the others in admiring the day's achievement. The work team had erected a dozen stair-like stages to load soldiers and gear onto the elephants. These stood in clusters around the area planned for the elephant pens. Another crew had previously constructed a ditch-like area to house them, which would apparently be enough to keep the animals in place. An earth ramp accessed the pen area.

He and Falco walked back on the same road they had taken in the morning.

At a crossroad, he could see to the end where the west gate closed.

Gallio in his full pack staggered into sight, collapsing to hands and knees.

"By the gods," Varro said. "Has he been running all day?"

"He had to have been allowed some rest," Falco said. "Or else he would've died by now. No one can do that in full gear for ten hours."

Yet Curio appeared behind him, haggard but not as exhausted at Gallio. He kicked at him from behind, but Gallio remained on his hands and knees. Curio knelt beside him, seemed to whisper, then hauled him up. Gallio staggered ahead, then collapsed again. Curio repeated his efforts, but this time had to kick and beat Gallio until he struggled up and lurched ahead. Both vanished from sight.

"You were right," Falco said. "Tertius is as bad as Latro was. Only it looks like he wants to kill Gallio."

4

The day Varro had his wheat rations restored, he offered a whispered prayer to Ceres. The others of the contubernium did as well, all seated around the morning campfire fresh from their march. Panthera and Curio sat together and the three recruits—Cordus, Otho, and Sura—lined up beside Falco and Varro.

Only one spot remained between Curio and Otho, and that was for Gallio.

"This is going to taste sweet," Falco said. "Better than anything in a long time."

"How much longer will you two be on construction duty?" Panthera asked. He then slurped from his bowl.

Varro, enjoying the honey-sweetened porridge, wiped at his mouth with the back of his wrist before answering. "We'll be done today, actually."

"Don't be so sure we won't have to build something else before they let us go," Falco said with his mouth full. "Every day they say we're done, then there's something new."

"I think this is it, though." Varro and the rest fell silent. No one wanted to say what Varro knew had to be said. So they sat and ate, while the soldiers from other barracks them did the same. Some called over to them, making friendly small talk that died in the cool morning. The sky was the color of dry stone and the sun was nothing but a dull haze. The camp had a muted and gauzy hum of early morning activity.

At last, Varro decided he had to speak.

"Gallio is getting out of the hospital today."

He did not want to look to Curio, since this was not his responsibility. But he was Gallio's closet friend. Varro might be his next closest. However, after Centurion Drusus recommended one man organize each contubernium and Varro assumed the role, Gallio had grown distant and even resentful.

Varro's statement thudded into the dirt between all of the others. Each man looked to his bowl, and Curio shifted, visibly agitated.

"His legs are recovered," Varro said. "Tertius said he'll be good enough to march again."

He hated being Tertius's mouthpiece to the group. But this was the news he had to share. The day of running laps around the camp had cracked Gallio's shins. When Curio dragged him back to the barracks that night, he and Varro had to carry Gallio to the hospital. The Greek doctor hissed at the condition of Gallio's feet, but sent Varro and Curio out.

"I haven't had a chance to visit Gallio," Varro said. "I've been so busy with construction."

Falco shrugged and nodded toward Varro to indicate he shared the same excuse.

Of the three recruits, only wide-eyed Otho offered any kind of excuse. "Well, he hasn't really got to know us very much. It didn't feel right for us to go see him alone."

Now Panthera and Curio both looked away. Panthera was the first to stand up and clap imaginary dust from his thighs.

"Well, we've all got our days ahead. I've drawn guard duty for the late evening. I need to get some rest before drills and the start of my night."

With that announcement, Panthera ducked into the barracks and the contubernium broke up. Before he and Falco went to their construction site, he caught Curio as he followed Panthera inside.

"You'll make sure Gallio gets back?"

"Why is he my problem?" Curio pulled away. "He doesn't want to see me. Not after what I did to him."

"That was Tertius's fault. If you didn't keep him running, then we'd all be in trouble. And I know he'd make it worse on us." Varro clapped the shorter man on the shoulder, but he simply shook his head and turned into the barracks.

"A fine mess Gallio has made for everyone," Falco said as they followed the road to the elephant pens.

"What do you mean by Gallio? Optio Tertius made him run until his legs broke, and he made Curio force him on. And not a word from Centurion Drusus either. He's fine to let his second ruin the relations between his soldiers. That's not the purpose of having us live and fight together."

Falco snorted. "Well who started the whole thing? Gallio has done nothing but complain since he got stuck in the gut months ago. I think he wanted a crown for that, but didn't get it. So now he's been dragging his feet ever since. And he resents you for showing leadership."

"You think so too?" Varro asked. They passed another centurion, who eyed them as if they were both involved in some criminal undertaking. But he continued past.

"Of course I do. He's always got something to say under his breath. I bet he wanted that job."

"Then he should've said something. No one volunteered when the time came."

"No one would listen to Gallio," Falco said, waving his hand.

"He ran away when we were ambushed along with the others. And did he have any good ideas when Centurion Drusus got netted? No, you led the way. So Gallio can go get fucked if he thinks I'd listen to anything he wants to say."

"See, that's not right," Varro said, stopping them in the road. "We shouldn't be fighting like this. We've got to stick together to get through this war alive."

"You and I have to stick together," Falco said, slapping Varro's chest with the back of his hand. "That's always been the deal."

"Well, I'm afraid of what Gallio will be like once he returns. None of us even visited him. I feel terrible for it."

"We're busy," Falco said with barely disguised impatience. "He knows what life is like. We're worked dawn to dark and have no time for fine wine and pleasant conversation. This is the army."

"He visited me when I was in the hospital."

"We hadn't started our real responsibilities then." Falco plucked him by the shoulder and they started along the road again. "And if we're late to the site you know we'll be in the shit. So let's hurry. Worry about Gallio when you see him next. We might not live so long for that to happen."

"Such a positive person, you are."

They put in a long, final day of work at the elephant pens. They had constructed watering trenches under the baleful eye of their hook-nosed team leader. The entire time he shook his head and cursed elephants as "giant piles of shit that drop more piles of shit. They're going to cost us the war just by smothering us in their shit."

Varro and Falco both tended to their shovels and offered no opinions. That was the veteran response to such cursing, and it worked well. Yet by the end of the day, their team leader's mood improved when he proclaimed their labors finished.

"The easy days are done, boys," he said, looping his thin and powerful arms around Varro's and Falco's necks. "Back to marching and drilling. Just remember what I said about elephants. Don't let them step on you."

"Of course, sir." Falco had become a model soldier after his initial failure with their team leader. He now seemed to favor Falco above the rest of the team.

"Say, I've got some good wine. Not the vinegar you get; the good stuff the officers handed out when Apustius sacked all those towns. You boys remember that? Come by my barracks and join us for a cup. We've ended work early enough for a drink or two."

Their team leader indicated the orange stripe on the western horizon. The sky never loosed the rain it had threatened all day, leaving behind clouds to blaze in the final rays of light.

"It's not dark," Falco said. "So we've no need to be back at our barracks yet."

They followed their team leader along a different road and met with his fellow triarii. Some knew Varro's father, and offered him condolences. Others had never heard the Varro name. For his part, he did not know how to handle the recognition. His father had been involved with the traitor Decius Oceanus and Optio Latro. Perhaps some of these men were victims of their plans. The thought soured Varro's mood.

Yet Falco enjoyed the wine and the chance to hear stories of the veterans' battles against Hannibal. Most were glad to share what they knew, and encouraged both him and Falco to great deeds.

"Better a dead hero than a living coward," said their team leader. "But best of all is a living hero. So aim for the best, boys."

The advice flowed with the sweet wine, for all had drunk generously. But none were foolish enough to become drunk. The team leader stowed the wineskin before anyone could ask for more.

They left as the first torches lit the roads and the watches changed. Panthera would be at one of these posts, Varro thought, and he recalled Gallio. A long day of hard work had vanquished his worries, but now the fear returned as he and Falco walked the roads back.

"Varro, listen, we've not had a minute alone for a while. We've got some business to discuss."

"What business?" Varro did not pause, but Falco stopped at a darkened alley between barracks.

"It's only the most important thing in our lives, yet you forgot it."

"Most important thing? Well, you can't think about women for now, Falco. Most of the slaves we've captured are men and —"

"I'm not talking about rolling in the hay with some whore." Falco waved both hands as if a bee had attacked his face. "Just step off the road a moment, and we'll talk. Gods, you are so stupid sometimes."

They both checked the roads, finding only pairs of shadowed figures of relieved guards returning to their barracks. Varro followed Falco into the shadowed alley.

"The necklace, you fool," Falco said, turning on him the moment he slipped into the darkness.

"Well, what about it? We split it half and half."

Varro had claimed a thick braid of gold chain from a bandit chief, yet had lost it in the woods when he was nearly killed there. Optio Latro had found it instead and claimed it for himself. However, a mysterious benefactor retrieved it and left it with Varro as he slept one night. The chain was as thick as Varro's thumb and worth a fortune to him, at least.

"It can't just sit in our packs until someone finds it," Falco said. "Can you imagine what Optio Tertius will do?"

"It's booty," Varro said, shrugging his shoulders. "All soldiers get a claim on booty. So why not us?"

"Because it wasn't sanctioned by the officers." Falco flinched at his own rising voice and ducked his head down before continuing.

"You don't think Centurion Drusus or Tribune Primanus want us to have more gold than they do? The officers give us the leftovers, and this chain is no leftover. It's a prize."

"Well, it's not like it can be any place safer than in our packs." Varro scratched his head, thinking of a better place to hide their fortune. Yet under Falco's scrutiny he could think of nothing.

"Any officer can turn those packs inside out if they called for it. Every time Tertius inspects the barracks or our gear, I feel like my heart is going to explode. I think about it all the time. I mean, Panthera slept all day right next to a fortune. What would he do if he knew the chain was there?"

"He'd probably turn it in to the officers," Varro said, considering the questions seriously. But Falco batted his shoulder.

"Listen to me, we've got to get that chain out of the barracks and someplace where only we can find it. We need to bury it, or else hide it where we can come back for it."

"We should just keep it with us, maybe sew it into a hem on our tunics."

"Creative but stupid, Varro. You don't think Tertius would notice? The first time you washed your tunic everyone would notice the chain. We're risking too much by keeping the chain in our packs. But carrying it around is too risky. I was hoping you'd have thought of a hiding spot by now. You're better at planning than I am."

"That's true, but I've not really worried for the necklace. Maybe we can create a false bottom to the packs where we can hide it. There's nowhere we can go to sell it for coin, and really, I don't want to sell it. I need it for the farm when we get home. You do too."

"Don't instruct me on what to do with my money." Falco folded his arms and looked around. "But that's probably the best idea. Listening to the triarii tonight made me wonder if we'll ever get out of this army. Their farms are all falling apart and going up for sale while they're away. We need to get rich during our time here, and the gold chain is the best start we have on it."

"I agree," Varro said. "That chain must be worth at least as much as our two farms and maybe more. It will make us rich enough to stay in business when we're out, especially if there's more loot to be had before we go."

"Your great-grandfather didn't burden you with any vow against getting rich, did he?"

"Shut up, Falco."

They both laughed then turned to exit the alleyway.

And ran into Curio standing at the end of it.

Varro shouted and leapt back into Falco, crashing into his chest.

"Jupiter's thunder, Curio. What are you doing?"

Varro's racing heart slowed as he collected his wits. Short Curio stood backlit at the end of the alleyway. His expression was hidden in the shadows, but he seemed confused.

"What were you two talking about?"

Falco pushed out of the alleyway into the main road. He bumped Curio aside as he did.

"We were talking about how I hate people who spy on my private conversations."

Curio did not acknowledge the threat, but looked quizzically to Varro.

"Really, what were you talking about?"

Varro shook his head. "Nothing to concern you. It's business between old friends. You know we've known each other since birth? There's just some things we need to work out among ourselves. Nothing to bother the rest of you with."

"Yeah, like two brothers," Falco said, squaring up to Curio. "We've got our own business both before and after the army. Now what are you doing besides spying on others?"

Curio looked between them. Varro tried to keep a pleasant,

open face. But he felt the heat throbbing there. Curio definitely heard a good portion of the talk. He smiled like a man who only half understood a joke, but was willing to play along for the moment.

"It's after dark and you've not come back. We figured you were at the worksite still, but no one is there. Panthera asked me to go see where you were at."

Varro realized he probably volunteered for the search to avoid having to face Gallio, who must have returned by now.

"We had a drink with our team leader before heading back," he said. There was no shame in the truth. "We were on our way before you came along."

"You were hiding in the shadows, whispering to each other." Curio's smile widened and he held up a palm. "But like you said, you two have your own issues. Anyway, we all better get off the roads before an officer finds us out here."

Varro let Curio lead the way back. He and Falco sharing a dark glance behind him. How much did Curio discover, and what would he do with that knowledge? Varro did not fully trust the little man, so quickly promoted from the velites by Optio Latro. He seemed to know more than he let on. What if he worked for Varro's enemies? He didn't even know who these enemies were or why they cared a whit about him in the first place.

At last, they arrived at the barracks. Curio's pace visibly slowed, but they all ducked inside to the guttering lamplight. All the others were in the bunks, but no one was asleep.

Gallio lay on his bed. His left leg was still braced with a length of wood and white wrapping. Gallio had laced both hands behind his head and smiled.

"Yeah, the left leg was worse than the right. But I can return to light duty. I'm excused from heavy marching for another week. I guess I marched enough for a year already."

He laughed and propped himself up on his elbows.

"I'm glad you're back," Varro said. Falco echoed the same sentiment as he sat on his bunk to remove his sandals.

"I'm glad to be back. I've been to the hospital enough. And the doctor looked at my shoulder too. It's going to leave a lumpy scar, but it's healing."

Curio climbed into his bunk above Gallio without saying more. The others sat back on their bunks, now satisfied that everyone was present and none of them could be held accountable for their being out after dark.

"I'm sorry I didn't come visit you," Varro said. "I feel terrible."

"Me too," Falco said, shoving his sandals under his bunk. "They worked us all day."

"Don't worry for it," Gallio said. "I'm fine now."

He broadened his smile. But Varro felt it a strange and crooked thing, like a plaster cast over his face. In fact, Gallio had somehow managed to turn a smile and pleasant words into something more akin to a threat.

"Yes, old Gallio is back in line. Let's just forget everything I've said before and start over."

"Sounds great," Falco said, rolling into his bed. "Welcome back."

"I'm happy to be back. Really happy."

Gallio lay back down on his bunk and put out the bronze lamp. The room fell into quiet darkness.

Varro climbed the ladder to his bed then fell into a night of vague and uneasy dreams.

5

The woods loomed ahead of Varro. Rain had lashed the area for two days, leaving the ground spongy underfoot. He was apprehensive of the conditions within the woods. The sky was still clogged with wooly clouds and the sun lost every battle to escape them. As he trudged forward with the rest of the century, he imagined a dark world of gray spirits all wreathed in dead leaves and smelling of loamy earth. He shuddered at the thought, then touched the pugio at his hip.

The pugio was a gift from his mother, which had come down from her brother's time in the legion. It had been blessed at the temple of Mars in Rome, and Varro considered it a charm against all evils. It helped to use the pugio in battle as well, which he decided would keep the charm fresh. He had no idea how long a god's blessing endured on an item. Did such things curdle over time like goat milk, or were they as enduring as the sun?

The century spread out in a loose formation as they approached the woods. This was a foraging expedition and not a march to battle. Men talked to each other in low voices, sometimes laughing. Quite contrary to his nature, Drusus did not insist on the usual protocols of marching formation and silence. The only indication they were a complete century was Drusus leading from the front and Optio Tertius herding them from the rear. Otherwise, their contuberniums were now forage teams.

"I hate the woods," Varro said to Falco at his right.

"You've mentioned that enough to never mention it again. Don't complain so much. It doesn't suit you."

"Every time I go into the woods, something awful happens."

"Not every time," Falco said. "You've had some good shits off in the bushes, haven't you? Look, don't start talking like we're marching to our deaths. Even Drusus is in a good mood. Everyone is, except for you."

Varro wondered if truly the entire century was in high spirits and he was alone in his dark mood. They had endured nearly a full week within or just around the camp, marching in rain and drilling in mud. All of this inflicted extra work to keep themselves and their gear in condition. Every normal duty had been burdened with the miserable rain. Varro had spent a night of guard duty huddled under a leaking, makeshift roof for so long that he felt he must go mad or freeze to death. He had slipped in the mud so often during combat practice that Optio Tertius's vine cane had left welts across the backs of his legs. "Learn to fight in the mud, you fool, or it won't be a vine cane striking you but a Macedonian blade."

So perhaps he did feel the weather more keenly than the others, who jaunted toward the brown and gray woods ahead.

The cavalry had returned from a week of scouting and reported no encounter with Philip's army. Yet he must be close, for word had come Philip was bringing battle to Galba and planned to drive him back to Rome. News of the cavalry's failure to locate Philip buoyed the spirits of all the fighting men. As much as they trained to fight and kill, and as much as men talked about the glories and crowns they would earn, no one really wanted a battle.

They would all be happy to camp out until their terms were served then go home alive. Perhaps only Galba and his tribunes were upset at not locating Philip.

Varro scanned the line of his companions. No one had complained as much as he, including Gallio, and all appeared in high spirits. Little Curio laughed with Panthera as Gallio hobbled along beside them, also smiling.

"Have Gallio and I changed places?"

"I was beginning to wonder the same thing," Falco said. "He's been a brighter spot than you, and you've noticed Tertius hasn't let up on him either. His leg isn't fully healed but he pushes on. So if anyone should complain, it'd be him. But he's just fine and you're as sour as leftover wine."

Varro looked again to Gallio. His left leg remained braced. He ambled with a stiff gait that tormented him during their marches in the rain. But he had maintained a fresh smile and good words for everyone. He even laughed after Optio Tertius berated him for not keeping pace.

"It's just one broken shin," he said. "Thankfully I have another one. Good thing marching in the rain is considered light duty."

Everyone was glad to see his humor restored. Curio, who had stayed apart from Gallio, no longer acted guilty around him. They were friends again.

Varro had indeed traded places, for ever since Gallio's return he had felt a strange uneasiness that would not depart. Maybe he dreaded the inevitable encounter with Philip's army. It would be his first major engagement on a battlefield where the Macedonian phalanx could be brought to bear in its full terror. Maybe he worried for his prized gold chain after Falco had made such dire predictions of its loss. He still had thought of no better place to hide it than stowed with his pack.

They arrived at the edge of the woods, where mule-drawn carts parked to await their loads. Centurion Drusus waited to gather all the men to himself then detailed everyone to their respective areas.

"We'll mark the trees deemed suitable for lumber and collect what firewood we can. It'll be wet still, but you all know what to look for. Catch game for yourselves, if you can. But unless a rabbit jumps into your hands, I don't want you chasing down animals. And remember, just because the cavalry hasn't found Philip does not mean he's far off. Be alert."

Here he looked to Varro, his creased forehead gathering what little shadow the flat daylight threw.

With their assignment given, Varro and the others picked their way into the woods. Wet branches grabbed at Varro like the clammy hands of the ancient dead. The loam scent filled his nose as expected and he wanted to retch.

Falco snorted a laugh at his side. "You act like you've fallen into a latrine."

"It feels like I'm stepping on a carpet of worms. This is disgusting."

"Looks like Optio Tertius isn't with us," Gallio said. "So this day is already better than most."

Curio laughed as did the recruits. Panthera was already patting the trunk of a tree.

"This one looks straight without a lot of branches," he said. "We should mark it."

He drew his pugio and began to carve an X into the bark at eye level. One of the recruits, Sura, joined him.

"Nothing good ever happens in the woods," Varro muttered to himself as he watched his footing. The rain-slick leaves were treacherous and rocks seemed to have risen out of the mud like budding plants.

Yet they worked deeper into the woods, pulling out suitable firewood and marking trees. They picked slowly, as they had the afternoon ahead. They formed collection points for the firewood.

Through the gray glaze of light between the trees, Varro heard others of the century calling their finds to each other.

"At least it makes the place feel less wild," he said. He and Falco had just marked a tree and now were beating the underbrush for firewood.

"Hey," Falco whispered. "I've been thinking about our problem."

Varro wrapped both hands around a cold and slick branch and pulled it from the underbrush. The so-called problem had become Falco's code for their golden necklace.

"You want to bury it out here."

"You thought of it too? We're always coming out here to forage. It'll be safe and we'll always have an excuse to come back to check on it."

The branch popped out, releasing a spray of dead pine needles and dirt. The branch was long dead and would burn well once dried out.

"Your idea has a few problems. First being we might never come back here again."

"We're here all the time."

"This is only the third time I've been here. I know, because I hate coming here. And besides, we're not going to spend the whole war in this area. We've already relocated camp once, or we could be assigned to garrison duty in one of those captured towns. How will we find this place again once we're gone?"

"Well, we'd have to come get it before we move." Falco fell quiet, his heavy brows furrowing. They shook through bushes and patted rough tree trunks before he finally sighed. "Shit, Varro, why don't you come up with an idea? Do I have to think of everything?"

"You're thinking too much. It's safest with us."

Soon they fell into their work and time passed silently and unmarked. Varro had been absorbed in his own loathing for the damp and gloomy woods and did not realize the contubernium had wandered apart. He saw Panthera and Sura marking a tree and called out to them.

"Let's gather together," he shouted across the distance. "Time for a rest, anyway."

Panthera nodded and soon all of them met in a clearing. Shadows in the distance indicated where others of the century worked, and Drusus's voice carried as a thin echo among the trees. Their pile of firewood held no more than a dozen branches.

"Getting harder to find good kindling," Curio said. "We're cleaning out the woods completely."

"But plenty of trees for lumber and firewood," Gallio said. He had sat on the only stone large enough for a man. He stretched out his braced leg and rubbed his shin with a grimace.

"Is it getting worse?" Varro asked. He preferred to lean against a cold tree rather than squat in the slimy mud like the others.

"It's sore all the time, and the dampness makes it worse. Don't worry about me. I'll be fine."

He kept is leg straight and winced at the smallest movement of his foot. Curio hovered around him, whispering questions that Gallio waved away with a chuckle.

They passed a short rest in quiet conversation, mostly around the weather and how bad the cavalry must have had it riding around in the rain searching for Philip's army. But no one wanted Drusus or Tertius to discover them idle. With heavy groans and tired stretches, they stood to return to their duties.

Gallio slipped off his stone, hopped and gritted his teeth, then collapsed with a curse.

Everyone paused, staring at him. Varro hoped he would stand again, but he remained on his side, holding his left leg and hissing through his teeth. At last, Curio rushed to kneel beside him. That brought the rest to crowd around him. Varro leaned over Curio's shoulder as he made to remove the bandages around Gallio's leg.

"No, don't!" He seized Curio's hand and shoved it back. He

talked through gritted teeth. "I heard something crack and I went down. I need the support of that splint."

He hid his eyes in the crook of his arm, and he squirmed with the agony of his leg.

"He's been working that leg too hard," Curio said. "He shouldn't have been forced to march or to be on his feet all the time. Now his leg is fully broken."

He swiped at the ground in his frustration, then stood again.

"We've got to take him back to one of the officers," Panthera said.

"I can walk. Just not on that leg. I don't want to get all of you in trouble." Gallio paused to groan, but removed his arm to look up at his companions. "Can you imagine if you all showed up with me? Tertius would ask why it took seven men to carry one man back. Then you'd all be in trouble."

Varro could hear those words in Tertius's voice. Gallio was right, especially if he could hop on one leg with support from another. He only needed a single man to take him back.

"I'll take him," Curio said, then crouched once more beside Gallio.

He rolled onto his side, as if attempting to get up on his own. Curio helped him rise then Varro and Panthera both steadied him. He groaned and yelped, but eventually stood while leaning on Curio's shoulder.

"I'm not sure if I'll be back," Curio said. "I may have to see him all the way to the hospital."

"Hold on," Varro said. "I'll take him instead."

"It's all right, I've got him."

"Yeah, this is best," Gallio said. "Let's go."

"No, you never know what Tertius is going to say, especially if Curio takes you in. For all we know, he might accuse the two of you of using Gallio's leg to get out of work. Let's spread out Tertius's punishment to others. I'll take you, just in case."

Gallio, still gritting his teeth, laughed. "Or you want to get out work?"

"I wouldn't mind getting out of the woods, to be honest. But I'm serious about Tertius. We're better off talking to Drusus, but you never know. Officers stick together."

Curio bent his mouth and finally nodded. "Maybe you're right."

"I'm fine with you taking me," Gallio said. "Tertius isn't that unreasonable, is he?"

"I think he is," Varro said. He slipped into Curio's spot and now supported Gallio with his shoulder. "Besides, it looked like you were crushing little Curio."

The others laughed, and Gallio hopped around to adjust to Varro's support. Together they turned toward the path back to the carts at the edge of the woods. Gallio hopped a few steps, then turned to wave at the others.

"Farewell, fools!" He laughed, tipping his head back.

"Get going," Falco called after them. "Enjoy your rest while the rest of us work ourselves sick."

"Get better," Curio called. "We'll see you back at camp."

Gallio offered a final wave, then drew his breath. "It's going to be a long hop back. Let's get going."

Not being sure-footed from the start, Varro struggled with Gallio unbalancing him. They aimed for the light between the trees, but Gallio's hopping skewed their path. Varro kept guiding them back on track.

"I'm sorry for this." Gallio said each time they had to readjust.

"It's not your fault. You've been doing everything you can to keep up."

Together they fumbled ahead, lurching toward the edge of the woods.

"I'm sorry, Varro. All this motion hurts so bad. Can we just rest a moment?"

"Of course." He balanced Gallio on his shoulder while searching for a place to let him down. "On that fallen log. Can you sit there?"

"It looks fine. Please, just a moment is all I need."

He let Gallio slide from his shoulder onto the log. His braced leg extended and he winced as he settled onto the log. Varro steadied him until he nodded to indicate he could sit unaided. Gallio removed his helmet and scratched at his hair. Varro did the same, feeling instant relief from the leather chin strap and the sweat accumulated beneath it.

"Gods, that hurts. Thank you, Varro. There's space here." He patted the log to his right side.

"My feet are cold and sore," he said. "I've earned a short break."

He set his helmet on the ground beside his feet.

"The air feels good in my hair."

"That's right," Gallio said, smiling through his pain. He had a strange, ashen cast to his face and blinked rapidly.

"How bad is it, really?"

"The bone didn't break the skin. I'll be fine."

But Gallio's voice wavered and his hand seemed to reach unconsciously for his leg.

"Tell me the truth. You look sick."

"Do I?" Gallio chuckled, but then he wiped his face with his other hand. "Really, I think it is bad. The pain has been worsening for days and when I heard that snap. Well, I thought I was going to pass out."

"It needs to be set as soon as possible. We should hurry."

"Something doesn't feel right," Gallio said, squirming atop the log. "I think all the hopping has loosened the wrapping and shifted the brace."

"I'll tighten the wrapping for you." Varro crouched and Gallio swiveled his leg to him. He hissed when Varro began to unroll the bandages. "I just need to loosen them enough to readjust the splint. I'll try to be careful."

He unspooled the dirty and yellowed wrappings. They were soaked with sweat and splattered with mud. Such a dressing would never do for an open wound, but could serve to brace a bone. He paid careful attention to Gallio's reaction, pausing when he flinched, working hand over hand to gently undo the layers of cloth. He did not take his eyes from his work, but imagined Gallio biting his lip against the pain.

"I'm really sorry about this, Varro."

"Don't mention it. You'd do it for me."

"I wish it could be another way. But I just can't think of one."

"There's nothing else for it. Someone had to take you back. I guess we could've carried you on a shield. That might've been better, now that I think of it. I've almost completely removed this bandage. It doesn't hurt?"

"No, it doesn't. I'm sorry, Varro."

"Why do you keep apologizing?"

Varro looked up from Gallio's leg in time to see something driving down on him. It filled his vision with black shadow.

Then it collided with his head, heavy and blunt, exploding into white sparks of pain.

He collapsed back, reeling and feeling hot blood run down his face. Cold earth enfolded his back. He thought he heard someone sobbing. But his vision was fading in from white haze.

"I'm sorry." Gallio said.

Then something slammed over his head and he crumpled into numb blackness.

6

Varro's vision swam up from blackness, through murky brown, to finally arrive at a fuzzy, circle of light. What he saw made no sense, being all a jumble of lines and jagged shapes interspersed with spots of pale gray light. This all rotated in a slow procession around the circle of his sight. He lay still, studying this until he realized the circle expanded and shapes within it were clarifying.

He now felt a strange mixture of heat and cold on his left cheek. A copper flavor rolled into his mouth. Blinking slowly, he realized this was blood and earth. He was on his side, staring off into the woods. The reason for this view or the blood made no sense to him. Why was he prone and bleeding? He blinked again, deliberately, hoping some reason would float up in the buzzing, chaotic mess of his thoughts.

But he felt like sleeping instead. He closed his eyes again, content to wait until another time to ponder these mysteries. Yet something jerked him from behind. His arms were behind his back, which pressed him deeper into the stinking dirt. He did not like the smell of it. Why? Where was this place? Something soft but coarse wound around his wrists, binding them together at the small of his back. He could not understand why this would be.

A desperate, weeping voice spoke to him. But nothing made sense. He was sleepy and wanted to close his eyes. Let this person bother him another day. Yet the person crying behind him seemed to demand his attention. Varro felt himself flipped over and his head rocked and spun with the sudden motion. He felt sick.

"Varro? I'm so sorry. I don't know what else to do."

He blinked his eyes open and tried to make sense of the blurry world sliding around him. Someone crouched over his face. He recognized the man, but could not remember his name. He was a friend. But where did he know him from?

"This is the best way," the man said. "So Tertius and Drusus won't blame the rest of you for my desertion. I had to hit you hard enough so they would know this isn't your fault."

"It's fine." Varro wanted to add a name, but couldn't think of it. He smiled at the man, who seemed so distraught. His face shined with tears and his skin was pale.

"It's just too much. They don't care about us, Varro. Every little thing could get us killed by our own leaders. I'm more afraid of them than I am of the Macedonians. And what are we doing here, anyway? I thought I could do this, to be a hero for Rome. But I can't. Not for monsters like Tertius and Drusus or any other officer in this damned army."

"It's fine," Varro repeated, still at a loss for the man's name. What he said bothered him. He wanted to do something, but could not think of what it should be. He could not think of anything.

"It's not fine," the man said. "I hope you and the others don't face punishment for me. You probably will. I'll have to live with that guilt. I'm going to live, Varro. But I won't if I stay in this army. Rome eats its citizens and leaves nothing but a handful of chewed bones to remember them by. I'm going to find Philip. I'm never going back to Rome. We're never going to meet again."

"It's fine." This was the sole sentence Varro could think to say. He really did not want to speak, but to sleep. The hot fluid rolled down his cheek, and he tasted it fresh and salty on his lips. Sleep would make it all better.

The man laughed, but not with humor. He turned his head aside.

"I should kill you myself and spare you what the officers will do." He began to sob again, choking off his words for a few moments before he composed himself. "But I'm not a monster like Tertius or Drusus. Maybe they'll let you go. I hope they do. Goodbye, Varro."

The man stood on both legs. This seemed significant to Varro, but again the reason for it remained obscured like the sun behind thick clouds. Something hot and fierce burned within him, but it could not penetrate the wooly blanket enveloping him.

The man kicked Varro down again, harder than needed, so that he sprawled out on his side. His vision rolled and flipped as if he were in a capsized boat. The rocking and swirling continued longer than it should have. But once this feeling ebbed, he realized he was alone in a woods and lying on his side with arms bound behind his back.

He lay still and time passed, whether hours or seconds Varro did not know. Yet as time elapsed, memories of the cause for his condition returned. It was a slow process, like shards of a shattered vase being reassembled a piece at a time. Each piece popped into place and brought with it a new anger and fury. The clouds smothering Varro soon burned away as fierce, bright anger behind them burst into Varro's mind.

Gallio had duped him, feigning an injured leg. He had led Varro to remove his helmet, and finally brained him with a rock. The bindings at his wrists were the wrapping for Gallio's so-called broken leg. It was all wound tight with the brace. Varro's hands were numb and cold.

Though he thrashed and struggled, he realized nothing would undo the binding. Yet his legs were free. Gallio had not doomed him to die in the woods as prey for hungry wolves. He struggled to regain his feet, but dizziness plagued him. He crashed repeatedly onto his shoulder, each time causing his bindings to bite deeper into his flesh. At last, he crawled to a tree, then wormed his way up the cold trunk until he stood straight.

He pressed against the rough bark to brace against the rocking ground. The blood from his head caked to his face and around his mouth. Flakes broke off as he muttered curses.

"Gallio, you stupid bastard. You're going to get us all killed."

While he pressed to the tree, he searched for indications of where Gallio might have run. To his untrained eye, any direction could have served except toward the gathering point. He doubted Gallio had any plan beyond escaping into the woods. He would avoid the sounds of other soldiers, and probably try to hide until nightfall before moving off.

After several failed attempts to stand free of the tree's support, he at last held his ground. Each step forward was leaden, but he would rather proceed with care than rush and injure himself in a fall. Since he had no hope of trailing Gallio in his condition, his best chance was to reach the edge of the woods and alert the soldiers waiting to load up the day's forage.

Twilight was coming. Light struggled to reach the floor of the woods. Drusus might have even sounded the whistle to recall everyone while Varro was unconscious. He had no idea how long that lasted. But since he remembered Gallio binding him, he might have only blacked out a moment. Memories remained distorted and he wondered if he would even make sense during his report.

When he finally fell out of the trees into the clear he was a good distance south of the wagons. He shouted for attention as he tried to run to them.

A group of soldiers, older men from the triarii, met him halfway. To Varro's horror, in the lead of them was Optio Tertius.

"What happened to you?" he asked. Varro stared at his optio as if he had been asked a question with no answer. "You're tied? What is this about?"

Tertius spun him around while one grim-faced triarii grunted at his examination of Varro's head.

"The boy took at least two solid hits," he announced, holding Varro by the jaw in a warm, rough hand. "Maybe more if we clean it up and get a better look."

Varro's hands slipped free and fell to his sides. Both flooded with blood, burning hot needles crawling under his skin. He rubbed them together out of instinct. Tertius appeared before him, holding the cut wrapping and splint in hand.

"Give me an explanation," he said in an even voice. "Did you run into Macedonian scouts?"

"No sir," Varro said. Then he paused.

At the least, Gallio's life depended on his next words. His life depended on it. Perhaps even the lives of his companions could be forfeited with his statement. Unknowing of Gallio's deserting, they would emerge from the woods only to face the dreaded fustuarium, being beaten to death by their fellow soldiers.

"Varro, I asked you a question. Can you answer?"

Contrary to expectation, Tertius looked more concerned than angry. He stared directly into Varro's eyes.

The sincere gesture moved him, however briefly, to spill out what must eventually be told.

"Gallio has deserted, sir."

Tertius's eyes flickered with rage and the triarii behind him moaned and cursed in disgust. But the optio said nothing else, and Varro continued to describe what he could of Gallio's deceit.

"And so I have come here as fast as possible, sir. We may still have a chance to catch him."

Now Tertius gave a cool smile.

"Catch him? What would you do if we find him, Varro?"

Varro swallowed hard. It was a good question, and a bad answer might imperil himself as well as the others. He struggled to focus on Tertius.

"I would catch him so that he can be submitted to the consul for trial. I would catch him so that I might be first in line at the fustuarium."

Tertius nodded, then ordered the triarii with him to gather others and begin the search.

"You need medical aid," he said, nodding to Varro's head. "Get to the carts and wait for my instructions."

"Sir, I want to search for him. I left my helmet back there. Sir, it was expensive and I don't want to lose it. Besides, I can show you where he fled from."

"We'll find your trail. Don't worry for your helmet. We'll find that as well."

"Sir, Gallio fooled all of us. I'm certain not even Curio knew of his intentions."

The optio's expression flattened. "We'll determine what happens to all of you later. I believe you, Varro, if that means anything."

He blinked, unsure of this understanding and almost compassionate man who he had reviled only hours before.

"Sir, it means quite a lot. I still want to join you. Gallio might listen to me, and if we can get the others involved, he might be more likely to give up his hiding place."

"Very well." Tertius examined Varro's wounded head then looked into his eyes. "But your eyes are not right. I've seen that look a hundred times before. You'll do more harm to yourself than good."

"I might not live so long for it to matter anyway, sir."

To his dismay, Optio Tertius did not disagree, but simply motioned for him to follow.

To Varro, it seemed Gallio's desertion was an enormous problem worth mobilizing the entire century. But besides the four triarii who had the light duty of guarding the carts and organizing the forage, no one else joined them. "Sir, he'll slip us if we don't have more men."

They were now beneath the trees and darkness swept over them. With Varro's already fuzzy vision, he could not see the path ahead. He followed Tertius exactly.

"It's not about catching him, Varro. He's just one soldier in enemy territory. He has chosen a lingering death by running away. We're doing him a favor chasing him down. At least he'll be dead by tomorrow if we can find him. No need to drag everyone else into this. Forage is more important."

Varro swallowed hard at the thought. Indeed, death was all Gallio had chosen. Varro could not understand that choice. The enemy would show no mercy, and neither would he get aid from the locals. He could never return to Rome now and expect to live. His best hope would be to join brigands like the ones they had faced throughout Illyria and Macedonia. It would be a pathetic and hard life, and also a short one.

Despite feeling nauseated and dizzy, Varro managed to follow Tertius to where he had been ambushed. The triarii also gathered on the point.

"My helmet," Varro said, pointing to the dull bronze glint beside the log where he had sat with Gallio. Its three black feathers stood proudly from the top.

Tertius retrieved it, handing it to Varro. Then he lifted a heavy, wedge-shaped rock from the dirt. He whistled low at it, weighing the rock in his palm.

"This is what he hit you with. You're lucky the edges were not sharp or this would've split your skull. Are you sure Gallio was your friend? I'm surprised your neck didn't snap under the weight of this."

Varro struggled to focus on the stone in Tertius's palm. Two of the triarii studied it as well, then laughed at Varro.

"The lad's head must be at least as hard as that rock."

They shared a laugh with Tertius, who threw the stone back behind the log where Gallio had pried it up. It thudded into the brush. Varro did not join the laughter, but tried to think of which way he had been facing when he fell. At least he was certain Gallio had not run that way.

Tertius began calling out the names of the contubernium while cupping his hands to his mouth. An officer required powerful lungs to be heard amid the chaos of battle. His voice boomed and echoed without answers. But by his second repetition he received calls back.

Varro stumbled around the small clearing, unsure of what he could do to help. But the four triarii bent to their work, and soon one uncovered footprints.

"Get following them," Tertius said. "I've got to gather up the other contubernales."

The triarii set off like eager dogs. Varro wondered what they would do if they caught Gallio. There might not be anything remaining of him to stand trial.

Awkward moments passed as he and Tertius waited for the others to converge on their position. The optio folded his arms and stared blankly ahead. For his part, Varro trembled both from the weakness imparted by the blow to his head and fear for what would befall them. Tertius's understanding might be a tool to keep him under control.

Falco was first into the clearing, and his smile was short lived. He looked between Tertius and him, and his heavy brows knitted together. Panthera and Curio arrived next and both pulled up short when they saw Varro's condition. The remaining three recruits joined and Tertius now addressed them.

"Gallio pretended his leg was broken. He smashed Varro with a rock and nearly killed him. Now he has deserted. I want your help in drawing him out. He's probably hiding in the woods someplace."

"I could've guessed," Falco said. His face darkened then he stepped up to Varro to study his head. "How did he do it?"

Varro did not get to answer before Tertius snapped at him.

"Never mind the details. Pair up and start searching. There's not much daylight left. Curio, you come with me. The others, pair up as you will."

"Looks as if I'll have to take care of you, lily." Falco pulled him closer, then cupped his head down to look at the wound. "You got crowned pretty good. A rock?"

"What else," Varro said. He looked to Curio, who stared up at his optio with a mixture of fear and anger. Panthera seemed to want to go with them, but instead took Sura to leave the other two recruits as the final pair.

"Take him alive if you can," Tertius said. "He should be made to stand judgement. But don't be kind to him. He's no longer your companion."

They set off in different directions. Varro remained unsteady on his feet. Falco had brought Varro's scutum, but he could only carry it on his back, being too unbalanced to have it pulling him forward.

"The triarii found his trail," he said, pointing where they had gone.

"It doesn't matter," Falco said. "Gallio is smart enough to hide it. He probably just fled in fright, but once he recovers he'll disguise his path."

"Still, let's follow it."

Falco led him along a trail that eventually came to a creek. They paused there and Falco laughed.

"And here's where Gallio's trail ends. He ran downstream for sure but probably found a way off the path that would hide him well. Let's go."

"I didn't know Gallio was so good at this."

"Common sense doesn't take much, lily. Of course, you don't have any."

They followed the stream. Varro could not focus on much beyond keeping his balance. Falco straddled the tiny creek in places, looking as if he understood the land better than Varro.

"When did you get so good at tracking people in the woods?"

"Like I said, just a sense I have."

But shortly after Falco's boast, Varro caught a white flicker ahead from the triarii who were deliberately picking around the area near the creek. Falco had just been following them. Varro cocked his brow to his friend, who ignored him and pointed ahead. "Seems like they've found what I've been looking for."

The four veterans looked up at their approach, but did not say anything. They were intent on finding Gallio's tracks. Falco and he joined them, each stooped to look for signs in the mud. Varro could not lean forward for long or else it seemed the earth was reaching up to grab him.

At last the triarii gathered together, shaking heads and muttering.

"Looks like they're giving up," Falco said. "I'm not sure we'll catch him."

From behind, Falco saw the others of his contubernium searching. Again, each one was hunched over bushes trying to figure out Gallio's direction.

But inspiration hit Varro just as sunlight flickered low in the woods.

Like the brigands, Gallio was not hiding under a bush.

"He's in the trees," Varro said, turning to Falco. "That's why there's no trail."

Falco's eyes widened in realization. Then he turned to look into the canopy of golden leaves and pine branches. The triarii followed along. Soon they were spread out, all looking up rather than down.

Varro now felt as if he would collapse backward. It seemed he was best if he stood without any incline to his head. He abandoned his search for Gallio and rested against a cold trunk. The woods were now dim enough that torches would soon be required. In the distance, a whistle blew. Drusus was recalling everyone to his position, and probably infuriated that Tertius and his men had left their positions.

"That's it," Falco said, straightening his back. "The little bastard got away."

"Gallio!" Varro shouted. "Listen to me. You're going to die alone out here. Come down and face your punishment. Better to make it a swift death than a lingering one."

"That's right," Falco shouted up into the dim light falling between a net of branches. "I'll give you the first strike. Smash your skull like an egg. You won't feel thing after that."

"Gods, Falco. We want him to surrender."

"You can have the first blow, if you want. He did nearly break your skull."

Varro rolled his eyes, but together they called out for Gallio. Falco continued to look up into the trees, wandering farther from the others. Varro and the triarii pulled together.

Tertius called out for them to regroup.

"I guess he did escape," Varro said, then sighed. He did not want to see his friend die, or to be the one to execute him. He deserved it, of course. For his selfishness endangered everyone else. But neither did he want to think of Gallio starving to death or else torn to pieces by a wolf pack hunting in the woods.

"There you are!" Falco began slapping a trunk, looking up. With Varro's shield on his back and his own on his arm, he looked like a turtle. But his face was dark enough to blend in with the gloom.

"Come down, you shit! You're surrounded."

Varro and the triarii turned in surprise, then rushed to join Falco.

But something streaked down out of the trees, slamming Falco flat.

It had been Gallio, who leapt down and used Falco to break his fall. He now clambered atop his shield, shoving off of it then springing away toward the edge of the woods.

Varro could not run. His first steps felt as if he were sliding on spilled olive oil. In a half-dozen more strides he crashed onto his side. He cried out, his curses matching Falco's distant swears.

One of the triarii hauled him up by his pectoral straps.

"Come on, boy. He's your prize!"

With the triarii's support, he hobbled off toward the chase. Gallio was younger and faster, and did not wear the heavy chain shirts of the pursuing triarii. Through his blurry and swimming vision, he saw Gallio sprinting into the clearing with three men lumbering after him. Falco had only just recovered as Varro passed him.

When he and his supporter both reached the edge of the woods, they found the three triarii had stopped.

At first his fuzzy vision could not discern what had caused them to pause. The golden grass ran away up a short slope to where the sun was poised to vanish. He strained to see what all were looking at.

When the blurry scene did resolve into definite forms, he saw Gallio running with both hands in the air.

A line of horsemen, perhaps a dozen, sat on their horses and watched him approach. All had javelins clutched in hand and ready to cast. But they did not threaten Gallio.

They instead looked across the field to where Varro, Falco, and the triarii had halted.

Gallio reached the line, hands raised and flailing. He pointed back at the woods and his indistinct but desperate begging echoed over the grassland. Within moments, one of the horsemen dismounted, then lifted Gallio onto another's horseback, but not before relieving him of sword and pugio.

"Well, fuck," Falco said with bitter finality.

The horsemen turned their mounts without any hurry or alarm. One by one, each horse and rider vanished over the rise, taking Gallio with them.

"Good-bye, Gallio," Varro said.

"And hello, Philip," Falco added.

7

The wrapping around Varro's head itched under his chin. His skin there was prone to irritation, especially from shaving or the strap of his helmet. But these bandages were especially aggravating. He sat on a chair while the doctor pulled down on his eyes and examined him.

"You seem to have avoided a dozen complications that could have plagued you from this blow. Your neck is fine. Teeth and tongue are fine. You remember all the important things in life. You are lucky beyond what is believable. You must offer thanks to the goddess Fortuna."

"I will," Varro said. "But my vision is still blurry."

The doctor laughed. "You complain? You should be dead and not talking to me. But with rest, you will see straight again. Just keep that gash covered and clean, and you will be fighting in no time."

Varro stared at the far wall of the hospital where an assistant worked over a prone soldier on a bed. The edges of his sight were grayed like dust accumulated in his eyes. He blinked hard twice but nothing changed. Again the doctor chuckled.

"Do not hit your head again, and you shall be fine. But I warn you, if you see spirits or hear voices speaking when you are alone, then you must come to me. Do not go to the temples first, for I have seen their efforts worsen cases like yours."

"I will come see you, Doctor." Varro nodded dutifully. If he saw spirits he might likely die from fright before having a chance to see either doctor or priest.

An assistant led him across the small hospital room to the door. He smiled happily, though the man was a Greek slave, the same as the doctor. They enjoyed a life better than some citizens, so why not smile? Varro nodded to the assistant as he stepped outside to the morning light.

Falco waited for him, arms crossed and leaning next to the door.

"Isn't it just like the army to patch you up for your own execution?"

"Don't say that, Falco. Optio Tertius explained everything to Centurion Drusus, and he will speak to the tribune."

"But it's the consul who decides, isn't it?"

"We're not locked up," Varro said as he joined with Falco in returning to their barracks. "So we will definitely not be executed."

"Funny how you go from believing every officer would enjoy nothing better than your death to believing our officers will intercede to save us. Anyway, we're not locked up but we're all confined to our barracks with posted guards. Our weapons are being held in reserve. We're not locked up because there are no cages of us, not because they're all laughing this off after a night of too much wine."

"But you're here alone."

Falco shrugged. "I don't pretend to understand what the officers want. Tertius sent me to fetch you back. Where are we going to run to, anyway?"

Varro looked toward the stockade walls, so recently erected where nothing had stood before. This was more a test of his vision than pondering his situation. He did not want to think what Gallio's actions would mean for him and the others. He had no control over what happened next. Everyone dies eventually, unless you are as lucky as his great-grandfather was to live over one hundred years. As a boy, he imagined he would live as long. But his first battle swept those illusions aside. He might not live to see twenty. Or tomorrow.

They arrived at the barracks to find three guards from another century posted outside. They gave narrow glances to Varro and Falco, but stepped aside to let them enter. The sudden shift from light to dark dazzled Varro's sight, but he clearly heard the fearful mumbles from the small bunk room.

Everyone was on their bunks. Panthera sat on the edge, nervously swinging his feet. Curio lay on the top bunk and faced the wall. The three recruits mimicked Panthera, sitting on their bunks and wringing their hands.

"We hardly knew him," Sura said. "Why should we die for what he did?"

"We're not going to die," Falco said as he sat on his own bunk. Then he stood again and took Varro's arm. "Here, use the bottom bunk until your head is better. You might fall off the ladder and hurt yourself."

Falco's astonishing kindness silenced the room. But Varro simply inclined his head and accepted the offer. The bed was refreshingly cold. The doctor's assistants had scrubbed him thoroughly and the clean feeling along with the welcoming softness of the bunk made him forget his worries. But only for a moment.

"What do you think they'll do?" Otho asked. He was the biggest of the three recruits, almost a match to Falco. He shared the same heavy brow. Yet somehow despite the heavy brow, Falco's intelligence showed in his eyes. Otho just looked slow overall.

"You'll be stuffed into a bag of vipers and thrown in a lake," Falco said. "Haven't you heard, that's the punishment for treason."

Otho groaned and covered his face with meaty hands. But Varro clucked his tongue.

"Don't make it worse, Falco. The consul will do as he pleases. We'll explain ourselves and try to make him understand the situation. Just focus on what you can do and don't worry for it."

"Easy for you to say," Falco said. "You'll survive a fustuarium by breaking every club with your head. The rest of us don't have heads of stone like you."

Varro surprised himself with a laugh, touching the wrapping enfolding the crown of his head.

They passed the rest of the morning with either worried predictions or heavy silence. Varro noted Curio remained curled up and silent on his top bunk, almost as if he were trying to vanish. He had been most deceived by Gallio. That he had wanted Curio to escort him indicated Gallio thought the smaller man might be easier to overwhelm.

Or that they had plans to escape together.

Varro wondered all morning what he should tell the consul. Would he pick up on this detail? He did not trust Curio. Moreover, he likely knew at least that Falco and he had a valuable secret or even knew about the hidden gold chain. A cunning man might use the opportunity to remove Curio altogether. But Varro shook his head against the thought. He had no proof for his suspicions and no one else had raised it. Falco would be the first to speak out, as he trusted Curio the least of anyone. Yet even he lay quietly on his bunk.

By early afternoon, Optio Tertius and Centurion Drusus summoned them out of their barracks. Both men wore a look of utter contempt. Varro did not blame Drusus. This was his second audience with Tribune Primanus and a first with Consul Galba, both for the poor conduct of Varro and the contubernium. While

Tertius stood a head shorter than Drusus, his strength seemed to outshine the larger centurion.

"You men will be seen by the consul this morning to hear your testimony regarding the desertion of your companion, Lars Gallio. Follow me, and do not speak unless addressed. Keep your eyes down. I mean you especially, Varro. Mind your untamed tongue today."

Varro straightened in surprise. He did not consider his tongue untamed nor see himself as a troublemaker. Yet Falco smirked at him as if to confirm Tertius's concern.

A column of princeps from another century, strangers all, surrounded them as they filed down the main road to headquarters at the center of camp. Soldiers stopped along the road to stare and shake their heads. Some spoke loud enough that words like "traitors" and "cowards" penetrated their line of escorts. Tertius and Drusus marched at the head, and Varro kept his eyes on them rather than those lining the road.

At last they stopped at the parade ground outside of the headquarters. Consul and tribune were not yet present, but chairs and tables with refreshments had been prepared for them, along with their staff of servants. Varro knew they both made a show of living in tents while their soldiers slept in barrack houses. But both their working and living quarters were as extravagant as anything in Rome. A dingy, stinking barrack house did not compare to the opulence of the highest officers' accommodations.

Drusus called them to attention, then he and Tertius stepped to the side. All seven of them lined up, with Varro at the center, Falco to his right, and Panthera on his left. The cold morning sun did little to warm Varro's exposed skin. He had not even worn his wool cloak, instead standing in his plain tunic with arms and legs exposed. At least the wrapping around his head covered his ears against the breeze.

The arrival of Consul Galba and Tribune Primarus brought all the guards and officers in the parade ground to attention. As instructed, Varro cast his eyes down rather than straight ahead. Still, he had never been so close to the consul before. During his orations, Varro was always in the rear with other hastati and velites. Nor had he ever been assigned guard duty to the consul, for that was an honor usually reserved for the triarii or sometimes the princeps. So he studied Consul Galba in the few moments he had.

He was a solid man, more like a soldier than his soft Tribune Primanus. He was middle-aged with iron-colored hair that was defiantly full and wavy. His thick brows remained cocked in an expression of keen judgement. As he stood before his prepared chair, his predatory eyes swept across the line of soldiers. It was like he cast a javelin at each man. Varro felt pierced when Galba settled on him. In fact, he seemed to stare overlong at Varro, enough that he had to drop his eyes.

Both consul and tribune sat, but all others remained at attention. Slaves and servants fluttered around them, filling cups or fussing over their comfort. Consul Galba's tunic was a startling white with a purple stripe along its hem to distinguish his senatorial status. A young girl waited on him. At first, Varro thought nothing of the slave, other than she had wide and beautiful brown eyes. But he realized she constantly looked to him whenever not occupied with the consul. Whatever her reason, she was not shy about it nor did she seem friendly. In fact, Varro wondered if she sneered at him. Even in his current predicament, a slave should not display such arrogance. In any other setting, he would have demanded an apology.

Then Consul Galba spoke. His voice was clear and full of authority, with an accent of high Roman authority that only the greatest politicians could hope to produce. Varro guessed these leaders of Rome trained themselves to speak as if they were voicing the will of Jupiter himself.

"I have learned the facts of Lars Gallio's desertion," he said. "As is customary, Lars Gallio is convicted of treason and will be subject to execution upon his apprehension. If the gods favor him, they will see he dies before returning for justice at my hands. For there is nothing more odious to me than the crime of desertion. To abandon one's country and family, to abandon one's fellow soldiers who serve without complaint and offer their blood for the preservation of Roman society, such an act is disgusting. There is no forgiveness for one who has turned his back on Rome."

Galba leaned back in his chair, then sipped wine from a silver cup that caught a spark of light. Varro was close enough that he saw his own distorted reflection in the polished silver. But the consul set the cup aside then leaned on his knees.

"Now the question remains, what is the fate of his companions? Men who should have known their brother planned to abandon them. I tell you this. I am wrathful to the condemned, but I lead with an open heart. Another consul would make you all examples in Lars Gallio's place. What have you to say in your own defense? I will hear your arguments, one at a time. Keep them brief and make them with consideration. You've had all night to prepare."

Both Consul Galba and Tribune Primanus tilted their heads back as if straining to see to the bottom of a deep gorge. Varro certainly felt as if he were at the bottom of a well where the water rose with each of his breaths. Centurion Drusus now stepped out before them and indicated Cordus, the youngest recruit, at the far end of the line.

"Explain yourself to the consul. Keep it short or I'll silence you myself."

Cordus and the other recruits offered little more than pleas for their lives that seemed to disgust Galba more than convince him. Panthera wasted his moment apologizing for their foolishness. Drusus cut him off.

When the order arrived at Varro in the center, Drusus pointed him out, but Galba raised his hand.

"I would hear his statement last."

Drusus's heavy brow furrowed but he continued on to Falco.

"Sir, Lars Gallio completely deceived us. He had made up his mind to desert long ago, but hid this intent behind a pretense of accepting his lot in life. He never lapsed in this pretense, sir. There is no way any of us could have known he would actually desert."

"Yet you knew he was dissatisfied," Galba said. This was the first time he had shown any interest in their reports. Tribune Primarus seemed to wake up from sleeping with his eyes open, and refocused on Falco.

"Sir, in complete honesty, no one is ever satisfied while enlisted. As I see it, sir, we are here to serve Rome. Our satisfaction has no place in this duty. Yet it is not uncommon to complain outside the hearing of the officers. Gallio's complaints were not unique."

Centurion Drusus's fists balled and his face reddened. But Consul Galba laughed heartily, and waved Drusus on to Curio.

"Sir, Lars Gallio was my best friend, or so I believed. He wanted me to accompany him during his escape rather than Varro. He probably believed I would be easier to overcome. Even I did not know he planned to desert."

Galba's lightened mood swiftly faded with Curio's testimony. He curled his lip then drank again from his cup. Varro doubted he was mad at Gallio's deceit of a close friend but instead disappointed in an uninformative report full of self-pity. Varro would have shaken his head if he had been so daring. Only Falco had offered any cogent reasoning to get them out of trouble. It would all be with him to sway the consul.

As Galba finished his wine, he handed the cup to the slave girl. She stared at Varro with a venomous light in her beautiful eyes. In fact, it seemed as if she might call out a curse to him, but Consul

Galba interrupted her. He spoke to her with gentle words and a smile utterly contrary to the judgmental twist he normally wore.

After their brief exchange, the slave girl backed away to join the others waiting behind him and the tribune. He turned to Primanus now, as Centurion Drusus waited at the center of the parade ground.

"What do you think, Primanus? You've heard all but one man's testimony."

"I've heard excuses and pleas for clemency. I have seen this lot before and not long ago. They had a number of excuses for fleeing from battle. They are a disgrace to our standard, and I would see them all subjected to the fustuarium as an example to others. The excuses of one more soldier will do nothing to change my mind."

Galba nodded. The slave girl behind him tilted her chin at Varro as if vindicated for some crime against her. But Varro had no moment for her. His mind raced with what he should say next.

Centurion Drusus cleared his throat then addressed the consul. "Sir, with respect, each man was to have his say."

With an impatient wave, he motioned that Varro should speak. Yet despite his apparent indifference, he seemed vexed. Varro could not place the consul's mood, but Galba's eyes narrowed and the corners of his mouth tugged down. He leaned back on his chair and hid his face, drinking from his silver cup.

"Sir, we should all be subjected to the fustuarium as is customary when a contubernale deserts. This is well known to everyone."

Drusus, who had been staring off at a distant point, whipped his head around. Varro saw both Panthera and Falco flinch at the edges of his sight.

"That is true," Galba said, setting his cup with a clack to the table beside him. "Are you asking for this punishment?"

"No, sir. I am recognizing that we are all aware of the danger we face. These men are frightened, sir. They are also inexperienced. They cannot be expected to provide any useful testimony in their own defense. Of course, under these circumstances we all will beg for clemency."

In defiance of his optio's orders, he lifted his gaze to Tribune Primanus and met his eyes. His small, heavily lashed eyes widened in surprise at this bold gesture. But Varro did not push the moment, and let his gaze fall to his feet.

"You are not frightened?" Galba asked.

"I would be a fool to not be frightened, sir. But neither do I fear death. Sir, in the matter of Lars Gallio's desertion, we are responsible for failing to understand his real intentions. While military custom dictates we should be executed as an example to others, I would ask that the consul and tribune consider the real affect this would have on morale."

"All right, Varro," Centurion Drusus said. "Enough with this."

"Centurion!" Galba sat forward in his chair, real anger now flashing beneath his knitted brows. "I would hear this soldier's words."

Drusus saluted and stood aside. Tribune Primanus leaned forward as if he hung between a curse and collecting himself. He looked sidelong to Galba, who in turn started directly at Varro. He extended his hand to him.

"Continue. What do you estimate would be the effect on morale?"

"Sir, prior to Gallio's desertion, I worked construction with a team of veterans and many have come directly from fighting Hannibal. These men are at the limits of their patience with army life and discipline. They have sacrificed their families and farms to continue to serve in what many feel is a cause unworthy of Rome."

"That is outrageous!" Tribune Primanus shot to his feet. Had the tribune a sword, he could have slain Varro. Yet Galba twisted on his chair and cocked his brow.

"Tribune, as hard as it is to hear, this may be the best report of the truth we can get. Please sit and let him finish."

Primanus sat again, fussing sharply with the hem of his tunic and making unvoiced curses.

"I'm sorry to cause dismay, sir." Varro lowered his eyes again. "This is the sentiment I've heard and know is not limited to the few I've interacted with. I believe, sir, that our executions would only reinforce their bitterness and lead to possible rebellion. Particularly as we were deceived by Gallio and did all that we could to find him before he went to the enemy. Sir, if I could capture Gallio myself, I would drag him before the century and strike the first blow in his execution. But for myself and my companions, we are still prepared to serve Rome loyally and with our lives. Let those lives be spent facing Philip rather than at the hands of our fellows."

Primanus snorted. "My legion will rebel because a handful of unknown recruits were executed according to military law? I applaud the creativity, Varro. But your argument is hardly convincing."

"Sir, a full cup needs only a drop more to overflow."

Now Centurion Drusus growled at Varro, and no one stopped him. Varro's pulsing neck pushed against the wrapping under his jaw. The wound at his crown throbbed with a blunt ache. He would say no more or else risk overflowing the tribune's cup, which seemed to brim with anger. Yet he did risk glancing up once more.

Galba folded his arms and lowered his head in consideration. Varro caught his slave girl biting her lip as if in anticipation, fixated on Varro with undisguised hate.

"I have heard everyone," Galba said. "Now I must determine a satisfactory outcome."

"Sir, may I speak?"

Every head turned down the line to find Optio Tertius stepping forward. Centurion Drusus was already reddening with a fresh burst of rage. Yet Galba diffused it with a wave of his hand.

"You were present, Optio. I should consider your words as well."

"Thank you, sir." Tertius looked to Varro, his expression flat and emotionless. "I believe everything Varro has said. He and his companions were deceived, as was I, at Gallio's rehabilitation. They made every effort to find and capture Gallio before he escaped with a mounted enemy scouting party. I ask the tribune and consul to consider this in your decision. The Macedonians must be close, and we will need all capable soldiers to fight them. I can attest these men, though mostly recruits, will acquit themselves in battle."

"You make a heavy claim," Primanus said, his heavy lashes drooping.

"Sir, I have trained these recruits myself. The others have been tested in battle."

"And they have fled battle," Primanus said with a sniff.

Tertius, having said more than Varro would have ever expected, did not answer. Instead, he saluted again and returned to his place in line without looking to the others.

"Very well," Galba said. "I've spent enough of my morning on this matter. I am prepared to pass my judgement."

Varro's breathing came short. Galba stood from his chair, and the tribune joined him. Galba studied each man, again pausing on Varro with a brief smirk.

"I would pardon these men," he said in a lower, conversational tone. He turned to his tribune and touched his shoulder. "I know you feel otherwise. But will you reconsider?"

Of course the tribune could not defy the consul. Varro felt a tightness in his chest dissolve and he might have collapsed in relief were his life not dependent on remaining as unseen and unheard as possible.

"I understand the consul's will." Now the tribune sneered at Varro and the others. "I agree to their pardons. But there is a condition I would impose."

"A condition?" Galba said, retracting his hand to his chest.

"If I may, sir?" Primanus stepped forward to Varro. "You claimed you'd execute Gallio yourself if you could bring him before me. Very well, I will consider you pardoned from execution on the condition that you bring me Gallio or his head. Until such a time, your offense will be merely suspended. If during this time, you commit one more offense of any kind—any kind—you will all be subject to death by flogging."

"That's impossible, sir!" Varro said. "What if the enemy has killed him already? Even if he's alive we'll never find him."

"Those are the conditions of my agreement," Primanus said, but turning to Galba. "That is, if the consul agrees. This preserves their lives but also ensures we do not set a dangerous precedent, sir."

Galba's wry expression faded and his critical countenance returned. He narrowed his eyes and answered in a tired voice.

"I agree."

8

Chapter-8

Varro interposed his shield before Falco's strike. The wooden practice sword slammed against the scutum to send a shock wave up Varro's arm straight to the wound on the top of his head. He stepped back, rather than follow up with a strike that Falco expected. So he paused, staring at Varro from beneath his bronze helmet. He still had not replaced the feathers, but had at least removed the stumps from their holders. With the sun behind him, his expression remained hidden in shadow.

"What are you two doing?" Tertius appeared behind Varro, shouting loud enough to ring his ears. "Are you going to kiss? Falco, this is the enemy. Do you kiss the enemy? No! You stab him through the gut. One quick stab and spill his innards all over your feet. Then you do the same to the next one foolish enough to stand before a Roman soldier in battle."

Falco stood to attention. Varro turned to face the sneering

optio, his vine cane poised to lash Varro's exposed hamstrings. Denying him the opportunity only heightened his rage.

"Are you going to tell me Varro's delicate little head kept you, Caius Falco, from executing the form you have been drilling twice daily for a year? Is that your excuse?"

"Sir," Falco stammered. "He looked pale."

"Pale! By Mars's red eyes, man! If the enemy had a cold would you help him blow his nose? Strike! Let Varro block it if he doesn't want to get hurt."

Tertius lashed his vine cane and it slapped against Varro's scutum.

"The two of you aren't even sweating. What kind of drill is this?"

"Sorry, sir." Varro and Falco both spoke at once. Tertius shook his head.

"Keep it going. I want to fill a silver cup with your sweat. So that it overflows."

Tertius smirked at Varro, who blinked at the obvious taunt from the morning's audience with Consul Galba. Then the optio flicked his vine cane behind his back and turned his wrath to the others in the century who drilled in the surrounding field.

"Sura, are you holding your gladius or your cock? I am going to break your wrists if you don't improve that stance."

Varro and Falco stared after their optio. Varro jammed his finger beneath the wrapping under his chin and scratched.

"How are we supposed to sweat when it's so cold outside?" Falco tapped Varro's leg with his heavy wooden sword.

"I can't believe he spoke for us," Varro said, resuming his stance. He kept his left foot forward which put his leg in the curve of his shield. He held his wooden sword, twice as heavy as a gladius, ready against it.

"A lot of good it did." Falco struck again. Varro knocked the sword aside but found Falco had withdrawn to the protection of his shield. So he skipped sideways to find an opening.

"The tribune would have killed us. So that's better than what might have happened if he hadn't spoken up."

Varro struck, clipping the edge of Falco's shield. But his larger and stronger friend had been expecting this. He slammed into Varro, sending him crashing to his back. Out of instinct, he pulled the shield over his body. Falco set his foot to it, and jabbed his exposed right shoulder. The dull point dug into his flesh.

"You'll bleed out from that one," Falco said. "My round, as usual."

The cold ground seemed to spin around him for a moment, but Varro simply laughed and extended his arm for help up. Falco's grip was warm around his wrist.

"How are we going to find Gallio?" Varro dusted off his tunic and got into stance again. But Falco was a blurry shape wavering before him.

"You don't look good," Falco said. "The doctor didn't want you doing this so soon."

"Tertius doesn't care what the doctor said. I don't care what he said. We need a plan to find Gallio. It won't be long before one of us makes a mistake. We're all new to army life. We're bound to make a mistake of some sort before Gallio turns up."

"Gallio's not turning up," Falco said. But he had dropped his guard and now stepped in closer. He was no longer as fuzzy, and Varro read the concern in his face. "That little shit is gone and left us all to die. I can only hope the Macedonians tortured him for information before killing him."

"How could he be so selfish?" Varro staggered back, and Falco caught him.

"All right, I don't care what Tertius says. This drilling will kill you if we keep at it." Falco steadied him with both hands. "Let's get you to the barracks."

To Varro's surprise, he found Tertius allowed the excuse with a curt nod. All the hastati of the century were at drill this morning, directly following Galba's audience. Those not absorbed in their drills stared after them as they left the field. Varro heard whispers and read the disgusted expressions. He stared ahead and blocked them from his mind.

The barracks were empty and he and Falco were alone. He helped Varro remove his gear then assisted him to the lower bunk. The warm softness of the bed welcomed him.

"Back home I would've complained about a bed this hard," Varro said, closing his eyes. "But here it feels wonderful."

"The army has a way of making shit smell like perfume," Falco said. "I guess they do it by making everything else smell worse than shit."

Falco left him and began digging through their packs in the front room. Without saying as much, Varro knew he checked on their gold chains. He returned, his hobnailed sandals clomping against the floor.

"Tertius didn't say I needed to return. But I suppose I should do the right thing."

"Don't get us in trouble. Say, did you see Galba's slave girl this morning?"

"Varro, I was busy seeing my life pass before my eyes. You were examining his slaves?"

"Not specifically, but there was a young girl there with beautiful eyes. She was staring at me with such hate. I don't know why, but I swear she was waiting on Galba's orders to see us executed. I think she was bitterly disappointed when we walked away from that audience."

"So what? She's just a slave. Anyway, it seems everyone outside of the contubernium is disappointed we didn't die. That makes your argument about soldiers uprising seem weak."

Varro waved his hand away. "It was all I could think of at the time. But that slave, why would she want me to die? It makes no sense."

Falco shrugged. "Nothing has made sense for quite a long time. Why try to force it? Rest your broken head. Worry about your next meal. Keep out of trouble. That's all we have to do. And survive the war. Simple, really."

After Falco left, he had another hour to ponder the slave and the events of the morning. Galba and Primanus seemed at odds with each other over more than just the fate of Varro and his companions. Yet Galba was consul and the last word in command. He outranked Primanus both in the army and in Rome. Also, Galba seemed to know Varro, which he found strange. Did he know of his father's involvement with Decius Oceanus and his mysterious patron? Centurion Protus had warned him of larger things that happened beyond Varro's small world. Was this a glimpse into that?

When the contubernium returned in an hour, Optio Tertius ducked into their barracks to address all of them.

"Be on your best behavior. For now, Gallio's position will remain unfilled. That could change, but as you can imagine, it would be unfair to the replacement to share your fates. But he would. So, think hard on how you'll find Gallio."

"Sir, you know we cannot find him," Varro said. "Why would Consul Galba agree to that condition if he wanted us to live? He might as well have just condemned us."

Tertius cocked his head. "As clever as you are, you don't see your way out? You disappoint me, Varro. Though maybe Gallio smashed that cleverness out of your head."

"Sir, I'm not sure there is a way out. The Macedonians won't waste time training Gallio on how to fight with a pike. They'll use him for intelligence then kill or enslave him. We'll never find him."

Tertius rubbed the back of his neck.

"Well, the gods might be kind. Though I agree with you, Varro. The chances to find Gallio are vastly slim. But if all of you aspire to great acts of courage and heroism, I think the consul would make a full pardon no matter what his tribune may want."

"What kind of acts, sir?" Cordus, the youngest of the recruits, stared hopefully at the optio.

"The kind that no one expects you to survive. You'll know the moment when it comes, for it will go against your basic sense of self-preservation. Basically, if you think doing something would kill you but would advance our position in some way, then do it. Do that often enough, and I'm sure you will be pardoned."

"Or dead," Falco added.

Tertius laughed. "Or that. But death is everywhere. Don't hide from it, for it will find you eventually."

The optio left them on this strained note. Varro understood the optio's intention, but wondered if Galba would ever hear of their deeds. If Primanus, paradoxically the very man who selected him for this legion, stifled those deeds, then death was assured. Mistakes were inevitable but glory was not.

Varro enjoyed a day of rest and marveled at Tertius's acceptance of his injuries. He had driven Gallio with such zeal when his leg was broken, Varro wondered if the optio had suspected it was not as injured as Gallio claimed.

The next day, Philip the Fifth of Macedonia arrived with his army.

It coincided with the arrival of the war elephants from Rome. The camp was as close to chaos as Varro had ever seen it, which by civilian standards would be undetectable. Yet the soldiers gossiped and strayed from their posts to glimpse the magnificent beasts filing in from the north gate or else to stare south to the hill where Philip set up a massive infantry screen to protect the construction of his fort.

"The battle is coming," Falco reported to him on the second

day after Philip's arrival. Varro was still resting on his bunk, but no longer needed to wrap his head. "Rumor is he has twenty thousand infantry and about two thousand cavalry. We're outnumbered, lily, in case your head is still too addled to figure it out."

"I bet those elephants are equal to a hundred men each." Varro had heard their distant trumpeting and tried to imagine what they would look like up close.

"They're the most enormous beasts I've ever seen, and ugly tempers. But what good would a gentle monster be on the battlefield? Anyway, it's amazing that Philip couldn't find us until Gallio joined their scouts. Then they show up the next day."

Varro waved his hand and puffed at the implied accusation.

"They had practically found us when they stumbled on the forage party."

"No, your head was scrambled, so you don't remember right." Falco sat on the empty bunk opposite him, then looked out the door to where the rest of the contubernium lingered outside. "Everyone is blaming Gallio for leading the Macedonians to the best spot to build their camp. Those scouts were leaving when Gallio rushed out to them. They hadn't found us, but barely missed us in the woods. Gallio fixed that for them."

Varro snorted and turned his head. "You overestimate Gallio's worth. He's just one of us. What do we know about anything? I doubt I could find my way back to camp. Gallio is no better."

"Well, you underestimate everyone else, lily. I think you're the one lacking directional sense. I don't want to believe it either, but Gallio's desertion and Philip's arrival are a bit too well matched. Even if Gallio didn't lead him here, everyone thinks he did. That's what matters."

Turning back to Falco, he studied his friend. Shadows from his brow ridge hid his eyes. But Varro read the tension in his posture.

"Is it bad?"

"Someone spit at Otho. Luckily Panthera prevented a fight."

"By Jupiter! A fight would be just the thing to send us all before the tribune again."

Varro sat up in his bunk. His head no longer spun at sudden movements or changes in position, though he still wobbled.

"That's why I'm saying this is serious trouble. Word is spreading fast that a deserter led Philip here, and that it was Gallio."

Varro rubbed his face with his palms, leaving it covered so his hot breath flooded his face.

"Philip was going to find us eventually, or we would find him. What's the problem? Didn't we come all this way to fight him?"

"I agree. But it's one thing for us to catch him unaware in his camp. It's something else when one of our own leads him practically to our gates overnight. Now we're surprised and on the defense. Consul Galba hasn't issued any commands to mobilize for two days. I don't think he was ready for this many enemies in a fortified position right at our gates."

Letting his wet breath bathe his face, Varro pressed his palms into his eyes. He did not want to imagine Gallio committing such a deep betrayal. Yet what else could he use to bargain for his life? Varro moaned and scrubbed his face.

"Tell me about it," Falco said. "I'm sure once the fighting gets underway everyone will forget about it. But until then, we've got to keep the testy ones in our contubernium under control."

Varro let his hands fall to his lap, refreshing his face with the cool air of the bunk room. Falco leaned on his knees, still staring out the door.

"And who are the testy ones?"

"All of us except Panthera. Look, maybe you should speak to Tertius about keeping us out of sight for a while. He seems to like you. If I asked, he'd have me clean out latrines with a spoon."

"I don't know about that. He's just eased up because Gallio almost killed me."

Falco now turned to him, raising a skeptical brow. "How are you feeling? It must be great lying on the bed half a day and doing actual light duty."

"I get dizzy still, but I think I'm ready for full duty."

They fell into a brief silence. A shadow flickered from the door, drawing both of them, then Curio appeared in the room.

"The cavalry is going to harass the Macedonian screen. Word just came down."

"Good for them," Falco said, waving aside the news. "All the rich men can go catch some javelins for us. Maybe the Macedonians will use them all up before we get out there."

"I wish we could go with them," Varro said.

"Remember, lily, all the peace and nonviolence stuff. You don't want to volunteer for killing."

"What?" Curio, being a late addition to their contubernium, did not know Varro's past. Now only Falco and Panthera knew of his vow to his great-grandfather.

"Never mind it," Varro said. "I don't want to get out and kill. I want to capture someone we can question. If Gallio led the Macedonians here, then they'll know it and might also know what happened to him. It's all fresh in their minds and Gallio's fate might still be undecided."

"What does it matter what happened to him?" Curio asked. "We're not able to bring him back. He's probably enslaved by now. What a fool."

"I agree," Falco said. "We're not going to find him even if he did lead the Macedonians here."

"But knowing his fate is better than not knowing," Varro said. "And if he is alive still, then there is a chance we can bring him back. I know it's not much of a chance, but anything can happen."

"That's true," Falco said. "I could be elected to the Senate too. But the actual chance is impossible. Maybe you ought to rest your head for another day."

The three stared at the floor. Varro studied his toes, which were dark with dirt. He needed a good bath but had neglected it during his recovery.

"We could still go out with the cavalry," Curio said in a small voice.

"We'll steal some horses and ride out?" Falco slapped his knee. "If I steal a cavalryman's horse, then I'm going to ride it back to Rome."

"Not with the cavalry," Curio said. "Velites will accompany them. I still have friends among them. There aren't any officers organizing them other than the cavalry, who wouldn't know one from another. We could join them."

"That is madness," Falco said. "And I think Tertius will notice we're missing."

"It's a harassing action," Varro said. "We won't have to stand ready. If things turn against the cavalry they'll just ride back. I think Galba is trying to buy himself more time for a better plan."

"This is where I imagine an officer screaming in your face about knowing what the consul is planning." Falco stood from the bunk. "I want nothing more than to drag Gallio before the tribune and restore my honor. But I think Optio Tertius has a better plan. Let's do something heroic rather than the stupidest thing we can imagine. How about that?"

"I'm the only one who can reasonably be missing," Varro said. "I'm still supposed to be in this bunk. I'll take the risk."

Falco put his hands over his head.

"It doesn't matter if it's just you. We'll all be in trouble and we'll end up in a line of our friends who will club us to death. Varro, this is nonsense."

"Now's the time to find out what happened to Gallio. It's fresh in their minds. And I have a feeling if it's just me who goes, Tertius will cover."

"You have all sorts of feelings," Falco said, sneering. "But not all are worth heeding. If Tertius covers then he becomes part of the plan. He'll be in line with us getting his brains bashed out, which he would not do for us."

"Curio, can you help me get in with the velites?"

"We have to act now," he said. His youthful face seemed to brighten. "You only need some javelins to look the part."

"Then let's go." Varro stood up, pushing Falco aside. "We'll be swift, and if the gods are kind, I'll find out about Gallio. Pray to Fortuna for me."

9

Varro pushed the wolf head off his brows as he stood in line with the hundreds of other velites assembled by the south gate. The fur lining itched his head and hung low over his eyes. The long wolf body hung as a heavy cloak. He decided he preferred his own helmet to the velites kit. They stood to one side of the equites, the cavalry comprised of Rome's wealthiest citizens. High atop their horses, their proud and shining bronze helmets gleamed in the sun. He had no contempt for these men as was common for poorer soldiers of the hastati. They were fighting the same enemy and enduring the same hardship. They were paid more and many were only interested in accumulating the necessary glory to secure a senatorial position in Rome. But this natural order did not bother Varro. This was how Rome grew in prestige.

The young men around him were his own age. In total, the harassing force comprised seven hundred velites and half as many cavalry. The velites were poor and young. Varro had originally been assigned to their number but was pulled into the hastati by Optio Latro. In truth, he was financially better off than these men, at least as long as he remained owner of his father's farm.

"I feel naked without a scutum," Falco whispered next to him. "And the little shit charged me two obols for this fucking rat fur hat."

"It's a wolfskin and you look bold in it," Varro said, smirking.

"Two obols," he repeated with more force. "That's a whole day's pay. Did your man ask for as much to take his place?"

"We're asking them to take a chance. Two obols is more than they make in a day. They deserve it and more still."

"I thought Curio would set us up with some of his friends and not brigands." Falco sniffed. "Two obols."

"I didn't ask you to come with me." Varro scanned the other velites. Most chatted with their companions while some stared ahead with a look of dread.

"Well, I had to come with you. What if you get hit on the head again? I'll have to carry you out of that mess."

"We're velites, Falco. We're going to throw javelins and run away. Then we can look for wounded enemies to drag off and question while the cavalry confuses everything."

The chatter of the assembled troops ended when Consul Galba appeared. He too was mounted on a horse and dressed in a muscled pectoral. The red horsehair crest flowing from his helmet lifted in the wind. His critical eyes swept the ranks of cavalry. For the lesser velites, Varro was glad Galba spared only a glance. Still, he let the wolf head slip down over his brow to obscure himself.

"Philip is no doubt expecting a harassing action from us. Proceed halfway to his screen position then entice him forward. He will expect you to make a quick attack then fall back and regroup. Do not play to his expectations. Drive him from the field and let him know the power of a Roman soldier."

The soldiers all shouted, and Varro joined as well. Along with the other velites, he raised one of his sheaves of javelins in the air.

The cavalry drew their swords, not the gladius of the foot soldier but the longer Greek pattern swords. They hailed the consul, then the officers ordered them to march out the gates. Other soldiers cheered them on from the sides. Varro looked for his contubernium or officers. He did not see them in the roaring crowds.

"I didn't see Drusus or Tertius," Varro said as they followed the cavalry out.

"Doesn't mean they didn't see us," Falco said, pulling the wolf head down.

They marched hard toward the screening enemy in the plains before the hill where Philip constructed camp. Varro could see the ragged edge of a stake wall and he knew behind the screening soldiers, men were hard at work creating a ditch. Keeping pace with the cavalry was easy for him and Falco. Their legs were thick with muscles from marching into hills in full gear and pack. But the velites were skirmishers and did not train as hard. Many lagged behind, and cavalry officers constantly fell back to ensure they kept up.

The line halted nearly a half mile from the enemy. The senior cavalry officer, the praefectus, arranged the lines and decided on the strategy. It seemed he intended a more conventional battle, exhorting the cavalry to hit hard and cut down the men on the ground rather than hit and run. The velites were to close after casting javelins rather than run, then use every opportunity to break open the lines.

"These are not Macedonians but Cretan and Illyrian mercenaries," he said. "They will not stand and fight to the last. But we shall show them no mercy today."

The men cheered. Varro ensured he and Falco remained at the center mass of the velites. But soon they were arranged into a long and loose line that would precede the cavalry. The snorting of horses was now loud from the rear, and straight ahead he heard the shouted orders of the enemy officers.

"It doesn't feel right being out here with just a fur cloak," Falco said. "These javelins are as light as sticks and this sword is a child's toy."

"We're not here to fight," Varro said, lowering his voice. "We'll fight as we must. But we need to concentrate on getting information from the enemy."

Falco rotated his shoulder and his neck, then looked around the assembled velites.

"This is a lot looser than being in a maniple. I guess we just do what we want. Throw some javelins and get out of the way. It's not bad, really."

Velites were never intended to stick in a battle, but served as simple harassers. Some, such as Curio, would distinguish themselves in individual combat with an aim for a promotion. Most would throw their five javelins then get aside and help carry the injured from the battle lines.

Yet today promised to be a different battle for the velites. Many would have their chance to distinguish themselves in combat.

They stood in their loose formation ahead of the ordered blocks of cavalry. Varro shifted between watching the vague shapes of enemies in the distance and turning to the ranks of cavalry behind him. These men wore heavy chain shirts like the triarii did, though most were much younger. Ranks of red horsehair plumes pointed west in the light breeze. Their horses were brown or black, though some were spotted with white.

"You're going to break your neck looking behind," Falco said. "Or draw attention to yourself."

"They look magnificent. I've never seen so many horses lined up like this. Who could stand against their charge?"

Falco shrugged and shifted his weight as he stood waiting for enemy action.

At last the enemy line in the distance began to advance. They could not leave the Roman challenge unanswered.

Varro knew, but did not see, the enemy had sent men forward to scout them. Once they realized they faced a skirmish force, they were emboldened. Varro readied his first javelin, which was nothing like the heavy and light pila he carried to battle. These were long and flexible with sharp iron points. Most would not penetrate good armor, but would stick in shields to make them unwieldy. Some would find their marks in flesh.

A decurion, the cavalry version of a centurion, trotted his horse to the front of the velites. Atop his black horse and wearing scoured mail, he gleamed in the midmorning sun.

"Advance to contact,' he said. "Strike and hold the center and the cavalry will crush them from the flanks."

"Hold the center," Varro repeated, shaking his head. Falco grumbled.

"That's asking much of men armed with sticks and toy swords."

But the velites raised their fists and shouted with joy. Most were eager to prove themselves and claim an enemy life.

They began to close with the enemy, moving at a jog. Varro's hobnailed sandals swept over the dry, dead grass. It was an expanse of amber soon to be stained red. Yet the velites only grew more excited as they neared the ever-darkening line of mercenaries arrayed before them. The jog grew into a run when individual enemies resolved from the dark line.

Varro recalled the bristling wall of pikes the Macedonians had used in their last-ditch defense of their town several months ago. But these were soldiers from Crete and Illyria, and they carried round shields of bronze and heavy spears. Their eyes were hidden in the shadows of their bronze helmets which flew plumes of horsehair. Strange beasts decorated their shields.

"Stick close to me," Falco said. "Don't run off."

The mass of velites now reached the extreme range of their

javelins. Each man clutched four in their off-hand and one in their casting hand.

Shouts rose in the throats of all the velites. Varro screamed with them, casting his first javelin at an enemy with a horse head painted on his shield. He seemed impossibly far off, but the light javelin launched from his strong arm caught the wind and flew.

The man stumbled back into the crowd of his fellows. Varro did not know if it was his cast or another's to take him down. He readied his next javelin as he sprinted over the grass. He overtook wolf-headed velites on either side. Falco whooped and cast his javelins at his right side.

Three more of Varro's javelins sailed into the bristling mass ahead. The elation of flying above the ground and sending death at his enemies began to dissolve into a more practical fear of running into a wall of shields supported with spears.

Yet hundreds of other javelins streaked pale and gleaming overhead. The air rippled with their flight. The velites screamed with joy and the enemy screamed with pain as the shafts clacked over shields and helmets. Varro saw the gap collapse before him. Stricken men had fallen dead simply standing before an attacking enemy and never raising their spears.

The final wave of javelins arced into the wide blocks of enemy infantry. The clank and thump of their landing was loud in Varro's ears as he cast his final javelin then drew his sword.

Rather than fall back as a velite attack should, hundreds of wolf heads leapt screaming into the staggered lines of enemies.

"Mars be with us," Falco shouted, drawing his sword. "And Pluto greet the enemy!"

Varro and Falco reached the enemy line at the front of the charge. The constricting heat and ear-shattering roar of battle enveloped him. His ears throbbed against the crashes of swords on shields. Before him, white eyes looked out from dark-bearded faces. Blood sprayed across his sight. His sword arm moved of its own accord. Without his shield, he still punched and stabbed. Only now he bloodied his own knuckles on shields and armor.

These mercenaries were not heavy infantry, and so the velites were an even match despite their lacking shields. Varro felt terribly exposed without one covering him. The terror of being run through with a spear fueled his own attack.

For he did not lack examples of the fate awaiting him from one well-placed enemy spear. At his feet, wolf-headed men rolled and held their punctured guts in place as blood poured between their fingers. One velite hunched over with hands to his face, though half of it had been sheared off to reveal his teeth. A simple helmet and cheek-guard could have saved him. But poverty ensured velites had nothing but the gods to defend them.

He and Falco worked in mutual support as they would in a maniple. But this was less like the ordered, mechanical slaughter the centuries delivered. This was a crazed brawl carried only on the fervor of the velite attack. In the swirling, spinning chaos, Varro found he and Falco were out of step with their supporting solders. He risked becoming enfolded and cut off.

Rather than press ahead, he and Falco held their ground and let the velites catch up. Varro had no concept of how much time had passed since joining. He was sprayed with blood and his wolf head dripped gore into his eyes, blurring his vision. Yet the cavalry had not charged yet. Nor could Varro see behind, for to turn back would invite an enemy spear.

The enemy line fell back, whereas it had expected to hold firm against an initial javelin volley. They had probably anticipated a cavalry charge which they would then surround and pull down.

"Looks like you've got your pick of men to interrogate." Falco backed up to him as the enemy receded. The fear in their eyes faded as they understood the velites did not intend to retreat. They were hardening for their own counterattack.

Between Varro and the enemy, bodies had piled up. But the

mercenaries had not backed up far enough to risk grabbing one of the twitching or screaming wounded. Some velites still had javelins, which they cast with terrifying accuracy into the enemies on the ground who cried from their wounds.

"We've got to reach the edges of this battle." Varro used his moment to search both ends of the line for a lighter passage, finding neither clear.

"Why did you pick the middle anyway?" Falco shook his head. "Just pick a flank. The cavalry are going to hit them any moment."

Varro realized the rumbling thunder he heard was the pounding of hooves, and the steely eyes of the enemy were not for the velites before them but for the cavalry striking their flanks.

"Forward!"

It was the husky roar of an officer, but Varro could not place him beyond somewhere over his left shoulder.

The sky had darkened as if the gods drew a blanket of clouds to hide the carnage from their sight. Varro did not run forward, but instead cut across the line to find the right flank. He crashed into velites racing ahead with bloodied swords and faces bright against the gathering darkness. Some had lost their wolf furs and now looked no more than serving boys in red-stained tunics waving thin swords. But their work had been brutally efficient and they overflowed with lusty confidence as they smashed into Varro cutting across the line.

Now he saw the racing cavalry. Sleek and muscular horses galloped past the tide mark of bloodied corpses. Their mighty hooves shuddered the earth and their brazen riders cried the glory and power of Rome. Their red plumes trailed behind their proud heads.

Varro could not see them strike the line. Too many men obscured their view. But he saw their standard held high overhead and heard the scream of horses and men when the charge bashed into the flanks. It was the slam of a giant hammer upon a massive anvil. The wave of force crumpled the mercenaries to the center, squeezing them into the wave of velites.

Across this line, Varro and Falco stumbled and crashed to the edge of the right flank, freshly demarcated by earthen divots from hundreds of hooves.

"Gods see the glory of Rome," Falco said. "Look at this."

Varro, who had kept his head down to avoid tripping over a casualty, now looked to the thicket of combatants.

The cavalry did not hit and run, which again the enemy would have expected. Instead, their horses drove deep into their flanks. Horses screamed and kicked, destroying friend and foe alike. The Macedonian mercenaries, resisting the weight of hundreds of heavy cavalry on each flank, bent to the middle where velites sold them bloody death.

"They'll route unless reinforced," Varro said, his voice a calm contrast to the rage flowing all around them.

"Let's get to work," Falco said, then began flipping men over with his sword readied to strike.

Varro picked over gruesome sights. He found seven fingers neatly arranged in the grass so that all the tips touched together like the petals of a bloody flower. Yet whoever had done this died soon after, for all around were corpses. He moved past this, trying to ignore the severed hands or hunks of flesh left behind. Most men had perished to a simple puncture wound. But Varro flipped over enough horrifying cuts to ensure a lifetime of nightmares.

Varro spotted an enemy whose ribs heaved as he lay on his side. Keeping an eye on the battle with a rear rank no more than a javelin cast distant, he wove a path to the man. Falco split off to seek others among the wounded sprawled on the ground.

He flipped the enemy onto his back and looked down into a dark and sweaty face framed with black hair and beard. Blood leaked between his gritted, yellow teeth. Varro touched the point of his sword to the enemy's throat.

"Answer my questions or your death will be painful." Varro stumbled with the threat, as he had no intention to torment the soldier. He had to hold to some scrap of his vow to his great-grandfather.

The enemy gnashed his teeth and growled in a foreign language. It did not sound like Greek, though Varro was no expert on the languages of these lands. He pressed the sword point deeper into the enemy's neck.

"Do you speak Latin? Do you understand me, at least?"

A flow of what had to be curses rose on a cloud of sour breath and steamed Varro's face. He tried twice more, but to no avail. In the end, he shoved the man down. It would be a mercy to kill him, but Varro would not do it. He would not risk an appeal to mercy to justify murder. How long before such an excuse would cover all sorts of brutality? He did not trust himself and searched elsewhere.

The injured were more numerous than the dead. He glanced to the battle, which still shuddered with horses and men churning in madness. But the cavalry charge ground down the enemy mercenaries such that they were lost behind the ranks of Romans. Varro increased his pace, scurrying from one injured enemy to the next.

"Do you speak Latin?"

Of course none of them did or would admit to it. The flaw in his plan, he realized, was to believe Latin was the language of civilization. Surely everyone knew a bit of it, or else how could trade and politics function? But these men dying in mud churned of their own blood were commoners like himself. They knew their mother's language and nothing more.

Finally he flipped a man and received an answer in Latin.

"I hoped you would find me. I heard you near."

The man lay atop a bloodied wolfskin that Varro did not see until pulling him over. He was younger than Varro, perhaps by several years. He should not be serving in the legions, but the tribune must have been deceived when selecting him. His short brown hair was matted with sweat, and blood covered the side of his face. Varro scanned down his body, then quickly looked up when he saw something slimy and purple hanging at his gut.

"I will die soon," the velite said. "I'm afraid of judgement."

Varro crouched beside him and sought the young man's hand. He found it cold and slicked with blood. Taking it to his chest, he massaged it as he knelt beside him.

"Fear no judgement, friend. You've fought bravely today. You will find your brothers in the Elysian Fields and you shall rejoice."

"I was slain because I was afraid." The velite's eyes began to flutter closed. Varro had to lean closer to hear his weakening voice and to ensure his own words reached the man's ears.

"We are all afraid. I am afraid. The centurions are afraid. Consul Galba is afraid. Only those safe in their beds far from the battlefield can be fearless. We endure the fear for Rome and her citizens, and we return her glory. What is your name?"

"Vel Lutorius."

"Do you have anything you want to tell your family? I will return home soon, and I can deliver a message."

"Tell Floria that I am sorry, and I forgive her."

"I will tell her. Where can I find her?"

The young velite smiled at him, then his hand grew limp and his eyes unfocused. Varro set the flaccid arm at Lutorius's side.

"You were a brave man, Lutorius."

A rough hand grabbed him from behind, spinning him around. Varro fell back, cursing and reaching for his sword. But a hobnailed, sandaled foot slammed it into the mud.

"I'm not the enemy, lily." Falco towered over him and pointed with his own sword across the field. "Our real enemies have broken. Decurions are reforming the lines. It's over. None of these fucking bastards speak Latin. Who would've guessed?"

"Macedonians might have spoken Latin," Varro said, still staring at Vel Lutorius's placid face. "These are foreign mercenaries."

"We need to get back before we're missed, then clean up without being caught. The day's not over for us. But this stupid plan of yours is."

Across the brief distance, cavalry soldiers marshaled their horses and raised their swords in triumph. The velites looked like a pack of wolves with their own shining blades held up to the shafts of sunlight falling between the gathered clouds. In one voice they shouted victory, the power of it shaking through Varro's head. The enemy force flowed back toward Philip's distant camp in complete route.

"Gallio is over there," Varro said. "It seems like we should just be able to fetch him back in one swoop."

"Forget him," Falco said. "Gallio is lost and we've got to find our own way out of the tribune's shadow. Now, let's get in order so we can escape our own foolishness."

Varro stood up from the fallen man at his feet.

"What a waste."

But he was not sure he meant his attempt to find Gallio as he stared at the smooth face of the young man who had sacrificed his life to inconvenience Philip the Fifth of Macedonia.

10

With cheering soldiers surrounding him as he emerged from the gate into the camp, Varro forgot all his anger and frustration. The cavalry had preceded the velites into the camp, being the first to receive the fresh adulations of their fellows. But the cheering did not soften for the young, wolf-headed skirmishers following behind. Varro waved back at the men who called out to them. Smiles met him on every side.

Until he turned to Falco, who brushed down his waving arm.

"Are you trying to get Centurion Drusus's attention, or are you looking to speed up the execution by finding the tribune instead?"

His face warmed at the rebuke and he lowered his head.

"I forgot myself. Falco, you must feel it, though? We were never so close to death as that moment. The two of us with no shield or armor and only a sword against all those enemies. I cannot soon forget that thrill!"

"I'd rather forget it. Give me a shield and a formation over running around with my balls hanging out for an enemy spear. We got asked to do the impossible today."

"But we succeeded," Varro said, the heat clearing from his face. "And we led the way."

"Let's hope no one wants to recognize us for it."

Varro stumbled and his heart raced. Falco cursed his clumsiness.

"No one saw us." But Varro's mumbled denial vanished amid the enthusiastic celebration.

They assembled in the parade ground and now awaited dismissal. Velites had no dedicated officers in their own ranks and so waited for a decurion to issue the order. Consul Galba and his tribunes, including Primanus, stood upon a short stage to greet them. The mounted cavalry officers fortunately eclipsed them from Varro's view. He let out a short breath of relief. The decurions leaned their heads together as they spoke, their long red plumes bobbing from their bronze helmets.

Then to Varro's horror, these decurions began to call out their own for distinguished acts of bravery.

"No one saw us," Varro repeated. Falco now looked at him and his face shaded purple. He cocked a thick brow and nodded slightly to three velites staring at them and smiling.

"What are they looking at?" Varro asked. But others turned and smiled as the decurions called forward men for citations for bravery.

Someone nudged Varro's left arm. He turned to a round-faced man with a splash of dried blood under his eye like a teardrop.

"You two led the charge. You ought to be recognized." He whispered as if conspiring to commit a crime. Varro shook his head, pulling his wolf head lower out of instinct.

"That's not true. We just ran faster than the rest. We weren't leading anything."

The round-faced man closed his eyes to the protest. "Nonsense, the two of you went right into the heart of the enemy line. You made the opening for the rest of us."

As Varro denied any exceptional behavior, he also saw the officers of the centuries that had dispatched their velites to the battle. The bear-like Centurion Drusus and his stout, stern Optio Tertius stood at the fore with their muscled arms folded over their chests.

"Drusus looks especially pleased," Falco said.

"He looks like he was forced to eat spoiled fish."

Now the velites were to be recognized, and Varro's heart flipped when three rows of his companions turned back to smile at him. It felt as if the sun had scattered the dark clouds to shine on him alone.

Being mounted, the decurion commanded a total view of everyone before him. His eyes easily swept to where the turned heads pointed. He smiled, deep lines forming on his cheeks as he pointed to Varro and Falco.

"There you are. The two tall velites who delivered a mighty blow to the enemy. Come forward."

Centurion Drusus and Optio Tertius shifted closer to the decurion's brown horse. They stood shoulder-to-shoulder with folded arms.

Warm pats fell on Varro's back and others encouraged him forward with a gentle push.

"Don't be so humble," said the round-faced velite with the teardrop bloodstain. "They'll probably make you both hastati if you can afford it."

The admiring men in their wolf-head cloaks encouraged them as they passed through their ranks. Hundreds of others strained to see them over the shoulders of their peers. A warm hum passed through the velites for it seemed none of the others would be recognized, but all were glad at least two of their number would earn a measure of fame for them.

Varro and Falco popped out before their officers and the decurion. Only the decurion smiled, and both centurion and optio frowned as if being presented an open sack of dog shit.

"You two led the charge and penetrated the enemy line. Such heroism must be recognized."

"These two are mine," Drusus said, his expression never shifting. He held Varro's gaze in utter contempt. "I'll ensure they are recognized appropriately."

The decurion leaned back at the interruption. Ostensibly of equal rank with Drusus, the decurion came from far greater wealth and power than any infantryman.

"That is well. But their acts should be made known to the tribunes and consul. It is an honor they earned."

Drusus waved his hand, at last looking up to the decurion who cast a shadow over him.

"In due time. The men have just been through a fucking battle. They had to march there and back. So let them rest. I'll see to their rewards."

The decurion's smile snapped from his face and a bitter frown replaced it. But an argument before the men would be unseemly for a cavalry officer.

"Very good, centurion. I'll leave them in your care."

"Sir," Varro said. His voice cracked but he squared himself to the decurion. "Sir, if I may report another act of bravery."

The decurion smiled as if indulging a child. "If the centurion feels the men can endure standing a moment longer, I will hear it."

Drusus remained unmoved with folded arms, scowl, and eyes full of rage.

Varro blinked and turned back to the mounted officer.

"Vel Lutorius joined us on that charge. He was killed, sir. I hope his bravery will be noted."

"I will issue a posthumous commendation for his courage."

"Thank you, sir."

The velites in hearing range cheered the added recognition and some clapped Varro's back for speaking up for a fallen companion. But the warm glow departed with the shadow of the decurion, who dismissed the assembled soldiers back to their officers.

Centurion Drusus and Optio Tertius sidestepped to where the decurion's horse had stood to interpose themselves before Consul Galba and the tribunes.

"You two will be coming with us," Drusus said in a low, threatening voice. "And get rid of those wolf heads. By the gods, you're hastati."

Varro tugged off his wolf pelt. The cool air rushed over his head and back, bringing refreshment but for the dried blood flaking off his hands and face. He knew better than to say anything, as did Falco who followed orders and lowered his head.

Drusus led them, and Tertius followed behind. With each step forward, Varro expected a wicked snap from Tertius's vine cane. Yet it never came, and his hobnails simply crunched on the dirt road behind them. All around men returned to their posts or other duties. After the horror of combat, the strangely prosaic sights and sounds of the camp at rest seemed unreal. The scent of a cooking fire somewhere made his mouth water and he swallowed. Idle conversations along the roadside floated cheerful and bright into his path. No more the screaming of dying men and horses, or the horrific odors of spilled blood and entrails. His hands were still numb from the smashing of sword on sword or fist against bone. But here he strolled down a road safe and at peace.

At least until they arrived at headquarters.

"In the office," Drusus said. "Optio, wait outside the door and be certain we are not disturbed. I'll call for you shortly."

Tertius's eyes flicked across Varro and Falco, then he saluted and took his position. Drusus entered the dark room, waving them forward without looking back. Once inside, Varro's eyes adjusted to the dim light of the tiny work space. Centurion Drusus removed his helmet and pegged it on a rack. He then dropped into his desk chair and stared at them. Varro clutched the wolf fur in a white-knuckled grip and stared at the dark far wall.

"I can't even begin to wonder at what stupidity the two of you were up to this morning. I don't really want an explanation. However, I cannot rightly strangle the two of you with my bare hands before finding out what you thought to achieve by your actions. So tell me."

Varro continued to stare past Drusus, but felt the weight of Falco at his side. As this was his idea, he had to take the responsibility.

"This was my plan, sir. Falco was just along to protect me. He had no—"

"Let's stop there," Drusus said with an overly patient smile. "I don't fucking care whose plan this was. Just explain what you were about so I can get to tearing your heads from your shoulders."

"Sir," Varro straightened his back and drew a breath. "I wanted to find out what happened to Gallio. I thought, sir, that while his betrayal was fresh the enemy soldiers might be able to describe him to me. They could tell me what happened to him."

Drusus blinked, his expression flat. His rugged forehead creased as he drew his brows together.

"And what did you expect to have happened to Gallio?"

"I'm not certain, sir. Perhaps they would make him a scout, or else sell him as a slave."

"Or just kill him once his usefulness was finished?"

"Yes, sir, that as well. But if he is alive, then there is a chance we can still bring him back to face justice. That is what Tribune Primanus wants us to do, sir."

Drusus pressed his thin lips together and folded his hands behind his round head. He looked to Falco.

"Is this really what you two were doing? Going out to find enemy soldiers to question about Gallio's health?"

"Sir, that was our plan. We needed to do this while Gallio might still be remembered by the enemy."

Sliding his laced hands to the top of his head, Drusus looked between them.

"I suppose I can understand why you'd want to find out what happened to Gallio. So, how did you do it? Who helped you?"

"No one, sir," Varro said without hesitation. "We approached two velites and paid them for their gear to disguise ourselves."

"Just you two tacticians, eh? None of the others in the contubernium of shame know what you were about?"

"No, sir."

Varro hoped Curio had not betrayed them. Yet he also realized he could hardly be in more trouble than he was now.

"So, what did you find out?"

Drusus remained with his hands folded atop his head, smiling between him and Falco. Varro dared a glance to his friend, whose red face betrayed his anger and embarrassment.

"We were not able to learn anything, sir. The enemy did not speak Latin."

The centurion leaned forward and burst out laughing. Varro felt his face growing warmer as his officer continued laughing. At length, he wiped at the corner of his eye with the back of his wrist.

"I forget how young the two of you are. You really should've been velites. Of course they don't speak Latin. Do you two speak Greek? That has to be the funniest thing I've heard in a month. What a plan, Varro. Makes me think of you in a whole new light."

Varro shifted as if he wanted to turn aside from the humiliation. He had risked so much on a faulty assumption. If he had included the others in his plans, then one of them might have pointed out this obvious flaw. Haste had cost him and Falco as well. If he survived the day, he vowed to never make that same mistake again.

Drusus recalled Tertius after he stopped laughing. The optio entered, his dour face a stark contrast to the centurion's lingering snickers.

"See Falco back to the barracks. I have to speak to Varro a moment longer. Since we're covering up this whole business, we cannot properly flog these idiots. But I will leave it up to your creativity to ensure Varro and Falco have something more substantial to reflect upon than their embarrassment alone. In other words, leave a mark for them to remember this day."

Tertius saluted, then nodded that Falco should exit. He did not glance at Varro, who felt as if his shield had been torn from him in battle. When the door thumped shut, he feared he might never step beyond it again.

Drusus stared hard at him, half-pronounced his name, then made a fist which he bit down on rather than speak. His eyes squeezed shut as his teeth sawed into his knuckles. At last, he ripped away his hand and shot up from his chair. He squared up to Varro, his round head inches away.

"If you did not have such powerful friends, Varro, I swear I would just as soon have you flogged to death."

Varro blinked and his mouth fell open to protest. But Drusus spun away, turning his back and again lacing his hands behind his head.

"Forget I said that." He shook his head like a dog fresh out of a pond. "I know Protus thought highly of you. There has to be a reason, for Protus was a good judge of men. Except for that snake of an optio he had. That couldn't be helped."

"Sir, I don't understand what you mean? What powerful friends do I have?"

Drusus's shoulders slumped and he let his arms fall aside.

"Did I say that, too? Then forget it as well." He scrubbed his face with the heels of his palms, then turned to Varro. He forced a smile over this grim expression.

"Sir, Centurion Protus told me all about Decius Oceanus. I did not think you knew about that. Did you know my father?"

"I did not know your father," he said. The redness in his face ebbed, as did the rage that had been swirling around him since the parade ground. "I know as much as Protus shared, and I don't want to know more. I am a soldier, Varro. I fight battles and am talented at it. Learn from me, and you might live to return home. And with your friends, you may go places I'll never see myself."

"Sir, I'm sorry to interrupt, but I have no friends like you describe. I come from a good-sized farm, but my family is of no account. My friends are all likewise, sir."

Drusus stared at him and smiled.

"As you say. Let's leave it at that. For today, it's fortunate we discovered you and Falco were missing. If Tribune Primanus had been alerted, well, I'm sure you know the consequences."

"Yes, sir." Varro remained at attention and shifted his eyes back to the rear of the small, dim office. He did not want to push the centurion with a direct stare.

"Also, when you lied to me earlier about not having help, you forgot that I already knew your plan. Why else would I have been waiting? You have to be more careful than this, Varro. You are swift to help your friends and feel great responsibility toward them. Men your age often do. But as you get older, you will have to consider yourself first. Friends are fine, but they do not always last. Particularly the friends you make at the start of a campaign. Do yourself a favor, and take risks for the men who are still with you at the end of the campaign. Few others are worth it."

"Thank you, sir. I will reflect deeply on all I've learned today."

"See that you do," Drusus said. "This is not a game, Varro. Army discipline is harsh. While exceptions are sometimes made, I've never seen them made twice for the same person. You will tire your friends and one day find yourself facing the fustuarium. Now, go see Optio Tertius for whatever punishment he has devised for your foolishness. You are dismissed."

Varro saluted and left the headquarters behind. He still clutched the wolf pelt in hand, and would have to clean it before returning it. His head swam with a dozen conflicting thoughts about who watched over him and why. Yet when he arrived at the barracks he found Falco standing at attention outside and alone. Optio Tertius squatted in the shade beside the door, then stood at Varro's approach.

"Good we didn't have to wait long," he said with a grin. "I've got some orders to carry out."

11

Varro followed Optio Tertius to the rear of the row of barracks. They stood in the late afternoon shade in the space between the stake wall surrounding the camp and their barracks row. The grass here was dead but fuller from the lack of activity. Still clutching the velite wolf pelt, he wished he could put it over his shoulders. The breeze in the shade raised goose bumps on his arms. Falco stood at his side, and the optio had them line up against the barrack wall. The solid barrack houses muted the sounds of camp life and its shadow stretched deep and purple. Varro stood to attention.

"I'm sure all the others are listening at this wall," Tertius said with a smile. "They're expecting screams for mercy, I'm sure."

Tertius flicked his vine cane before him, slashing hard at the dead grass. It passed across the dry blades and sent them scattering into the breeze. He stared at Varro with a wolfish grin.

"So, you are eager to fight the enemy? You'd do anything to get them to grips?"

Unsure if he should answer, Varro stared ahead and held his shoulders square. Optio Tertius narrowed his eyes then stood on his toes. His hobnails dug into the top of Varro's feet, radiating pain as he pressed his weight onto them. Tertius pushed to rise to Varro's eye level. Hot breath bathed his face.

"I'm not even sure how many regulations your broke today, but at least one is enough to see you flogged to death."

Varro stared through him. It was an empty threat, yet he dug his hobnails deeper into Varro's foot, grinding so that Varro thought the bones might shatter.

"But you've avoided that fate, haven't you? A special case, it seems. Well, aren't you the fucking luckiest piece of shit in this army."

Tertius remained with his feet pressed atop Varro's a moment longer. Then he backed off and snapped to Falco.

"But this tower of stupidity is not so special. No one watching over you, Falco. Probably because you're so ugly no one but your mother can stand to look at you for long."

Not daring to give Tertius a hint of an excuse to rebuke him, Varro stared ahead. He strained to see the optio leaning in to Falco. His vine cane hung from his hand clasped behind his back, flicking gently as he continued in his low, threatening voice.

"So, Falco, you had to take care of your friend? Did you think adding your stupidity to his would help? That's like cleaning spilled wine with more spilled wine. It becomes one big, fucking mess."

Tertius grabbed the wolf pelt from Falco, then snatched it away from Varro. He held them up in one fist.

"Did you two think of what would happen to the men who sold you these? Are you going to protect them and tell me you don't remember them?" He stood before Varro, shoving the fistful of furs closer at him. They smelled of sweat and blood. "They should be flogged as well."

Tertius threw the furs aside.

"But since this whole affair is covered up, they got lucky too."

Tertius now stepped back and folded his arms. His vine cane hung from his hand and pointed at his left foot, dangling with the stiff breeze. The optio looked between them, twitching his crooked smile.

"What kind of punishment will leave a mark for you to remember?"

Varro imagined pulling up his tunic and enduring a whipping to his buttocks or lower back. He was prepared to do as much when Tertius relaxed.

"Very well, here's your punishment, Varro."

"Sir!" He straightened his shoulders and his heart sped.

"You'll scour my mail shirt, sharpen and oil my blades. I'll supervise. I could stand some time off."

At last, Varro faltered and looked in surprise to Tertius. His angry expression did not fade.

"I know why you went out there today. It was foolish, but brave. The army requires brave fools to feed its success. I'm not going to break your fingers or leave a scar. I suspect your humiliation is scar enough."

Varro blinked, his heart still racing. "Thank you, sir."

"Don't thank me. It's Centurion Drusus's orders. I follow procedure, Varro, and I would be the first in line for the fustuarium if he had ordered it. I'm certain he won't ask after your punishment. If he's going to hand wave all your disobedience, then he shouldn't have wasted my time with this exercise."

"Of course, sir." Varro wanted to smirk at the optio's own show of disobedience. But another question floated out of his mouth before he could stop it.

"Sir, why were you so hard on Gallio?"

Tertius stopped in mid-turn to Falco. He remained with his foot forward, paused as if considering the answer. Then he completed his step and answered.

"Gallio was a troublemaker. He had an attitude incompatible

with the army, and I was not wrong about it. He ran off, and didn't care what happened to his friends."

"Sir, he might not have run off if you had been—well, sir, he might have had a different attitude if someone in authority listened to him."

The optio cocked his brow and smirked.

"You think he'd be a different man with a little more care? Indulge him a bit more?"

"He was bitter at being punished after leading a charge against bandits."

"He was bitter that he fled like a coward and was called out for it." Tertius's face darkened and his smile turned to a sneer. "He was bitter at not being lauded as a hero for doing his basic duty. He expected much and gave little. He wanted to run the century, probably the whole fucking army if he could. Such a man needs to be broken and remade before he's of any use. He was a poison to your contubernium. Trust me, Varro, better he ran now than when you're facing a wall of Macedonian pikes and every man needs to drive into it. He was the weakest part of the contubernium, and he was taking Curio along with him. My responsibility is to find those weakness and either strengthen them or remove them. As I see it, I did my job well."

Varro straightened to attention and stared ahead. He did not mean to insult the optio or sour his generous mood. He waited while Tertius stared at him until he was satisfied. He then turned back to Falco.

"And your punishment? If you're going to protect your passionate friend, you need to think clearly. Don't just run alongside and do what he says. Help him think."

"Yes, sir!"

Tertius stepped back, then studied Falco with folded arms.

"No punishment for you. But I suspect my news will help you mark this day, nonetheless."

Out of reflex, Varro looked to Falco. His friend remained at strict attention, his face red and staring straight ahead.

"I'm sorry to report, Falco, you father is dead. It's by luck the news reached the consul, but it is a firsthand account."

Falco did not shift, but remained at attention. An awkward silence expanded, until Falco tilted his head as if struggling with his thoughts.

"Speak," Tertius said. "You have a question, I can tell."

"Sir, was it for misconduct? Was he drunk?"

Tertius raised his brow and cocked his head. "Not at all. He was assigned to support the fleet that sailed to Cassandreia. He died in the siege there. I don't have the specifics. As it was not a victory for our men, details are harder to come by."

"He died in battle, sir? You're certain?"

"I'm not lying to you, Falco. As I understand it, our men pushed hard but did not have proper siege machines for the task. The soldiers did all they could. And your father gave the ultimate effort any soldier can offer Rome."

"Thank you for telling me, sir."

With this, Tertius nodded. He swished his vine cane at the pile of wolf pelts he had dropped. "Make sure these are cleaned and returned. And do not repeat this foolishness. You will not be forgiven a second time, and I don't care who says otherwise. And for finding Gallio, there's no chance. I doubt they'd put a deserter into battle with his old companions. The fool fled directly into slavery as far as I'm concerned, which is probably what they offered him for giving up our location instead of death. To get out from the tribune's shadow you're better off doing something heroic, like delivering King Philip's head. You've a better chance at that than taking Gallio's head."

They stood at attention until Optio Tertius vanished around the corner, leaving Varro and Falco alone in the shade behind the barracks. Varro rushed to Falco, grabbing him by the shoulder.

"Are you all right?"

Falco's eyes shined and his cheeks glowed red, but his voice was steady.

"I'm fine, lily. I just can't believe he was smart enough to get killed in battle rather than flogged to death for intoxication."

"I'm sorry."

Falco held up his hand and turned his head aside. "I don't want to talk about it. Things were difficult with my father."

Varro nodded, patted Falco's strong shoulder, and then started to retrieve the wolfskins.

"Well, there is one thing," Falco said. "Where is Cassa-dendarden-raria?"

"I don't know." Varro tried to imagine the strange place so far from home, but he only knew big cities like Athens. Even then, he wasn't certain of its location.

They returned to their barracks to reunite with the others. Each of them wanted to ask after their punishments, but none would ask directly. Falco, having just received news of his father's death, ignored everyone and went to lie on his bunk. In the end, Varro went to bathe and took Curio along to help clean the wolf pelts and return these without raising suspicions.

The day following the battle was given to rest, for Galba intended to take the infantry out to face Philip on the next day. The cavalry and war elephants would remain garrisoned.

"Lucky us," Falco said at the end of their night while relaxing on his bunk. "We get to fight again."

"At least we didn't have to face their pikes," Varro said. "I'm afraid of what that will be like."

"They're not using their pikemen?" Panthera asked. "What are they saving them for?"

No one in the bunk room had that answer, and once the lights were out they drifted off to sleep. Varro listened to Falco snoring above him. He still kept the lower bunk even after his head injury had healed. He still had bouts of dizziness.

The next day, the centuries were assembled and now it was time for the cavalry to cheer on the infantry as they marched out the gate. Galba and his tribunes marched with them this day, all mounted atop royal horses and clad in shining mail and bronze armor. To Varro, they seemed as marvelous as the statues and reliefs decorating Rome.

Varro marched the same path as the cavalry had followed, going to the same field. Parties from both sides had retrieved their fallen in the interim. But Varro knew gruesome surprises would hide in the grass. He recalled the strange circle of severed fingers, probably assembled by a dying soldier who was too in shock to understand what he did.

"Why are we in full pack?" Varro wondered aloud as they marched. Drusus and the junior centurion led their maniple. At the rear, the two optios herded the men ahead. "We're only going a few miles from camp."

"Does anything make sense?" Falco said. He had his pack sagging at his back, just like everyone else in the century. "Maybe we're not going back but marching ahead."

"Philip's camp is only about three miles away," Panthera said. "Where would we be going?"

Yet Varro had understood, as did everyone else, that soldiers always marched in full gear. Battle was too unpredictable and preparation for any possibility was expected. In Varro's pack he carried three days of rations, sharpened stakes for encampment, entrenching tools, all his kit for maintaining his weapons, and sundries needed to remain on the march for days. Atop all this weight, he wore a bronze helmet and pectoral, carried his shield on his back, and two pila in hand. Gladius and pugio slapped at his thighs as he trudged along, feeling as if he were sinking into the earth. He had a new appreciation for the simple wolf fur and javelins of the velites.

Marching came automatically to Varro. He had drilled so often that his legs pumped the required cadence to match the pace set by Drusus no matter how heavy the burden. As they drew closer to the battlefield, the centurions began to reorganize their maniples. They moved beneath dull, wintery clouds shedding a glare of sunlight. A half-mile distant, a line of Philip's men rose up from the horizon. Varro strained in silence to see what they faced, yet saw little more than an obscure line. He did not see raised pikes.

He would have cheered in relief, but now every soldier was to maintain strict silence so as to hear the commands of their officers. Drusus, looking like a bear in mail armor, shouted out their position and pointed with a strong arm to where Varro's century would form. Being part of the tenth maniple, they would be on the outer right flank in the rear position, meaning they would not engage first but remain in support of the other century of the maniple. He prayed the lead centuries of hastati would route the Macedonians before needing relief. Following the hastati, the principes would take over, and in turn be relieved by the veteran triarii if needed.

Varro hoped the battle would not come down to the triarii. He shuddered to imagine the carnage needed to eat through so many heavy Roman troops to reach the rear ranks.

The orderliness of their deployment imparted a calm to Varro he did not expect. While had fought several battles already, this truly was his first as a hastatus in a proper engagement. He should have felt more fear. Recalling how he worried for shaming himself in battle, he wondered who that person had been. That Marcus Varro was somewhere on a farm back home, hiding in his room and afraid of the world. The Marcus Varro he had become did not fear death and knew his duty. He did not relish killing, and would avoid it whenever possible. But Falco, Curio, Panthera, Sura, Cordus, and Otho all depended on him to be a Roman soldier. Today he would kill Macedonians and hope he and his friends returned to camp alive and unhurt.

The battlefield was anchored to a line of heavy trees. These were not the woods where they had foraged, but each woods seemed alike to Varro. They were all impenetrable masses of darkness that housed evil spirts and lurking danger. Wolves and bears dwelled beneath those dark boughs. Nothing good came from the woods. Varro eyed it warily.

The enemy line drew closer. Now Varro could see the swell of massed cavalry leading lines of men with round shields and gleaming swords. Yet no pikemen. These were light infantry.

He shared a worried glance with Falco, who simply nodded that he saw the cavalry as well. Being on the flank meant they were exposed to a charge, and without their own cavalry they had nothing to counter it. Varro did not understand how the Macedonians fought other than in deep ranks of pikemen. He assumed their cavalry would mirror what he had seen of Rome's, striking fast then regrouping.

His calm ebbed away as the enemy encroached. By the time they reached the quarter-mile mark, his heart thudded against his neck and his eyes were dry from opening so wide.

"Time to raise a noise," Centurion Drusus shouted. "Let them know we're here. Forward!"

In one voice, the thousands of Romans of every rank bellowed their war cries. The ordered blocks lurched forward, with screaming velites in wolf heads leading the way.

Varro's throat numbed with his screaming. As they jogged ahead, he readied his light pilum and banged it against his shield. So did all the other hastati. The crash and boom rippled across the open field like thunderbolts from Jupiter. Varro's pace quickened with his nerves and the anticipation of battle. Men swarmed all around, turning the air hot with their fear and popping his ears with their cries.

The enemy moved into their positions. Even over the shouts of the Romans Varro heard enemy officers shouting their men forward.

"Hold!" Drusus shouted upon reaching their appointed distance.

Varro stumbled short, his momentum flying forward from him. Yet the abrupt halt was part of his training, and he set himself like a stone in the earth. He turned his left shoulder toward the enemy and pulled his scutum close. Light pilum held ready in his right hand and his heavy pilum was in his left with his shield.

Yet the other maniple continued on with the junior centurion leading the charge.

The velites had already sown their javelins into the enemy ranks and filed off the field. Some remained to claim a trophy or else be seen in personal combat. Having just experienced the nakedness of battle as a velite, he admired these young men so desperate to make a name for themselves and increase their fortunes.

The hastati charge shook the earth. Drusus ordered another war cry to support the closing ranks. Again, Varro roared and slammed his pilum to his shield.

Then the battle was joined and the world erupted into shuddering thunder.

Varro held himself in rigid, shocked silence. To participate in battle was one thing. To see it unfold before you was unlike anything he could have expected.

The Macedonian light infantry nearly crumbled from the hail of pila. Their shrieks peeled over the heads of the closing Romans. The clash of the lines sent a visible shockwave through the hastati. They seemed to ripple as men jostled into their position. Their optio stood at the rear, shouting encouragement and ordering men into gaps. Varro could not see where the two lines pressed into their murderous embrace, but he knew when a Roman fell for someone at the rear squeezed into the spot.

Centurion Drusus stood ready, watching the battle as if it were a drill. Men bled and fell scant yards away yet he did not flinch or look aside.

The silence of his own maniple was nearly as weighty as the pack hanging at his back. Each man watched as the hastati shoved into the Macedonians.

Then they stumbled ahead.

The light infantry pulled back, answering the calls of their officers to retreat.

"Is it over?" Sura asked.

"Shut your fucking mouth!" Optio Tertius screamed from behind. "Hold steady and silent."

But that battle was not over. Drusus traded nods with his bloodied, sweat-slicked junior centurion then raised his sword.

"Advance!"

The same command repeated down the long row of hastati. This was Consul Galba's will, that they not lose contact.

"Our shift now," Drusus called. "We'll bring this home."

They jogged after the enemy in eerie silence. Varro's breath came fast and rough.

But as he advanced on the flank, his vision slashed across the ranks of enemy scrambling to reform their position.

And he saw Gallio.

12

"Gallio!"

Varro's shout trembled as he charged forward. If anyone heard him, no one reacted. Falco jogged at his side with his shield up and wide eyes just visible over the iron-topped rim. He did not have a moment to check his left for Curio's reaction. They cut across the first line of hastati that had bloodied the Macedonians into falling back. He had to hold his eyes on Gallio or else lose him. At this distance, his outline blurred into the mass of soldiers surrounding him. But Varro knew that outline and was confident Gallio now faced them.

But as the lines closed, the Macedonians pulled behind their shields, for they had already endured a pila volley and knew to expect the next one.

The Roman line spread out before the enemy, and Varro rotated to present his shield to them. This eclipsed the man he swore was Gallio standing in the front rank with his gladius and round shield. He had reached the distance for his light pilum and so cocked his arm and let it fly. Without waiting to see where it landed, he exchanged his heavy pilum into his free hand while advancing.

The Macedonians screamed as they died. The hastati screamed, but with the ferocity of attacking lions.

Yet before Varro cast his heavy pilum, the thunder of hooves erupted over closing battle lines.

The Macedonian cavalry flew like a javelin for the center of the legion's line, where Consul Galba commanded from the rear and center.

The explosive charge by a mass of cavalry stole Varro's attention. Being on the flank, he would have expected to be the target of the charge. But the cavalry ran straight into the heart of the line as if to shatter it on one go. The retreat had been a feint.

"Keep moving," Optio Tertius shouted from the rear. "Close the gap!"

Centurion Drusus and his signifer who carried their century standard did not pause. Varro could not do less.

He cast his heavy pilum in the last paces before reaching the line. It sailed from his hand to arc down into the black line of enemies. Men crumpled as the heavy spears crashed through their shields or broke open their helmets. The pilum volley devastated and disrupted the enemy formation long enough for them to close the distance to where their short swords would dominate.

"Gallio!"

Varro shouted and drew his sword into his right hand. But he no longer saw Gallio. The line of Macedonians had scattered away from the pila, exposing their slain companions impaled to the ground. Their dark faces glowed with confusion and fear, as light infantry had nothing capable of stopping the heavy weapons of the hastati. Perhaps Gallio had died in the volley.

The Macedonian cavalry slammed into the heart of the formation. Varro could not see it, but heard the overwhelming crash and the cries of men and horses. But he could only shift on his feet to present this shield to the threat before him and march into combat.

He met the front line in step with Falco and Curio along with all the other hastati of nine other maniples. While the center may have buckled, the flanks held firm. Varro punched then stabbed as he had trained for hundreds of hours. Enemy swords could not find a way under or around his scutum, which covered from eyes to feet. The wood buckled and shuddered as he punched one enemy to the ground, then stepped forward to use his momentum and drive his sword into the exposed body. To him it was as easy as trampling dead stalks underfoot as he advanced in time with his century.

Drusus fought at the fore with them, hewing a path through the foe. Varro's arms tired with the effort of punching and thrusting, then jamming against a resistant knot of opponents refusing to yield. For the Macedonians did not melt away this time, not while their cavalry tried to split the Roman lines. They still had hope and their officers held them in place.

Yet when Varro's ears rang with the clash of battle, his hands numbed with the ceaseless work of murder, and his nose filled with the horrific stench of blood and bile, the enemy broke.

Again they spun away, and Varro made a halfhearted stab at the final, faceless enemy retreating before him. Dead lay sprawled out on the grass in bright pools of blood. Some cried while holding their wounds. Others stared glassy-eyed into the gray sky.

Drusus ordered a halt, as the other century of the hastati would now advance again after their rest.

"Gallio!"

Varro searched the fallen enemy at his feet.

"Shut your fucking mouth!"

Optio Tertius's ferocity bathed him from the rear, but he continued to look into the face of every fallen soldier.

Falco narrowed his eyes at him, letting his shield droop to

expose his mouth hanging open. It was red with blood, though he had no visible cut. He shook his head at Varro.

At last, they began a slow advance again as the Macedonians retreated at an angle and in disorder. The temptation for a less disciplined force might be overwhelming. But Varro and every soldier in the Roman army knew to pursue without an explicit order was as good as exposing his throat to an enemy sword.

Picking a path through the dead bodies, Varro searched for Gallio. At his left, Curio did the same. Had he seen Gallio as well, Varro wondered. It had been a glimpse, but he was certain of whom he had seen. Gallio was not a stranger, but had become nearly as close as a brother over the long year together. Varro was confident he had seen him.

But now they had passed the tidemark of their last battle and the Macedonians were reforming a new line along with their cavalry.

As they were now closer to the woods, Varro cast a wary glance at the dark clump of evergreen trees laced with the gray skeletons of late autumn trees. He hated the woods and fighting beside them would be bad luck.

As he eyed the clump of trees with the same wariness he would a real enemy, he caught a hint of movement there. He blinked and saw more shapes. Realization spread over him like a cup of cold water poured down his back.

"Centurion Drusus! Look at the woods. This is a trap!"

Drusus spun around, his face splattered with blood and eyes brilliant with battle-madness. But rather than curse Varro, he followed his pointing finger.

"Sir, look to the edges. There are grays shapes there. They're moving."

Drusus halted the line and every head followed Varro's pointing finger.

He saw the faint forms of men amid the trees. They had

betrayed themselves with their pale tunics which caught spots of light that penetrated the cover of the evergreens. Varro saw their fuzzy gray shapes wavering like leaves in a breeze as they tried to see the shape of the battle.

"Varro, report this to the tribune. Go!"

The lines behind him broke apart to let him pass. As he popped out the rear, he saw the blocks of principes and their centurions staring at him. He looked for Tribune Primanus's standard and ran directly toward it, weaving amid the openings in the checkerboard formation.

Arriving at Primanus mounted atop his gray horse, he saluted.

"Sir, Centurion Drusus has dispatched a report. There are men hidden in the woods on the right flank. The centurion fears we are being led into a trap."

Primanus immediately stood straighter in his saddle. His attendants did as well. In the rear of the formation their own soldiers likely screened the enemy, for Primanus squinted and stared but at last sat back and shook his head.

"I trust the centurion's judgement. The Macedonians are behaving strangely." Primanus's heavily lashed eyes narrowed. He never once looked at Varro, and instead ordered his attendant to inform Consul Galba. He then stared back over the heads of his soldiers and issued Varro's next order.

"Centurion Drusus will take his maniple of hastati to flush out the enemy. The principes will reinforce your position and await my command. Be swift, Varro."

He raced back the same path and repeated his orders after reaching Drusus.

"Your sharp eyes reward us again," he said. "Now that I see them, I can't stop seeing them. Let's drag them out of their hiding places."

With concise, swift commands, Drusus had broken off the hastati maniple and shifted the principes to their former position.

They made a swift march across the open fields, aiming directly for the woods.

The enemy realized they had been discovered. Rather than flee, they emerged to meet the threat.

The woods disgorged perhaps a thousand men.

"This is where we die," Falco muttered as they proceeded forward.

But Varro dared not speak more. The soldiers were pelasts, each bearing crescent-shaped shields and thin javelins. They were much like the Roman velite, which Varro held in great respect for their personal courage. One thousand such enemies to their one hundred twenty hastati made a discouraging chance to prevail.

"Let's see if we can grab some of their javelins before the tribune sends up reinforcements." Centurion Drusus fell back in line with his century. "Testudo!"

Being in the front, Varro held his shield forward while his companions formed a wall and ceiling of shields to complete the formation. He could only see out the gaps where the shields touched. Also the necessity for close formation slowed everyone's march. Varro was not eager to close without reinforcements in support.

"Steady now," Drusus said. His voice echoed in the shaded confines of the turtle shell of shields surrounding them. "They'll want to see if they can pluck someone as a prize. But don't worry for it, men. Nothing is getting through this."

The first volley of javelins swished across the open distance then slammed down, immediately telling on Drusus's lie.

Iron points crashed into wooden shields, filling Varro's ears with sharp clattering. A man at the rear screamed as a javelin passed into the gaps and landed upon him. His collapse jumbled their organization and flashed sunlight into their protective darkness.

A javelin clanged off the iron boss of Varro's shield, vibrating through his forearm.

"Fill that gap!" Optio Tertius shouted. "Keep formation or I'll kick you out of it."

They continued to trudge forward. The javelins continued to fall. But despite one lucky strike it was no worse than enduring a hailstorm under a tile roof. The javelins' iron heads raked across the shields, sticking to some and shattering on most. The thud and scrape filled Varro's ears, but he marched forward.

The pelasts did not stand to fight, but retreated ahead of the massive block of men tramping toward them. Once engaged, they would be slaughtered. These men were not foolish enough to try, and unlike the Roman velite did not seem encouraged to fight for personal glory. They melted back into the woods.

"We're shaving them off like barnacles from a hull!" Centurion Drusus laughed as he led them down the line of ever vanishing pelasts. Being a farmer, Varro had no idea what barnacles were, but imagined they must be something easily peeled away. For a single maniple of hastati had chased off a thousand men with only the threat of an attack.

Drusus halted their advance, for to stretch too far might encourage the pelasts to swarm them from all sides. But Varro guessed another maniple might be moving up to cover their rear. From the narrow slit of vision in the fore of the testudo, he saw distant pelasts wavering before fleeing. Some at least appeared to consider their chances against heavy infantry. But no one was valiant enough to lead the attack.

Varro felt a strange sense of pride. Had those been Roman velites, they would have attacked without hesitation, even if they knew death was the likely outcome.

Drusus had them break into their normal lines now that the threat of javelins had been eliminated. During their reorganization, Varro saw the Macedonian cavalry retreating and their light infantry streaming after them. Consul Galba did not order further pursuit and so the field was won.

"Raise your swords to Rome," Drusus shouted. They raised bloodied swords in their battered fists and shouted victory. The shouts chased the Macedonians back across the wide field.

"We ruined their trap," Drusus said, smiling. "We broke them!"

With the enemy in full retreat, Primanus recalled Drusus's maniple to the line. Silence was still to be maintained, but with the relief of victory many could not control themselves. Neither centurion nor optio made more than token efforts to stop talk that grew too loud.

Falco lowered his shield and smiled at Varro.

"Good spot. The gods guide your eyes."

Falco's bottom lip was split and stained his mouth and teeth bright red. Varro nodded to it, and Falco turned his head aside.

"I hit my mouth on my own shield. It's nothing, lily."

With victory settled, the soldiers were allowed to search the dead for prizes and prisoners. The velites has mostly cleared their own wounded during the course of the army's advance. Varro and his contubernium had survived without injury, except for Falco's accident.

"Did you see him?" Varro asked of Curio as they both picked through the fallen. These men, if they were Macedonian, possessed little of value. So Varro just swiped his hand across their necks and fingers for anything of value, then moved on.

"I heard you call his name," he said. He knelt and began to pry at something on a dead enemy's shoulder. "But I didn't see him."

Curio stood up with a gore-soaked pugio as his prize. "Someone must've dropped his sword and had to fight with his dagger. I'd like to find a better sword, if I can."

Yet the officers did not allow unlimited time for looting. The enemy was still near and casualties had to be cleared for transport back to camp. Varro never found Gallio among the corpses before he was set to new tasks collecting salvageable gear from the field.

He tried to remember what he had seen, but now everything felt less certain. As he discussed this with Falco after finishing their tasks and awaiting new orders, Tertius joined them.

"Good job, Varro. Centurion Drusus will ensure you're cited for this. You're turning into quite a reliable hero."

"Thank you, sir."

"But I wonder about your eyesight, still," Tertius said. He rubbed his neck and looked back toward the distant Macedonian camp. "Gallio was not out there. I heard you calling for him. But it's impossible. They'd not put him in the front line of an attack, even a suicidal one. You're seeing things that are not real, Varro. That's not good."

"Yes, sir. I'll try to be more careful."

Varro followed Tertius's gaze. Somewhere behind the jagged walls lining that hilltop, Gallio hid from his former friends. He had betrayed his country and his companions, and left them to die for his own selfish impulses. Varro would find him and ensure he faced justice, and clear the blot on all their reputations.

No matter what he had to do to capture Gallio, he would find a way.

13

Varro stood before Consul Galba, who had changed into his tunic with its broad purple stripe. His critical eyes never wavered as he heard Centurion Drusus's recommendation for Varro's citation. When Drusus completed his brief but accurate speech, the consul offered a keen smile.

"Marcus Varro's vigilance is noted and commended. Without such sharp sight we may have succumbed to an ambush. A reward of one month's extra pay shall be made to him immediately. Centurion, see to the details."

Light applause from the hastati of the tenth maniple followed the announcement. The day was late and many were still fatigued from the battle. Some were injured and others dead. Varro accepted his accolade with a grateful bow and stepped back into the line of his fellows, fitting between Falco and Panthera.

The consul and his tribunes offered a smattering of encouraging talk. But Varro did not listen. As the red sunlight slashed the parade ground in half, he searched the rear darkness for the slave girl that had previously attended Galba. But he did not find her.

Despite all that had happened since, returning to this setting reminded him of the hateful glare from that slave.

The consul dismissed them, being the final group to assemble before Galba for their rewards. Varro was learning that where the army offered harsh punishment for the least infraction, it also offered generous rewards as well.

While the hastati returned to their barracks to prepare for the night ahead, Varro accompanied Drusus to receive his reward. He placed ten silver denarii into Varro's palms. The weight of the coins was welcome and he clicked the cold silver together. Drusus laughed.

"A good start on earning your way back to Tribune Primanus's favor. But you'll need to do something that no one else could have done. Another man might have seen those hidden enemies. Not taking away from what you did, but you understand my meaning?"

Varro understood. The tribune intended to ensure his shameful contubernium would be erased at the next mistake by any of its members and would not be easily dissuaded.

Returning to his barracks, Varro found the others excited for his award. Sura insisted on seeing the coins, then whistled as if it were a king's fortune. This brought laughter to the others, and they were able to sleep in a fair mood even with the camp on alert for a night attack.

Varro awakened at dawn. His joints ached from the trials of warfare, but being young and strong he slipped out of the bunk without complaint. A moment of dizziness accompanied his sudden motion. Vestiges of Gallio's attack still lingered, but he improved with each day.

Outside, the camp hummed with excited chatter. All the other hastati were still assembling, but everyone looked toward the main road.

"What's going on?" he asked of Panthera.

"Consul Galba is sending the elephants out to challenge Philip. The entire army is going in support."

Varro blinked. How had he slept through that news? He did not question this, but instead accepted a wafer of bread and a bowl of wine for dipping. Curio and Panthera were away, summoned by Tertius for some task.

"Looks like we'll see elephants up close today," Falco said. "We deserve it after building all that shit for them. I wonder if they're as bad as our old team leader thought."

Varro shrugged, then dipped the bread into the sour wine. It was a sizable hunk, but fuller with millstone bits than usual. He wasted a quarter of his bread spitting out the small stones.

The morning passed in frenetic activity. Mobilizing the entire camp meant leaving it completely undefended but for the barest of troops. They were to take all their gear as if they were never returning again. As they wore their armor before joining the marching column, Falco patted his pack still suspended from its wall peg and whispered.

"I'm glad we're taking these, really. You know some dog will come sniffing around when everyone else is gone."

Varro rolled his eyes at Falco, who stared out meaningfully from his heavy brow.

"Does anyone really think a hastati owns anything worth stealing? Especially since even stealing a wooden spoon would see you flogged to death?"

Falco patted the pack again, like he might the belly of his pregnant wife. "Still, I'd rather it be right here. If I fall, lily, you better grab my half. You know I'd do it for you."

Again he rolled his eyes, and they shouldered their packs, shields, pila, and formed up with the rest of the maniple in marching formation.

The elephants were more enormous up close than Varro imagined, even after having built the stands and howdahs for their riders. Twenty of these monsters would lead the column out of camp. They seemed docile enough standing side by side while teams of men danced around them. Their gray flesh was wrinkled and dry. Their tusks were long and fierce, and could probably pierce ten men each at once. Bronze plates adorned their skulls and reflected the morning sun while their massive ears flapped.

The two soldiers in each of the howdahs gazed down like lords from the backs of their monstrous steeds. Yet despite all the straps securing this small enclosure to the elephants' backs, Varro thought these wobbled enough that the soldiers would fall out.

The gates opened and the army marched out with elephants and Consul Galba leading the way. They left an envious skeleton force of the oldest triarii to maintain the camp perimeter. Had Varro's father been alive, he might have been assigned this duty. As he passed out of the gate, one of these triarii standing aside it caught his eye.

"Give King Philip a punch in the head for me."

Varro saluted and the soldier laughed.

"Wouldn't Philip have to punch you first before you could do anything under your peaceful philosophy?" Falco elbowed him as they marched into the grass field. The officers would soon enforce silence, but not while the army was still filing out of the gates.

"I think all these battles can count as the first punch."

Falco chuckled. "Good to see you've expanded your thinking. But we have a better chance of catching Gallio than punching Philip in the head."

Galba's consular army of two legions poured into the field between the two camps. Varro felt lost amid so many thousands with elephants and cavalry on their wings. Outside of Rome he had never seen so many people at one place. Even within Rome, he had never seen such numbers in organization. Though he could not see beyond his own column, he experienced the weight of this force enveloping him like a fist in an iron glove. He wondered how they could lose any battle. Yet the Roman army had suffered defeats and Hannibal had once ravaged Roman lands. But that was long ago to Varro's young mind, and today he marched with the mightiest army in the world. That pride lifted his step. He was a Roman citizen, and this march today was a sacred duty of a citizen.

They halted the advance halfway to the Macedonian camp, then assembled in battle lines. Varro's heart raced and his arms tingled anticipating the clash of shield and sword. Yet the Macedonians remained behind their walls.

For all his pride and the flash of patriotism, Varro was relieved when Philip did not field his army.

Galba ordered them to advance once again, repeating the whole procedure closer to the Macedonian camp.

"Feels more like a maneuver exercise," Falco muttered from Varro's right.

"Silence!" Tertius shouted from the rear. "I'll have all your teeth broken if I hear another word!"

They all stood ready and silent, facing the camp walls. The elephants trumpeted as their riders worked them up for battle. The cavalry on the flanks leaned forward on their horses, stroking the necks of the beasts as they stared ahead. Rows of velites in wolf pelts milled to the fore, but had no enemy for their clutch of javelins.

Yet again they drew up their line and marched forward. Centurion Drusus shared dark glances with the junior centurion of the tenth maniple. Both seemed frustrated at the enemy's reticence.

The camp sat on a high hill with steep slopes. Varro had been through one siege of a town and he would not soon forget the horrific sight of men set aflame by its defenders. But these walls were much like the Romans', sturdy but temporary. The ditch surrounding the base of the hill was just wide and deep enough to break up men and horses rushing these walls.

At last, the elephants moved up. Varro and a thousand other heads turned to watch the twenty war elephants amble forward. Their riders seemed to hold on for their lives, but they had spears and javelins in hand. Once lined up, they seemed to answer some order Varro could neither see nor hear. They surged forward.

The elephants charged across the ditch, stepping easily over it, and ran up the slope. The infantry and cavalry were ordered to shout their war cries. Varro joined in support, taunting Philip and his men to come out for battle. Their cries echoed to the clouds scudding above them. The elephants trumpeted as they mounted the final distance.

But they stopped at the walls.

Varro had expected them to crash through the walls and trample everything in their path. Yet now they stood before the walls, shaking their massive heads as if they too were frustrated at their denied battle.

Varro continued to call out with the thousands of other voices smashing against the Macedonian walls. But no answer came from Philip's camp. One elephant pressed against the wall, but its riders led it away. Not a drop of blood was shed. At the instant Varro's voice went hoarse, he saw Drusus's motion for silence. Cries fell away down the long rows of soldiers like the slowly ebbing cheers of an audience at the theater. Following this, handlers arrived on the hill to help organize the elephants' withdrawal. The Macedonians did not harass them as the elephants returned to their positions in the formation, which consumed nearly a half hour.

At last, they reversed their march, with Varro's maniple attached to a rear to guard against a surprise sally from the camp. Yet the Macedonians cowered, and the entire army marched with their heads shaking in disgust back into camp.

Despite the lack of battle, the soldiers celebrated. Varro guessed he was not alone in the relief at having been spared a day of fighting. Men died even in victory. So the release spread through the camp, softening when near officers who had anticipated a good fight. Centurion Drusus was one such officer. He and his counterpart reviewed the maniple before dismissing them. Drusus's round head was creased with frustration that shined as bright as the sweat from the marching in full panoply shined on his face.

"I call Philip a coward. He'll prove me wrong if he has some better ruse planned for us. But hiding from battle is pure cowardice. I despise that, especially in one who calls himself a king. So he's fine to attack Athens and make a mess out of the world as long has he thinks he can win. All he earned was shame and scorn today. What complete loss of dignitas."

Two centuries of the maniple nodded. Varro, like his companions, wanted to assuage Drusus's frustration so he would dismiss them to rest. Evening encroached with cool winds and pale light fleeing a purple sky, lengthening the shadows of the hastati assembled before their barracks row.

With a final huff and shake of his head, Drusus dismissed them. Optio Tertius oversaw the dispersal of Varro's century, giving him a curt nod as they filed off into their barracks.

Inside their crowded front room, they unstrapped their bronze pectorals, set their helmets and weapons on racks, and hung their packs. Varro removed his stakes and set them on the floor. These three sharpened stakes were used for reinforcing marching camps. Most men kept theirs ready in the pack, but Varro worried the sharp points would pierce the leather. Others lightened their packs so as to not stretch the straps suspending them from the wall pegs.

"Someone's been in my pack," Panthera said. "My patera is at the bottom."

Otho pulled out his bronze patera, the pan used in the field to cook and eat their suppers. He held it up in his meaty hands.

"Mine's here."

"I didn't say it was missing," Panthera said, digging into his pack. "I always keep it on the top, but it has been pushed to the bottom."

"Probably just shifted to the bottom from all the marching and fighting," Curio said. Yet Panthera shook his head.

"No, this is not jumbled. Someone carefully put everything back, but in the wrong place. I suppose since everything is here, I am not going to worry."

He placed it on the peg beside Falco's pack, keeping his bronze patera in hand.

Slaves outside the barracks door announced the nightly ration of pork. Cordus and Sura were already dragging out the cooking pot and trestle. Varro's stomach growled, earning a laugh from Curio.

"Your stomach talks more than you do."

The contubernium filed outside. But Varro remained behind with Falco, who had gone rigid after Panthera's observation. He remained staring at his pack, his heavy brows shading his eyes. But Varro did not need to see them to feel the tension.

"Keep an eye on the door," he said in a low voice. "I'm going to check on our packs."

"I'm sure Panthera was just mistaken. Anyway, our packs have been on our backs for a few days already. Everything is fine."

Falco set his pack on the ground, and began removing the contents. His three stakes clattered on the floor. Next he set aside whetstones and a flask of concentrated wine. He dug deeper and began shoving aside the other contents with increasing violence. Soon he was a like a dog digging for a bone. He upended the pack, thumping everything onto the floor.

"You all right in there?" Panthera returned, but Varro leaped into the doorway and blocked him.

"Yes, it's fine. Falco just upended his pack accidentally. Do you need help starting the fire?"

"Cordus has it going now." Panthera tried to glance over Varro's shoulder, but lost interest when Varro did not shift.

Tossing his arm around Panthera's shoulder, he guided him outside. The recruits had the fire started and the slaves had filled their cooking pot with water. They crowded around it, adding ingredients to the pork broth. Curio led most of the chatter, talking about the elephant charge and how he would've liked to see some Macedonians flattened.

But Varro turned his ears to behind, where Falco bumped and banged around the front room.

Another tumultuous thumping echoed out of the barracks, turning both Panthera's and Varro's heads. He put a hand to Panthera's back.

"You help get the meal ready. I'll go see what Falco's doing."

Inside Falco stood between two leather packs, both turned out and their contents scattered. The whites of his eyes shined from the shadows of his eyes' sockets.

"Both halves are gone. We've been robbed."

14

Falco seized Curio's pack from the peg and dumped the contents to the floor with the scattered mess of two other packs. Gear clattered and clanged, but Falco simply kicked through it.

"Are you mad?" Varro leaped to grab his friend and steal back Curio's pack. He snatched it away, limp and cold leather deflating in his hand.

"He must have hidden it somewhere else." Falco's crazed eyes searched the small room, his nostrils flaring. Varro shook him.

"You don't know Curio took it."

"I don't?" He sneered at Varro. "He was spying on us while we talked about it. Who else would know what we had?"

"The same person who returned it to me."

This paused Falco, but he snorted and rolled his head back. "Return it to us then take it away? That makes no sense."

"Nothing makes sense," Varro said, mocking Falco's tone. "Someone told me that once. So just calm down a moment."

Panthera now reappeared in the doorway. His smile faded to

concern as he saw the scattered contents of three full packs spread on the floor.

"Don't worry," Varro said. "Falco is confused about something he lost. A memento from his father. Just give me a moment with him and keep the others out, please."

Panthera's expression shifted again, this time to sympathy. While none of the others in the contubernium knew Falco's father had died, Varro had informed Panthera. It seemed he should know such news.

"I see," he said. "You'll clean this up? If Tertius comes by we'll be in trouble."

"Yes, yes." Varro spun Panthera around and guided him out the door. The scent of the boiling pork and spices set his mouth watering. Outside the others were bent over the cooking pot and filling their bowls. But he had to deal with Falco, who remained standing amid the mess with both fists balled.

"Curio stole the necklace," Falco said, hissing through gritted teeth. "And I'm going to find out where he hid it."

"You don't know that," Varro said. "Look, I'm as mad as you are. It's my fortune too. But we've got to go about finding it with more care than this. Whoever took it knows more about us than we do about him. There's more risk here than you think."

"I'm bigger and stronger than Curio. I'm the best fighter of all seven of us. There's no risk."

Varro clucked his tongue and started to gather up Curio's gear. "I'll put his pack together. Just fix yours then behave yourself. If you think it's Curio then we'll deal with him. But until we know, try not to be a complete fool."

Falco narrowed his eyes and curled his lip as he stared out the door to the fading light. But then he nodded and bent to collect his gear. Once they had completed restoring all three packs and hanging them, both joined the others.

"Saved you some scraps," Curio said with a bright smile. "We thought you weren't hungry."

Varro's hands went cold anticipating Falco's explosive response. Yet he laughed and squatted beside the cooking pot. He extended his bowl for Cordus to fill it.

"Generous of you," Falco said. "As I'd expect from a wealthy man."

Curio laughed but the others frowned in confusion. The broth along with slices of pork and cabbage plopped into the bowl, which Falco then stepped away to eat.

Varro accepted the last of the broth, finding it fuller with meat than expected. He wished it had more salt, but his stomach welcomed the warm flood of sustenance. He observed Falco and Curio from over the brim of his bowl. But neither gave any outward signs of awkwardness. Falco's comment must have been deemed a poor joke, for no one questioned why he thought Curio wealthy. That Curio himself did not question this led Varro to wonder if he had stolen their gold.

Night arrived with a gust of cold wind and a spangled indigo sky of stars. Beneath the impassive glare of the gods in their starry forms, the Roman camp settled for a night on alert. With Philip's camp so near, and his denial of battle during the day, they were to remain alert for action. Optio Tertius, completing his final rounds, stopped by as Panthera and Varro were burying their campfire.

"Sleep with your swords and shields ready," he said. Panthera laughed at this, but the optio glared at him. "It's not a manner of speech. It'd take no effort for Philip to launch a night raid being so close to our camp. Be ready for anything. Now, sleep well."

After he left, Panthera muttered about nightmares of Macedonians burning him alive in his bunk. Yet they completed their duties and the entire contubernium settled into the cool darkness of their bunk room. Varro pulled up his wool blanket, the roughness of it scratching his chin. The bunk above creaked with Falco's shifting weight. Across from him Curio lay on the top bunk over Gallio's vacant spot. One of the recruits had taken his bedding, probably Otho, to leave the bare wood frame and rope straps exposed. Varro stared at it, remembering how he helped construct the bed. This tiny room and all its furniture were the labors of him and seven other men. How could they build so much together, yet one betray them and another steal from them?

Varro's eyes drooped and sleep crept upon him as he stared into the darkness. Then he snapped awake when Falco's feet hit the floor. Despite just awakening, Varro's pulse raced as he realized Falco was going to do the stupid thing he expected.

"Curio?" he whispered into the dark. Varro heard his feet slide across the floor to the opposite bunk. His white tunic was a faint gray patch hovering in darkness. "Curio? Wake up. We've got orders."

Varro hesitated, worrying if stopping Falco would alert everyone else and require an uncomfortable explanation. He also wanted to dispel his doubt of Curio. Maybe taking him outside to talk made sense. But this was Falco's plan, and talking was not his way. A beating was more likely.

Sitting up too fast, his head swam and he had to fall back to keep the world from spinning out of control. Damn Gallio for that blow to his head! Now he heard Curio answer then also slip to the floor. Rather than call out, Varro decided to follow behind as the two exited the barracks room.

Rising slowly, he did not experience the swimming sensation and padded out after the two men.

"What's this about?" Curio asked as he stepped outside.

Falco answered by snapping a headlock on Curio, who squealed in surprise. Falco clamped his hand over Curio's mouth, muffling his shouts. The two scrambled around with Curio trying to break free and Falco trying to drag him off the road between barracks to the rear where Optio Tertius had recently reprimanded them.

As they scuffled, Falco lost his balance and fell toward the barracks. Varro jumped in to block him from knocking against the wall.

"Lily, glad you're here. Help me get him behind the barracks."

"Falco, what are you doing?" Varro hissed his question, but still grabbed Curio by his arms. He worked these behind his back. Better that he get everyone under control than let the two fight.

"This little traitor is going to confess to all he's been up to since he joined us," Falco said, grunting as he twisted Curio's neck.

The dangerous hold gave pause to the smaller man. With Varro pinning his arms and Falco locked around his neck, he went limp in surrender. Falco did not hesitate, but dragged him around the back of the barracks to darkness relieved only by the silver patina of starlight.

"All right, I'm going to let you go," Varro said. "Falco and I just want to talk."

Falco snapped his head up in surprise. His heavy brows drew together.

"Now's not the time for that stupid peace shit, Varro. The truth is only going to come if you beat it out of him."

"He's not our enemy. Treat him with respect."

Varro's concentration had slackened and his hold on Curio loosened. He was the smallest of the contubernium but by no means weak. His arms broke free and he slammed one fist into Falco's groin. The larger man doubled over with a groan, but did not release his hold.

Curio landed a second and third blow before Varro could react, and Falco at last staggered back from the battering to his crotch. He released Curio to defend himself. Hair tousled and face red, Curio glared at the both of them.

"You fucking bastards! You want a fight?"

"No, we wan—"

The punch sprawled Varro to the grass. He hadn't even seen it coming before his left eye burst into white stars that filled his sight. His head spun like he was trapped in a whirlpool from an ancient Greek legend. He felt as if he were sinking while his breath grew heavy and labored. Yet worse than anything was a terrible metallic ringing that shrieked within his head. The relentless scream made him ball up and hold his hands to his ears, yet to no avail.

The spinning and the ringing made him feel as if Curio had thrown him into another world of noise and darkness. He could do nothing but cling to the cold earth and pray the world would stabilize enough for him to open his eyes. But he dared not while everything spiraled around him.

Soon he grew aware of warm hands gripping him at both shoulders and both ankles. Yet even so he spun. Voices spoke, but the piercing metal wail filled his skull. He could not understand the words. The voices remained insistent and the grips held firm. Soon, the spinning and squealing subsided. He heard Falco's raspy whisper over him and felt his iron grip crushing his ankles.

"You fucking killed him, Curio!"

"He's not dead, just dazed." Curio's equally hushed and husky voice was filled with irritation. "Dead men don't kick and moan, you stupid shit."

Varro at last blinked his eyes open and Curio's red and swollen face looked into his. He raised his head, feeling dizzy and numb. He did not experience much pain, but his head felt as if it had been covered in a heavy woolen sack. Curio held his legs steady and his eyes flashed two points of starlight back at him.

"You were kicking like mad," he said. "If I let you go, will you stop?"

Varro groaned in answer, and both Curio and Falco released him.

"I didn't hit you that hard."

Putting his hands over his head, Varro squeezed his eyes together to regain his focus. "I've still not recovered from Gallio's attack. Now my own companions are going to kill me before the Macedonians have a chance."

"I'm sorry," Curio said. "But you attacked me first."

Falco protested and the two broke into a hushed argument of recrimination. Falco was certain he would never have children and Curio claimed the two were going to kill him unless he defended himself. At last, Varro sat up and hissed them to silence.

"This is all a stupid mistake," he said. "It's cold and dark and a patrol will pick us up any time. Let's just get to the point."

"There's a point?" Curio asked. He extended his hand to help Varro up, but Falco shoved in front to offer his hand instead. Varro looked at the pale hand, but stood under his own efforts.

"Yes, just answer one question." Varro had to grab Falco's shoulder or else fall over. His head swam and a faint ringing still rose and fell in his ears. "Did you go through our packs looking for something?"

Curio smiled, searching between him and Falco. "You dragged me out here by my ears to ask if I've gone through your packs?"

"Yeah," Falco said. "And you better tell us the truth. I know what you did. So just admit it."

"Admit what? I've got my own pack and gear to worry about. You two think I'd sharpen some extra stakes for you or what? Worried you'd lose the fun of cleaning your own gear? Don't worry for it, because I never touched your packs."

"That's a lie," Falco said. He stepped forward, but Varro still held his shoulder and pulled him back. He whirled around. "You believe that? He was listening in on us. Of course he knows."

"What do I know?" Curio folded his arms, his smile bent into a frown. "Are you talking about that day the two of you were planning something? Falco's been staring at me like I fucked his sister ever since. You know what? I don't care what you were discussing.

Don't drag me into your problems. Whatever you two are about, it better not get me in trouble. We're already in trouble for fighting out here, if we get caught. So can I get back to bed before that happens?"

"All right," Varro said. "He's innocent. It was someone else."

"I'm not convinced," Falco said. He pulled out of Varro's grip and folded his arms to match Curio. The tallest and smallest members of the contubernium squared off, both tilting their heads back in defiance.

"Believe whatever you want," Curio said. "I never touched your packs. Who has time for anything like that? Whatever is missing, you lost it yourselves."

"Don't mention this to anyone else," Varro said. "I'm sorry for what happened. I'll make it up to you."

"Apologizing?" Falco's voice rose and he slapped his hands atop his head. "He stole our gold!"

Varro stepped back in shock and Falco's belated realization froze him in place.

"Gold?" Curio asked, leaning in. "You were hiding gold in your packs? No wonder you're shitting yourselves. You stole something and it was stolen from you. Serves you both right."

"Hold on," Varro said. "We never stole anything."

Falco covered his face, shaking his head in his hands. Varro took Curio aside and explained how he had claimed the necklace from the brigand chief he defeated earlier in the year. He left out details of how Optio Latro stole it and its mysterious return after his death.

Curio placed the back of his wrist over his mouth to stifle a laugh.

"And you think I overheard you talking about it, and then decided to steal it from you. Well, it wasn't me. But I'll promise you this. You two idiots must've let it slip to someone else and now they've got it. So think about where you've discussed this and who might've heard. And there's your culprit."

Varro sighed, and he and Falco stared at each other a long moment.

"But now I know," Curio said. "And I can help you get it back. If I do that, of course, I'll want a share."

"We killed the brigand," Falco said. "So it's ours."

"It's not yours any longer." Curio smiled and patted Falco's shoulder. "If I help you get it back, then it's ours. Split it three ways, and it should still be worth quite a bit for all of us. I promise, I'll keep it quiet."

In the end, they could only agree with Curio. They slipped back into the bunk room as if nothing had happened. Except Varro's head spun and his ears rang. He fell asleep, deep and cold.

And he did not awaken the next morning.

15

Varro's mind hung somewhere between the world and a place of dark fog. He saw things in the fog that made no sense to him. It was cold and lifeless there, a peek into a world where no living man could exist. He certainly had not found the Elysian Fields. On the contrary, he realized he lay in a bed in the hospital. The assistants chatted in Greek, their voices low and companionable. Varro could not see them out of his foggy, fixed point of view. He could only look up at the wooden rafters.

Around him in the distance men shouted to each other. Hammers pounded on wood and mules brayed. He thought an elephant trumpeted. But the voices were closest, and he recognized the doctor's accented Latin. He spoke with another man, perhaps an officer as high as a tribune by his diction and the doctor's deference to him.

"It has been two days, sir," the doctor said. "But he has moments of clarity."

"And you believe this was a caused by a second blow to his head?" The unfamiliar voice was nearer than the doctor. Varro felt the weight of his presence at his side.

"There is bruising around the temple area that suggest knuckles struck him there. None of his fellows claim anything of the sort happened. My guess is he was struck during the recent combat and later experienced the affects. He has not fully recovered from his first blow to the head. To be struck a second time is nearly a guarantee of serious injury. Even death."

"Yet he was nonetheless put in line?" The stranger approached, his hobnails clomping on the floor.

"Of course, sir. He was capable of combat, but not of suffering another blow to his head."

The derisive laugh was close to Varro's ear. He wanted to turn to see the man, or else blink or speak. But he was frozen in place like invisible hands held him still.

"Such is the Roman way. We ask much of our citizens, and they bear it all without complaint. I admire such men. Can he hear me, do you think?"

"It is hard to say, sir. Even if he did, it is unlikely he would remember anything in this state."

"Will he recover?"

"He has already awakened and seems to have control over his body, sir."

"I mean, will he recover enough to be useful?"

"Ah, that I cannot say until he remains awake long enough for a full examination, sir."

Varro could hear the shrug in the doctor's voice. He was aware of the stranger's presence hovering close to his left side. A clean, strong scent reached Varro's nose. This might be the only way he could recognize the man in the future, and he marked it well. For whatever the doctor said, he was certain he would remember this encounter if only for its bizarreness.

"Keep me apprised of his progress. I cannot remain here long." The man paused, and leaned closer. "If you do hear me, Varro, and you do remember this, then know you will owe a favor. Until then rest well, son."

The doctor's and stranger's voices faded off. Varro again felt tired and sleepy, and the sound of hobnails on the floor echoed into the darkness which pulled him down once more.

The intermittent fog and confusion seemed to continue on until one day he realized he was sitting on the edge of his bed and speaking to the doctor. A sleepy-eyed assistant hovered behind him. The doctor, who seemed to have been speaking, now tilted his head with a wry smile.

"That is a new look? Do you know what you're doing, Varro?"

He blinked, looking between doctor and assistant.

"I'm wondering how many more times I'll see you before I die."

The doctor laughed, clapping his hands.

"Most don't see me more than once. But you are Fortuna's favorite son. It is as if a caul has been pulled from your head and you were reborn right before me this moment." He turned to his assistant, who nodded with admiration. "I want to do some tests. Are you able?"

Again Varro blinked, then shrugged. He felt as if he could do anything asked of him. A vague confusion clung to him, however. He remembered promising himself to remember something, but could not recall. His last clear memory was agreeing to split the necklace three ways if they could find it again.

The doctor instructed him to perform basic actions like moving his arms and legs and tilting his head in various directions. Nothing bothered him besides stiffness from having been immobile so long. He then quizzed Varro on basic questions for what seemed hours. Though he had a terrible headache, he answered every question.

By the end of the doctor's tests he realized he was no longer in a wooden hospital building. He was in an expansive tent. A spot of brilliance shined through the top of it, marking the sun at just past midday. The beds were the same, only spaced out differently with the doctor's main desk placed at the center. Varro searched around, finding a half-dozen other patients lying in their beds. The assistants migrated between them, leaning over to tend to their patients.

"What happened? The building is gone?"

The doctor pulled up a stool and sat opposite of Varro. He smiled and looked toward the tent flap where light spilled in, broken by the restless shadows of passersby.

"Consul Galba decided our camp was too close to Philip's and that it was unsafe to forage. So we pulled down our walls and buildings, salvaged what we could, destroyed what we could not, then relocated about eight miles more distant from our original camp. We are near a place called Ottolobum. There is more grain in the surroundings and a marsh and forest for additional forage. Philip's cavalry cannot reach our men here."

"How long have I been here?" Varro scratched his head around Gallio's old wound, looking to others in the hospital. They did not seem to suffer battle wounds, and so he guessed they were ill or otherwise injured out of combat. He hoped his friends had not gone to fight without him.

"Less than a week," the doctor said. "So we have erected tents this time, and more permanent buildings will wait. Perhaps with Philip so near now, Consul Galba can bring the war to swift conclusion."

"That would be welcomed," Varro said. He stared at his feet, now clean and smooth. With all the marching and fighting, he could never scrub the dirt from between his toes. He had forgotten what clean feet felt like. "The Macedonians didn't attack?"

"They harassed us while tearing down the former camp. But we have been left at peace since. Philip does not seem to have the stomach to fight."

Varro recalled the war elephants raging outside the ramparts of the Macedonian camp and the cowardly silence that greeted them.

"I am glad not to fight," he said. "But we'll never be sent home until Philip is defeated."

The doctor laughed. "Well, that day must come soon. Winter is at hand, and the season for fighting will soon end. I think Philip may settle into winter quarters, much as we thought to do until forced to pull up stakes. Still I have hope Consul Galba forms a plan to drag him out and spare us a winter in camp."

Varro thought of passing a winter in tents. At least with the others sharing it with him, they might keep each other warm. He laughed to himself. Never in his life would he imagine pushing up to Falco to stay warm through winter.

After further review, the doctor released him to report to Centurion Drusus or Optio Tertius.

"There is too much to do," the doctor said. "So I will clear you for all duties. But protect your head. You may wish to make an offering to Fortuna to watch over you. You have been twice lucky, and have prevailed on the goddess's favor too often. Your head will heal if you let it, but a third blow any time soon and you will not stand again. I am not wrong about it, young Varro. So don't disappoint me. I've no wish to find you in one of my beds drooling on yourself and unable to speak."

"How soon is soon?"

The doctor hunched his shoulders and faced both palms out. "Don't hit your head, Varro. That is all I can say. It is good advice for anyone. Now report to your officers before they curse me again for coddling you."

Outside the camp, the midday sun warmed him, but the chill never left the air and he wished for a cloak. He brushed the side of his head where he had been struck, finding it tender against his fingertips. Dressed in his cleaned tunic with no weapon or armor to carry, he felt like a civilian again. For an instant, he wished he was anywhere but this patch of dead grass on a hill in a foreign land. But he was stuck here until the war ended or injury or death ended it for him. He frowned at his choices.

"A moment of self-pity can be forgiven," he mumbled while taking the path to headquarters. A warm bed with no duties or dangers hanging over him had made him homesick.

The layout of the camp remained exactly as the others Varro had lived in during his enlistment. The roads, which were simple tracks cleared through the grass at this point, followed the same patterns. The walls were the same low ramparts and undoubtedly surrounded by a ditch on the outside. They had probably taken the same stakes from the old camp and replaced them here. He heard the elephants across camp. They were noisy beasts, given to trumpeting and thundering about their pit. Varro was glad he had slept through this reconstruction. Only the tents were different from the temporary buildings constructed at the last site. They would not likely build with wood again until certain the camp would hold another season.

Headquarters were different now that there were no offices. He asked directions to Centurion Drusus and found him with several others inside a larger tent. They stood together, arms folded in amicable conversation.

"And here is the hardest head in Rome," he announced to the others. "If you ever find yourselves lacking a battering ram, Varro's head would be a fine substitute."

The other centurions laughed, and Drusus excused himself to greet Varro outside the tent in the light of parade ground. Groups of soldiers and messengers crisscrossed the wide field, which was already flattened and battered from thousands of footsteps already set down in the early days of this new camp.

"So you managed to take a nap long enough to avoid all the work." Drusus clapped his shoulder and studied him. His round, creased head tilted as he judged Varro's health. "Any restrictions from the doctor?"

"None, sir. He says there is much to be done. I'm sorry to have been unavailable when the others needed me. Please help me make it up to the others, sir."

Drusus laughed. "Optio Tertius will see you do your share. Go find your contubernium and prepare for an offensive. We're going to finish the coward Philip and be home before winter ends."

His arrival back at his barracks was tepid. He passed Panthera and the recruits, who barely smiled and did not stop to ask after him. Falco met him before the gray and dirty tent bobbing in the afternoon breeze. It was one of long rows of tents.

"Don't take it personally. No one is happy sleeping on the ground with our feet in each other's faces. This tent makes our last barracks feel like a senator's villa."

The tent was crowded with bedrolls and their gear. At last their contubernium had been assigned two slaves as permanent attendants, and they slept behind the tent. Varro searched for his gear, which he found.

"There's no space for my bedroll," he said, looking wide-eyed to Falco.

"Like I said. Don't take it personally. But now we've got to crowd in for you."

"And there's one more member still to be assigned," Curio said. He sat on the grass just inside the tent twisting blades in his fingers. "I guess we didn't realize how good things were until now."

"I guess not." Varro stared forlornly at the interior and imagined the bunks he had derided as terrible only a week ago.

The next days passed with Varro and the rest resuming normal duties. They marched and drilled as they always had. Varro's head strangely felt clearer than ever. In a private moment, Curio took credit for the recovery.

"Think of it," he said during a pause in the sword drills. "Gallio let a forest spirit in your head when he opened it up. I knocked it out of you when it was already loose. Seems I did you a favor. You owe me doubly now."

"That remains to be seen," Varro said. He offered Curio a laugh, but still suspected the little man whom Optio Latro had introduced to them from the velites. Curio always seemed to know something he should not know, or at least appear as such.

After three more days, the Roman forage teams were now going out to the nearby forest. The marshland was still avoided, but would eventually be explored for anything of use. Bountiful hauls of grains from the surrounding area now filled the camp's storage houses. The move to Ottolobum had been an excellent decision. On this day, an overcast and blustery day presaging winter's eminent arrival, Varro and the others were assigned to forage teams going out to the forest.

By now everyone knew of Varro's aversion to woodlands, and at least Panthera seemed to agree with him.

"Varro's right," he said while strapping his bronze helmet under his chin. "Whenever we go to a forest something awful happens. Nonius was killed by brigands the first time we foraged in the woods. It's been terrible ever since."

The recruits did not know Nonius, but the three stared down at their sandaled feet at the mention of death. Varro scratched his head around the soft flesh were Gallio had struck him. The healing cut was relentlessly itchy.

"I've made my prayers," Varro said. "And I'd make an offering to Fortuna if I had anything to give. Hopefully this time will be different."

They joined a forage team of about five hundred men. While some would be collecting wood, most, including Varro, were to forage for game. Being the nominal head of his contubernium, Varro would organize their efforts.

The column of men marched out of the camp and followed a

freshly laid path to an established main road. The mood among the foragers was cheerful, for Philip had refused to show battle since the elephants had challenged his camp. Unlike Centurion Drusus's prediction, Philip seemed to be settling in for winter. Varro had hoped for that decisive battle and a swift end to this war. He would not need to find Gallio if the legions were demobilized, at least until he had to serve again at some future date. But others did not share his disappointment and so chatted happily on their long march to the pine forest. Their forage duty excused them from the rigors of marches, drills, and other menial tasks. Most men enjoyed time outside the camp, even if in full battle gear.

"With five hundred men tramping into the woods, I don't think we'll find much." Falco strode beside him, squinting into the flat glare from the gray sky. "Won't all the animals flee?"

"It's just supplemental," Varro said. "It's not like we're going to starve if we don't bring home carts of game today. And half the men are collecting walnuts."

"I wonder what winter is like here," Panthera said. "Will it snow?"

They debated whether there would be snow during winter. No one actually knew where they were, and so could not decide on the likelihood. They agreed that it was colder here and probably higher in elevation. So snow might fall some cold night. Varro had heard horrifying stories of men freezing in high mountains. But he doubted they were so high here.

Their debate lasted until they were once again under the oppressive branches of the forest. Varro immediately felt its damp darkness pressing upon him. Yet he had a duty and they beat the brushes for whatever they could find. After several hours of this, they had managed to catch three rabbits and two squirrels. They hung these from a long pole that Otho shouldered. While their catch was not impressive, if their success repeated five hundred more times, the foragers would return with a good supplement for winter reserves.

They had dispersed into teams, with Varro, Curio, and Falco forming the team to catch the game the others herded toward them. While they waited in a clearing filled with pale green light slipping between the pine branches, Falco's eyes narrowed.

"Well, Curio, what did you find out?"

Varro raised his brow in confusion.

"I didn't find out anything," he answered. "While you were taking a nap for a week, Varro, I tried to learn who entered our barracks. I've asked around, and no one saw anything. The only thing I can say is that no one else had anything stolen. So you two were definitely targeted."

"Turns out Curio here is a popular man," Varro said, his eyes still narrowed in suspicion.

"I'm just friendlier than you two." He pointed to Falco. "You're just an ass to everyone you don't know. And Varro walks around in a cloud half the time. I talk to people and try to make friends. You never know when you'll need a friend."

Varro scratched the edges of the scab on his head. "Did anyone other than Panthera say their packs had been tampered with?"

"I don't think the recruits are organized enough to say. No one touched mine. Probably whoever robbed you got lucky right after going through Panthera's pack."

"So they only knew us enough to know our barracks, but not identify our packs." Varro folded his arms and stared off into the gloom. He heard Sura shouting as he herded game closer.

"One pack looks like another," Falco said. But Varro shook his head.

"Only at a glance. Someone who really knew us and spent time with us would know the difference. Especially if they planned to steal what we carried in our packs. So this means whoever robbed us doesn't know us all that well."

Falco tipped his head back. "Great. You've narrowed it down to about everyone in the legion. So we just need to look into about ten thousand more men and we'll find our gold."

"Don't be an ass, Falco." Varro again scratched his head. "At least we know it's not one of our own or our officers."

"Unless they wanted to make it look like it wasn't them," Curio said.

This silenced everyone and Varro considered the possibility. Officers could've just ordered an inspection of their packs and then claimed the gold themselves. But who else could be so cunning to disguise their search?

"No, if the thief wanted to make it seem like a random robbery, he would've thrown everyone's packs around. Though that would make a lot of noise." He shook his head. "Just keep asking around and maybe something will come up. Now that I'm back I can help as well."

They nodded in silent agreement.

Then the alarm whistles sounded. Sharp and desperate blasts on wooden whistles shrieked from all edges of the forest.

Varro's hands went cold and he looked into Falco's stunned face.

"Forests are cursed."

16

Varro and the others emerged from the woods to find Macedonian cavalry swarming the collection points. Their horses thundered past in tight formation. Roman soldiers shouted as the cavalry raced through their thin ranks. Varro watched one thrust his heavy pilum at a rider, only to have his hand hacked off as the Macedonian swooped past him.

"I thought Philip wasn't coming out until after winter?" Panthera pointed at the masses of cavalry charging over the open ground.

"We're dead in the open," Varro said, ignoring the obvious answer to the question. "There's no organization for our side. We're going to lose five hundred men and then another five hundred who come looking for us when we don't return."

"Encouraging," Falco said, staring grimly from beneath his helmet.

They all huddled behind trees or bushes at the edge of the forest. Some of their fellow soldiers attempted to form ranks but the Macedonian cavalry broke these apart before they could complete a formation. The wagons were overturned and the dead sprawled in the grass beside them. The collected forage now mixed with the blood of its guards.

"We've got to get around them," Varro said. "If we go into the open, we'll be run down. But cavalry can't reach us in the forest."

"Good point," Curio said as he pointed across the field. "But those soldiers can."

Varro and the rest stared across the field to the dark ranks of Macedonian auxiliaries marching toward them. Their line had halted so their officers could organize a blockade of the best escape routes. Smaller units were already breaking apart from the main lines, their spear points raised and gleaming in the flat light.

"If we stay together, we're going to be obvious targets." Varro held close to a thin tree trunk and watched as small units rallied to resist the cavalry attacks. But the cavalry surrounded then cut them down. Small piles of bodies bled out into the grass where the cavalry had completed its butchery.

"If we can get around the cavalry, then we can skirt the infantry on their south side." Varro tried to recall the path they followed into the forest. It had forked off the main road. Rough hills and trees to the north and the marshland to the south made the road the fastest way to camp.

"But we can't separate," Sura said. "We'll get killed or lost." He looked to Panthera for support, who stared ahead at the unfolding chaos.

"That's going to happen if we stay here," Varro said. "The infantry is closing in. They're going to flush us out the way we flushed those rabbits Otho is carrying. Now's the time to make a run. There's no shame in fleeing this disaster. There's no organization, no officers, no orders. We need to alert the camp. If Consul Galba can catch Macedonians in the open, he could destroy Philip's cavalry."

The enemy infantry now began advancing under the flat gray sky. The cavalry had pulled back to regroup. As far as Varro could tell, the enemy had not lost a single man. The groans and cries of the wounded filled the space between them and Varro.

"We'll spread out and make ourselves small. Curio and Cordus are the two smallest. So go together and you might escape. Otho, drop those rabbits please. You're big enough to go alone. Panthera and Sura are a team, and me and Falco. We'll lead off, so that if anyone spots us it'll be me and Falco. The rest of you can take advantage of that distraction."

They rushed along the edge of the forest as long as possible. With the Macedonians reforming, the Romans attempted to organize themselves. As far as Varro knew, their forage parties had no officers. Yet the whistles sounded in attempts to bring men together. Varro squeezed the shrill notes out of his hearing. Having been completely surprised, the Romans had no chance to form a cogent defense and Varro knew this.

He stopped them at the edge of the Macedonian line. A small detachment of auxiliary infantry blocked this avenue, likely Cretans since they carried the same round shields Varro had seen in his previous battles. But the uneven ground here meant cavalry would not risk their horses, and also scattered trees, bushes, and folds offered a chance at hiding a few men.

"Allow us a short lead, then follow," Varro said. Falco nodded to him and both men exited the safety of their woodlands hideout. They held their shields on their backs. Varro was grateful his was painted green and black while Falco's was pure black. He worried for Otho with his sheer size and red shield. But such worries faded as the tree line vanished behind him.

The enemy was already spreading out to catch any stragglers. He and Falco were darting straight into this widening net.

"This was a dumb idea," Falco said, scurrying with a bent back next to him.

"We could've fled deeper into the woods," Varro said, hushing his voice as he steered for a cluster of bushes. "But then we'd be executed for cowardice. So death is everywhere, friend."

He couldn't speak more. When the Cretan infantry turned his way, he threw himself flat into the cold and dry grass. It snapped over his face as he wished he could melt into the earth. Falco thudded beside him. His eyes were wide and white under his heavy brow.

Varro's heart thudded against the ground, but the Cretans scanned past him and pointed to something more distant. He lay atop his two pila, the points a thumb's breadth from his face. He could smell the iron.

He looked behind but did not see anyone following.

"We can't bunch up," he whispered to Falco. "Let's get to that tree, and from there we can probably get around them if we follow the fold in the ground."

Falco nodded hard enough to set his bronze helmet wobbling. It flashed in the diffuse sunlight, and Varro felt a sinking feeling in his gut. He waited for shouts from the enemy, but when nothing came, he got on hands and knees.

The Cretans had settled their lines, had shields raised, and began to advance. He and Falco were out of their approach.

"We're going to make it," Falco said. "By the gods, I thought we would surely die."

"But the others are going to be caught." Varro still hugged the ground, shield pressing on his back and hands clamped around his pila. He watched the Cretans nearing, then looked back toward the trees. He saw nothing but dark vertical trunks shoving up behind the golden brown of the dead field.

"You said it yourself," Falco said. "Someone has to get through to warn the consul."

"We're not letting the others die."

"Who says they'll die?" Falco now pulled up beside him, eyes fixed on the advancing line. "They can't follow now, so they'll go back into the trees. It just makes sense. How stupid do you think they are?"

"They're not stupid. They're brave."

Both he and Falco fell flat once more and shimmied down the fold as the enemy line approached. They had dispersed their formation, each keeping his round shield forward as they marched toward the trees. Their footfalls vibrated through the ground as they passed Varro and Falco hiding in the grass. He heard the men grumbling to each other in their strange language. Their officers did not care what noise they made and this struck Varro as undisciplined, which might be something he could take advantage of.

"They're past us," Falco hissed beside him. Their shoulders touched as they both waited to see what would happen. "We need to go."

"We need to be sure the others escaped into the trees."

"Or what?" Falco's hushed voice did not disguise his irritation. "Look, I love the others too. But I love my own life better. There's only two of us and at least twenty of the enemy. And they have about ten times as many more friends nearby to call on. We can't do anything."

Varro scanned across the field. The cavalry was already charging back on the wings of the main block of infantry pointing into the forest. They meant to kill every forager and not allow anyone to hide among the trees.

Rather than answer Falco's complaint, he watched for his own friends. He trusted Panthera to get them organized and fall back. He seemed to have the most sway with the recruits. Curio would probably survive no matter what happened. Yet he had to be certain.

The unit of twenty Cretans stopped short of the woods, perhaps only two dozen yards. Varro guessed their task was to clean up any stragglers attempting to flee around the edges of the main body. As Romans appeared they would pick them off.

"See? They've fallen back to safety. Now let's go." Falco shoved his shoulder into Varro's then crawled back to hands and knees.

"All right," Varro said. "They will have to find their own way."

He joined Falco in rising as high as he dared. None of the Cretans faced them, but with so many other enemies around they might still be discovered.

The shrill whistles of the Romans had all but ended. Instead he heard the victorious hollers of the enemy and the thunder of galloping horses. From his brief glance, it seemed the Romans had broken and scattered in every direction. The eager cavalry no longer held a formation but chased after these unfortunate men.

As he turned to continue on, he heard a massive bellow from the woods where the others hid.

Between the gaps in the Cretan line, he saw giant Otho lumbering out of the tree line. Others were with him, though Varro could not see who they were. He realized all five of them must be charging the enemy.

"By Mars," Falco said, straightening up. "They're throwing their lives away."

"No they're not," Varro said, already slipping off his shield. "They'll not die today."

"Are you fucking mad?"

But Varro was already charging ahead. Seven heavy infantry versus twenty light infantry made for desperate chances. But he counted on his superior training and gear to carry the fight. He readied his light pilum as his legs flew across the ground. Falco cursed him from behind as he sprinted ahead.

With all the countless hours of practice, he knew the moment his foot landed within proper casting distance for his light pilum. It sailed across the gap and landed plumb in the center of a Cretan's back. The man collapsed forward and screamed.

Varro shouted his fiercest war cry.

Falco did the same, just behind him. His pilum flew after Varro's, easily piercing the lower back of another Cretan.

The pila storm from the fore landed among the twenty Cretans. The thump and scream of the shocked enemies drowned out the distant clamor of battle. Seven men lay dead before they could react. Some had whirled to face Varro and Falco, who had closed to the distance for their heavy pila.

The second volley devastated the surprised enemy. Torn between two fronts, the Cretans lost fourteen men. They had misjudged the fighting prowess of the average Roman soldier and now they were outnumbered, six light troops to seven heavy Roman soldiers.

Varro's gladius sprang easily from its scabbard. He met the rear line and slammed his shield into the back of one man, then ran him through as he fell. It seemed cowardly to pierce a man's back, but this was no fair battle. He met the rest of the contubernium in the center in one swift, startling display of bloodshed. Twenty Cretans lay in the brown grass, dead or else screaming for it.

"I knew you would flank them," Panthera said. "I knew our pila would carry the day."

"I sure didn't," Falco said, standing over an enemy writhing around the pilum stuck through his chest. "I can't believe it."

"Gather up any pilum that looks usable. But let's be quick." Varro pushed his bronze helmet off his brow and scanned the overall scene. The Cretans were breaking up in pursuit of Roman pockets. Being so far on the flank they had a minor advantage that any cavalry soldier could easily negate.

The grizzly work of extracting pila yielded only three. All the others had bent or would not release from the corpses. Curio worked on one where the Cretan still lived. He screamed and begged for death, but Curio laughed at him as he churned the massive spear in the enemy's guts.

Varro claimed a light pila for himself then pointed their way forward.

"We can follow that fold and stay out of sight for a while. But we have to get to the main road. I know of no other way back, and I suspect that is true for most everyone else."

Falco grunted. "I'm sure the Macedonians know that too. They'll have cut off that way."

"There's the marsh," Varro said. "It does touch the edge of our camp. We could chance it."

"And drown?" Young Cordus thumped his bronze pectoral. "I'll chance the road."

"We won't be alone on the road," Varro said. "Any Roman who escaped will head to the same place. We should have a better chance to break through any defense the Macedonians left behind."

Their decision made, Varro led the way into the fold. They hunched low, paused at every sound. But soon threaded their way far behind the Macedonians. They emerged on a small hill. Beneath the flat gray sky Varro felt exposed, like an eagle would swoop down and carry him off. The hill was not high, but he could see the flashing spears of the enemy troops turning to chase down the stragglers. The cavalry were out of sight, hidden behind trees. Yet by their nature they could only keep to the plains or roads.

"Here's the path to the main road," Varro said, indicating the track they had followed. "Once we gain it, we'll run with all our might back to camp. Let's pray their cavalry is distracted with other stragglers."

"Better still," Falco said. "Let's pray our own men come out to meet us. It's a long run back."

They followed the path to the main road, and as predicted it swarmed with Macedonian cavalry. Varro and the others fled the road to a small copse of trees at the outskirts of the marsh.

"We can't hide here for long," Varro said. The others crowded around them, huddling against their massive shields. "They'll want to flush out the flanks for men like us. We can't see around that bend in the road, but my guess is there are more Macedonians there. It must be a rally point."

Falco grumbled and hit his fist against a thin trunk.

"They're preparing for Consul Galba's response. They know he'll send men to learn what happened to us."

"And so the Macedonians will pick us apart and never have to face our full strength." Varro looked between all the blank faces. They waited for him to provide direction. Yet he had no better answer than anyone else. He wished he had not been so free in giving his opinions, earning him leadership duties that sat ill with him.

"We can't move ahead without facts," he said. "Curio and Cordus, you are the smallest of us. We're safe enough here for the moment. Scout ahead and learn what's happening up the road. Then we can decide how to get back."

Both Curio and Cordus stacked their shields under bushes, having no need of the cumbersome scutum shield while scouting. With grim nods to the rest, both silently set off along the road. They crouched low, dropping prone whenever cavalry galloped past. Soon they vanished out of sight.

"They really did it," Falco whispered from beside him. "Good work, Tribune."

"Don't jest now," Varro said, straining to see either of the two men. But they had gone past the bend. Satisfied he had made the right choice, he let his shoulders droop and he turned to the others.

Giant Otho stood full height, staring placidly in the direction Curio and Cordus had taken. The bushes barely reached to his waist and his freshly painted red shield faced the road.

"You fucking fool!" Varro stepped back in shock, pointing toward the road. "Do you want to be found?"

But Otho's answer came in the sound of pounding hooves. Three cavalrymen had emerged onto the track, and apparently spotting Otho, now drove their mounts for them.

Varro and Falco each had one light pilum. Curio had taken the third. He reflexively cocked his arm to cast, but the swift moving target charging at him was both narrow and unstable. Deciding he would only lose the pilum, he dropped his arm.

"Into the marsh! Spread out!"

Panthera and Sura had already fled ahead of them. At least Otho was brave if stupid and remained with shield ready.

Now they split up, each racing in a different direction.

Varro's heart pounded as he fled, the wild beating a match for the thumping hooves behind him. Fear of death carried him with the speed of Mercury. Yet the horse snorted close behind and his back prickled with the anticipation of a cold blade slashing open his spine.

The marsh was still distant, but Panthera and Sura had already reached its edge. He could not look to either side as he fled. His cheeks puffed as he heaved forward. The ground underfoot shook with the closing horse. The Macedonian cavalryman chortled with delight.

Then the horse screamed and a tremendous crash shuddered through the ground. Something struck Varro underfoot and sent him careening into the air. He screamed. The cavalryman screamed. And his horse let out a terrible, choking cry unlike anything he had ever heard. Snapping bones sounded like breaking branches.

Varro landed on his back, then rolled along the ground. His shield and pilum flew from his grip and his gladius tore away in the violent collision.

He lay in a pile beside the thrashing horse and Macedonian cavalryman. A light pilum stuck in the horse's neck and bright blood flowed over its slick brown coat. The rider had fallen but had apparently leapt from his saddle. For he already regained his footing and still held his thin, swooping sword.

The Macedonian cursed, all white teeth and bulging eyes as he leaped over his dying horse to fight Varro.

He pulled his pugio from its sheath with the same deft motions he would for his sword. This was his mother's gift, blessed at the temple of Mars, carried by his uncle on campaign, and the weapon that had slain Optio Latro. It would end this cavalryman as well.

Varro stepped back as the enemy landed. He slashed high for where Varro's head should have been. But he ducked and swooped in low. The Macedonian wore a chain shirt like Roman cavalry. But Varro knew such armor could be defeated.

He punched with his pugio using all his strength. He aimed below the Macedonian's extended arm, and the wide blade cut through the chain links. It plunged down to its hilt, spraying dark blood over Varro's hand and blasting him with a sour exhalation of his enemy's dying breath.

The Macedonian fell forward, carried by the momentum of his strike. He crashed into Varro, impaled on his blade, and threw his feeble arm around him like greeting an old friend. His sword tumbled out of his grip and he slid to the ground. Varro released his pugio so it would not snap.

"You all right?"

Falco arrived, standing opposite of the dying horse. It kicked and screamed but its violence weakened as its blood streamed into the dirt.

"Nice throw." He pointed to the horse.

"I was aiming for the rider."

Varro's sense snapped back from the precipice of near-death. He dropped into a crouch, expecting another attack. But Falco shook his head, his mouth hanging open from his exertions.

"The other two left. Didn't like their chances, I guess. Panthera and Sura got away. But Otho…"

Leaving the dying horse behind, Varro ran alongside Falco to where Otho lay in the grass. He looked as if he were an oversized boy staring at shapes in the clouds above.

A cavalry sword had cut off his right ear, slashed open a thick flap of skin from his neck, continued over the collarbone, and stopped at the top edge of his bronze pectoral. His skin had gone ashen and blood poured from his neck like dark wine from a decanter.

"I'm sorry, sir." Otho's voice was hoarse and weak. "I gave us away."

"I'm not an officer," Varro said, kneeling beside him. He placed his hand on Otho's. The meaty hands were like ice.

"Oh, sorry. You act like one."

"Do you have a message you want to get home? I can deliver it for you. Just tell me."

"Yes, thank you."

Then Otho's eyes unfocused and the blood running out his neck slowed to a trickle.

Varro stared at the dead man. He had spent no effort to know him and felt guilty for it.

"We should bury him," he said. "We can't just leave him here."

"I know we should." Falco's voice was patient and warm, and he placed his hand on Varro's shoulder. "But those two cavalry got away and will be back with help to finish us."

"What about Curio and Cordus?"

"I don't know. Maybe they've been caught already. But we can't stay. Cavalry moves too fast and we need a head start."

Varro knew this was true. He retrieved his pugio from the corpse and recovered all his weapons and shield. Then he and Falco fled into the marsh after the others.

17

If anything smelled worse to Varro than a dank forest, it was marshland. It smelled like rotting hair. He clomped along with Falco behind him, jumping from one patch of spongy earth to the next. In the short time they had been navigating the marsh, Varro had twice stepped into cold water up to his mid-calf. While the slimy residue was uncomfortable, he feared the depth of the water. One misstep and he might plunge to his death.

"I think we've gone far enough," Falco said. "We can't see the road from here. We should be safe."

Varro halted, setting his light pilum down on the wet ground. He kept his shield on his arm so its iron edges would not touch the water.

"I'd give anything to have my scutum bag now," he said. "My arm is sore from holding it."

"Well, Optio Tertius would tell you its fine training. Try to be positive."

Falco joined him on the flat mound of earth in the swampy expanse. Clumps of trees dotted the wide area, but it was mostly high grasses on small hillocks that rose out of the dark water.

Insects flew around his head, tiny and irritating things that couldn't be seen until they formed into cloud-like swarms. Waving these away did nothing to dispel them.

"I think I've found something I hate worse than forests."

Falco grunted. "Tell me about it. We've been walking in a straight line but I think we're still lost. Every direction looks the same."

Varro tilted his head to the sky. The glare caused him to squint, but the sun was nothing more than a diffuse splotch of brilliance behind heavy gray clouds. He was no good at determining direction, but he could at least guess the right way back to camp with a clear sky.

"I hope the others are all right," he said. "Why haven't we found Panthera or Sura yet? They were not that far ahead of us."

Falco shrugged. "Nothing ever makes sense. Maybe they drowned."

"Gods, Falco. Don't say it."

"I almost stepped into a deep drop and I'm trying to be careful. They were running for their lives."

Varro did not want to know what drowning in cold muck would feel like. He shivered at the thought.

"Do you think Curio and Cordus got through?"

Again Falco shrugged, drawing an exasperated sigh from Varro.

They set off again, neither acknowledging the purpose of their wandering. Were they searching for Panthera and Sura or trying to find the camp or just avoiding the Macedonians? Somehow Varro felt if he spoke these questions aloud it would somehow invite disaster. As the doctor had promised, he had prevailed on the gods too often. Now they would scorn him. He wanted to crawl along the earth, unnoticed by them, and solve the problems on his own.

Using his pilum like a walking stick, Varro tested the ground ahead. This made for slow but safe progress deeper into the marsh.

"Now I understand why we carry our packs into battle. A bit of wine wouldn't go wrong now."

"I'll never go anywhere without mine again," Falco said. "Too bad I didn't learn that lesson earlier. We wouldn't have lost our necklace."

"Are you still thinking of that now? Where are we even going, Falco? I'm just walking ahead."

"Well aren't you the leader? I'm just following along. I thought you had a plan?"

They stopped again. Varro scrubbed his face in frustration, then stared back at the sky.

"If we head west, we should eventually arrive at our camp. By that time, whatever is going to happen with the Macedonian attack will have happened. We just need to stay alive long enough to report back to Centurion Drusus."

"Wouldn't want to be late for that." Falco turned and pointed to their right. "All right, then you're not heading west. So go that way."

Varro blinked in astonishment. "If you knew we were going the wrong way, speak up."

"There's no wrong way if you don't know where you're going."

They continued on their trek, now moving with purpose. As they picked a path, Varro worried for Panthera and Sura meeting their end in this marsh. He thought of Curio and Cordus left behind. He thought of Otho dying before he could express his final wishes.

Then he thought of Gallio.

That little bastard was fighting for the enemy who had done all of this to them. He had run to them. The memory of that traitor fleeing toward the Macedonian scouts would never leave him.

"I know I saw Gallio in that last battle."

"Not this again."

"I'm going to find him, Falco. And when I get my hands on him, I'll have no mercy."

"Let's find camp first."

"He's dining with the men who drove us into this marsh."

"Something to eat now would be nice."

"All the gods hear me now. I will bring Lars Gallio to justice."

"I'd rather the gods bring us to safety."

"Falco, are you listening to me?" Varro whirled, his pulse throbbing in his temples. "Gallio is the worst kind of man. He is a traitor to his friends and country. I never knew I could hate someone so thoroughly."

Falco stared at him with a wan smile.

"I agree with everything you said. But we've got more practical problems ahead of us. I'm dying of thirst, but I doubt this water is good to drink."

Again Varro mourned his pack sitting back in camp. Three days of rations sounded good right now, just the amount stored in his pack. The water mocked his thirst as he again began a slow trudge west, or what he thought was west.

Judging from what he could tell of the sun's position behind the heavy clouds, several hours had passed since they had left the main road. Panthera and Sura were either dead or fled in a different direction. No sign of their passing ever showed. He had no idea how much longer they needed to reach camp. He simply prodded the earth ahead and moved forward.

Something appeared on the horizon. Varro saw it as a shadow flickering to his right. He spun toward it, bringing Falco along with him.

Clear above the horizon a mounted figure guided his horse through the marsh. The horse's head was down, and the figure leaned forward to encourage it.

Without a word exchanged, he and Falco ducked into the tall

brown grasses. They lowered their shields, and Varro readied his pilum. Both watched the figure drawing near. The rider was not Roman cavalry, and so had to be Macedonian. But Varro guessed the rider's presence in the marsh so many hours after their initial clash at the forest meant the rider was equally lost.

"He might speak Latin," Varro whispered. "He owns a horse, after all."

"I wasn't planning on having a chat with him."

Varro shook his head. "If we could capture him, we may learn something useful. Taking a prisoner back to camp would go a long way toward excusing our failure."

Falco's face darkened and he turned back toward the approaching rider. They knew the officers would call them cowards, particularly after having unjustly earning that reputation. The scale of this defeat might cover them. However, Varro wanted assurance the tribune would not have reason to punish the contubernium. Of course, by now only he and Falco might constitute its members.

They waited in hiding as the rider picked his course toward them. If he maintained the direction, he would pass within pilum range. Varro believed if he could kill the horse, then the rider would be easily overcome in the ensuing chaos.

Yet as the rider approached, Varro's eyes widened at his stature.

This man was no cavalryman. At the least, he was an officer. He sat dismount with pride, back straight and shoulders squared. His eyes squinted against the flat glare as he surveyed his path. He wore a muscled breast plate of intensely polished bronze, such that it gleamed from every point.

"He's a bit young for an officer," Falco whispered, drawing closer.

Varro nodded. For the man looked only several years older than himself. His wavy hair was full and flowing. He wore no helmet, but his hair held an impression where one might have sat on his noble head. A long purple cloak flowed behind him and over the horse's flanks. But this was stained with mud.

"Purple?" Varro blinked. In Rome, at least, that color was reserved for the highest classes. This man was of some importance.

He was also now within range of the pilum.

With a shared nod, he and Falco sprang from their hiding spot.

The rider had passed them so they attacked from the rear. Their throaty shouts broke the heavy silence of the marsh. The horse startled at the unexpected burst, and kicked out of reflex.

Varro took three steps, casting on the third.

Then slipping in muck and crashing to his side in the cold water. The fetid swamp water doused his face, flowing bitter and moldy into his mouth. He cursed and grabbed for his sword. He had landed on his right and pressed the iron blade into the water.

Losing no time, he staggered up. The horse bucked and the rider held on, screaming at the beast as he flopped around the saddle. Falco stood back, hiding behind his scutum against the kicking horse. The pilum had scored its left flank, leaving a brilliant slash of red. But the pilum itself had bounced off into the marsh.

Dripping with swamp mud, Varro retrieved his shield and drew his sword. It sucked against the sheath from the muck forced into it. Within a day this sword would be a rusted ruin. But for now, its edge was still sharp.

The two skipped around the kicking horse and held their shields forward. The animal did not flee, but the rider could not bring it under control. Varro at last noticed his pilum sticking out of the ground.

With two bounding but careful strides, he reached it, extracted it from the mud, then cast it again.

Bent and thick with slop, the pilum flew more like a thrown

club. It spun and struck the rider high in his back. He screamed and fell from the horse to crash into the water. The horse danced around him. The rider must have the gods' favor for the hooves splashed mud all around yet missed him each time.

Relieved of its burden, the horse turned then bolted back the way it had come. It sprinted away, leaving the cursing and screaming rider fighting the weight of his armor and waterlogged cloak.

He and Falco pounced on the man. The pilum had struck on its blunt wood side and so had only bruised him at worst. The rider slapped at them, trying to find his sword but pulling up a handful of mud instead.

Falco smothered him with his shield and pressed him back into the water.

"Give up or drown," he shouted. "I know what I'd choose."

"I surrender!" The muffled voice was full of rage and hate. But he spoke accented Latin, much to Varro's relief.

Falco removed his shield like swiping the lid off a cooking pot. The rider lay on his back, pressed into the soupy mud. He sputtered and spit water as he cursed them in a foreign language. His eyes were white against the brown muck clinging to him.

Varro and Falco each took an arm and hauled their prisoner out of his muddy stew. A disgusting slurp followed the rider's extraction from the muck. He sat upright, stunned at the filth that now bathed him. Mud encased his formerly shining bronze cuirass. Where the bronze showed, it was filmy brown.

They hauled him to his feet. Falco grabbed the rider's sword the same moment he did. Both men stared at each other, but Falco smiled first.

"A prisoner is nice but not necessary."

Both shoved against the other, but the captured Macedonian relented. He let both arms drop to the side. His once magnificent cloak now clung to his back, shimmering with brown mud.

"You would not dare to kill me." The man tilted his head back and sneered while Falco drew the prisoner's sword from its sheath.

"Friend, it takes no daring to put you back in the mud and stand on your head until you drown. Don't tempt me."

Varro kept his sword ready for trickery, stepping closer as Falco examined the muddied blade. It was long and swooping, a cavalry sword. Falco turned it around in his hand, then flung it carelessly into the marsh. It plopped down in the distance. The prisoner flinched at the splash, then stared ahead as if trying to ignore both of them.

"Does he have any other weapons?" Varro now moved behind their prisoner to ensure he would not attempt to run.

"A dagger. A very nice dagger." Falco whistled as he stripped the dagger from their prisoner's belt. "This has got to be worth my whole year's pay."

Falco held it to the side for Varro to see. It was a long, well-made blade. But it seemed more ceremonial than practical. Its hilt was gilt with gold and had a green gem embedded in the pommel. Falco spun it around and tucked it into his belt.

The prisoner snorted at Falco's claim. He mumbled in his accented Latin. "A year of your pay is no more than the cost of toy knife."

"Let's bind him," Varro said, he took the man's arm and bent it back. To his surprise, he resisted. They wrestled back and forth while Falco folded his arms and smirked.

"Enough!" The prisoner shouted as he pulled away. "I will obey. But you will treat me with respect."

He only turned his head aside, but Varro read the intense loathing. The man at last crossed his arms behind his back.

"You won't need this fine cloak anymore," Falco said. "I'll cut it up to make the bindings. Just hold still."

The Macedonian turned up his chin and stared away from Falco. Varro kept his sword pointed at their prisoner's back while

Falco sheared wet strips from the cloak to create bindings. He fought the heavy material and the process took longer than Varro expected. Their prisoner continued in his stony silence, sighing with impatience as Falco wrestled through his process.

"I hurt my leg in the fall," the prisoner said. "I cannot flee from you in this marsh. Must you tie me?"

"You really think we're stupid," Falco said. He tore away another long strip. "You want me to give your toy dagger back too? Go get fucked, you bastard."

Whether the Macedonian understood the curses, he seemed to understand Falco's tone. He lowered his head and sighed again. At last, Falco handed Varro long and thin strips to bind their prisoner.

"Make them tight so they don't slip when dried out," he said.

Varro wound them around in the manner Optio Tertius had taught him. Such training was not standard, but Tertius used odd moments to teach them skills that might be situationally useful. Binding prisoners was one such drill, and Varro was grateful for the lesson.

"That is too tight, Roman. My hands will die."

"You'll live," Varro said, tightening them still. "You're coming back to camp with us."

The prisoner chuckled.

"What's so funny about that?" Falco asked. He threw the ruins of the prisoner's cloak into the mud, then folded his arms. "You better have something good to tell our officers, or you won't be worrying for your hands."

The prisoner laughed again.

"Of all the men to capture me, it had to be two Roman country boys. Such uncultured fools."

Varro yanked up on the bindings, eliciting a surprised yelp of pain. He then shoved against the prisoner, pushing him away so that he staggered forwards. Freed but arms tightly bound.

"If you want respect, give some to us. You're a little over-proud for a cavalry officer."

"An officer?" The prisoner turned to face Varro. The mud had dried on his face, flaking off to reveal haughty and proud features. "Is that who you think I am?"

Varro shared a blank look with Falco, then nodded to their prisoner.

"Then introductions are in order. I am King Philip the Fifth of Macedonia. And who are you two fools?"

18

"A fine lie," Falco said. "But it won't get you any better treatment."

Varro stood before their prisoner. Even in this barren marsh, covered in mud and stinking of fetid water, the Macedonian held himself like a king. His sneer was cruel and the flash in his cold, hazel eyes revealed a confidence beyond reason given his circumstances. His hands were bound behind his back, but his spirit soared above them firm in the belief the gods would side with him over two Roman country boys.

"It's the truth," Varro said. "Just look at him."

"Looking at him makes no difference," Falco said, stepping beside Varro to jointly review the man claiming to be Philip of Macedonia. "Have you ever seen him before? Do you know the face of even one of our own senators, never mind a foreign king's? He's just trying to get us to go easy on him, or scare us."

"You should be afraid," Philip said. "My men will scour this marsh until they find me. You will soon become my prisoners."

Falco scoffed at Philip. "Look, why would you be riding

through the marsh without even a single guard at your side? We're country boys, but we're not brainless. You're just a lost cavalry officer who thinks all Romans are witless brutes. But I'm not fooled."

Philip narrowed his eyes at Falco and gritted his teeth. He turned aside to gaze out at the flat marsh, dotted with clumps of dark trees and muddy hillocks of waist-high grass. A line of birds attracted him, simple black dots against the sheet of gray clouds, and he followed these until they settled back into the horizon. Then he released a long breath.

"I let you Romans grow confident enough in your new camp that you would send out a large part of your force to forage. It must happen eventually, I believed. So my scouts reported your march into the forest. I gathered my cavalry and mercenaries. You know what happened then."

Philip faced them with a wry smile. Varro hated how he relished the defeat of five hundred Romans. But he let Philip continue.

"I set up in the main road, expecting stragglers to flow in this way, and Galba's response to appear there as well. He sent his cavalry, which went off on a wild chase and left me waiting a long time. When Galba's infantry finally arrived, I was ready. We dealt them a hard blow, but then became greedy."

Philip lowered his head and paused before drawing a deep breath to continue.

"You Romans fell back and we pushed after them. That shifted my lines and cost the discipline of my men. I have a new respect for your people. You turned around and slaughtered my men. My own horse was killed under me, and when I fell one of my cavalrymen offered his horse. I then fled into the marsh. As you two know, it was the surest path of escape from that road. And now I stand before you, a prisoner."

When Philip fell silent, only the thin buzz of marsh insects filled the air. Varro noted how swarms of bugs flew around himself and Falco, but did not touch Philip. This surely meant his claims were true.

"I believe him," Varro said. "By the gods, Falco, we've captured King Philip. Now that ought to be worth something to the tribune."

His voice was bright with the excitement of their windfall. But Falco folded his arms and scowled.

"All right, so he's King Philip. You think we'll get credit for capturing him? Really, Varro, you're too innocent. Before we even get into camp some cavalry officer will pluck our fat prize and take all the glory. Even our own officers would take the credit before us. We'll get nothing out of this. Nothing except all the trouble of hauling him back to camp."

"But the tribune will still know the truth," Varro said. He suddenly felt as if he were arguing with his father for permission to play outside after dark. "He'll at least drop his conditions against us."

Falco laced his fingers over the top of his head. His lips pressed together while he seemed to search for the right words.

"You and I see the world differently. You think everyone is kind. I think everyone is evil. If anything, bringing back King Philip will probably get us killed. Think about it. The tribune and his favorite pet officer will want the glory and fame for capturing him. So once they steal Philip from us, they won't want us around to tell the truth. So, we'll get the tribune's forgiveness along with a dagger in the back. They'll throw us in a river and let our bodies wash away with the proof that they didn't really capture the king themselves. That's what bringing Philip back means."

Varro stared in amazement at Falco. The heavy ridge of his brows cast faint shadows in the overcast light. His lips were tight and flat, and he offered a slow nod as if to confirm the doubts Varro felt.

"Listen to your friend," Philip said, his smile growing wider. "He is wiser than you. You have no place in the affairs of great men. Small men like you are their tools and cast aside when no longer useful. You would do well to free me."

"I didn't say letting you go was a good idea," Falco said. "We still have a duty to Rome. You're the whole reason I'm standing in this fucking marsh. I wouldn't have had to come to this country if you weren't such a bastard."

Philip laughed and it echoed through the marsh. But Varro paid it no attention. His mind turned on how to make the best of their situation.

"We will disguise him," Varro said. "He doesn't look like a king now. We can let the tribune discover Philip's identity on his own, and we'll look like we never even realized who we had."

"Doesn't change the fact that they'll want us silenced," Falco said. "Anyway, I say we kill him here. End this fucking war and leave his rotting corpse for these flies. Solves all our problems."

Both Philip and Varro gasped at the suggestion.

"Gods, lily, you're not really going to call that murder, are you?"

"I am!"

Falco roared, balling his fists and rapping his knuckles to his head.

"Why? It's the best choice. Just slit his throat and bury him in the mud. No one will ever find him. The war will end, Varro. Think of the thousands of lives on both sides you could save. That must count for something in your useless, idiotic philosophy?"

Varro drew a calming breath. The mighty confidence in Philip's eyes had wavered, but once he met Varro's it seemed restored. He even smiled as he waited on Varro's next words.

"The right thing to do is to present him to our officers as a prisoner of war. I will not murder a defeated and bound man, even if he is the king of my enemies."

"He's got more blood on his hands than anyone you'll ever know. He deserves death." Falco's entreaty echoed over the marsh, amplified by the water. It was a stark contrast to Varro's calm and measured words.

"I have bent my sense of honor to its limits. Yes, Philip of Macedonia should die. But it is not for me to decide. I will not do this, Falco. My vow is still worth keeping."

"It's not my fucking vow!"

Falco drew the golden dagger from his belt and stepped toward Philip. It was a halfhearted gesture and Varro easily interposed himself.

"I cannot allow it. It's murder, Falco." He spread his arms wide before Philip. Falco lowered the dagger then butted his chest against Varro's. They stared into each other's eyes, each resolute in their own beliefs.

"You'd fight me to save the king of our enemies?"

"I'd fight you to save myself from evil. I'm asking you as a friend. Let's deliver him to our officers. The war will still end and lives will be saved. We won't get the credit we deserve. But if we do not act like we want it, then we'll be spared. After a while, no one would believe our story anyway."

They remained locked together, neither side willing to look away. Varro recalled how often he had endured punishment at Falco's hands. How his face swelled with bruises because he would not fight back. He had been misguided then, too naive and too broad in his definitions of nonviolence. A season at war had taught him quick and harsh lessons on the distinctions between defense and murder.

He was no longer unclear. This very moment was what his great-grandfather had warned him against. He had foreseen the choice would one day have to be made, and was determined his youngest descendant would not err. This was the start of the red road promised Varro should he submit to anger and violence. He would be better to die with honor than sink into a myriad of excuses to cover his evil and bury him in shame.

At last Falco turned aside and stepped back with a growl.

"I'm blaming you if this all goes to shit."

Philip lifted his head back and sneered. Even with dried, flaking muck breaking over his cheeks, he radiated superiority.

"I must take back my words, Roman. You are a principled man. You speak with reason and passion. Yet I am certain your officers think little of your capabilities and your civic leaders even less so. It is a pity. Perhaps you should consider joining me. I have a place for capable men, and unlike your narrow-minded, fearful senators I do not inhibit a man's capabilities just so he remains in his place. I would let you grow."

"You are my prisoner," Varro said. His voice was soft and his hands trembled, but he still looked Philip in the eye. "And I am a citizen of Rome. There is no greater honor to be found in all the world."

They resumed their journey west, though Varro was less certain of his direction than before. The fight had spun him around, and the sun, now close to the horizon, still hid behind clouds. Yet he could take a general direction from the lengthening shadows. As long as these all pointed behind him, he was heading toward the camp.

Falco trudged along in sullen silence. Varro thought he might not speak again. Philip remained compliant and silent, though his eyes searched the horizon with increasing frequency as the light waned. The only sounds along their path were the sucking of their sandals against the mud or the occasional plop and splash of an escaping frog. Varro's stomach grumbled once again and the burning thirst returned. He called a halt to their march.

"Travel by night will be too dangerous," he declared as the sun threatened to vanish beneath the horizon. "I expect it will be cold, made worse by all the water."

Falco grunted and Philip simply glared into the gathering darkness.

"We can probably strike a spark off our swords," Falco said, his first words since their argument a few hours earlier. "But nothing is going to burn here."

"There is plenty of dead grass," Varro said. "And we might find kindling and sticks among the trees that will be dry enough. Let's use the remaining light to search. Even you can help, King Philip."

"You'll unbind me, then? My hands are numb."

Varro shook his head. "You don't need free hands to look for dry wood. It's in your interest too."

So they scoured the hillocks and found enough thick branches to make a platform over the ground, which they covered with dry grass and small twigs. Starting the fire consumed all of Varro's patience, but eventually they had a small campfire. The gods favored them with only a low breeze, but they still selected the best natural windbreak they could find among the hillocks.

All three of them huddled around the fire, sitting on thin piles of dead grass to insulate them from the damp earth.

"This is pathetic," King Philip said, sneering into the fire. The orange light and shadows broke his face into unsettling shapes. He leaned forward toward the small fire. "I am hardly warmed."

"It's the best you'll see until tomorrow," Varro said. "I'm sure you'll be well treated once Consul Galba receives you. Until then, just stay by the fire."

"Don't be so nice to him," Falco said. "He's our enemy."

"He's still a king," Varro said. "Anyway, what good will come of cruelty?"

"A fine man," Philip said, though his expression was mocking. "I am thirsty. I don't suppose you would have a flask of wine among you?"

They fell into silence, for no one had anything to eat or drink. The day's exertions had drained Varro of any energy to fish or hunt. But he was confident he had only a day ahead before finding camp. So he let his stomach growl. Only the snap of the burning fire was louder. Frogs croaked all around them, but the incessant buzz had subsided with the onset of night. The heavy clouds above ushered in thick darkness the moment the sun slipped below the horizon.

"You said you'd put me into your army?" Varro asked, breaking the silence. Philip looked up from staring into the fire.

"Return me to my camp, then you could name your position. Do you want to lead men? I would make you an officer and give you five hundred soldiers. I'd pay you well, too."

"A Roman deserter went over to your scouts, then shortly after revealed Consul Galba's position to you. Do you know this man?"

Philip stared vacantly, as if he had not heard the question. Falco gave a derisive laugh and lowered his head.

"His name is Lars Gallio," Varro continued. "I am certain he's the one who led you to our camp. I want to know what became of him. Did you reward him as well? Is he leading five hundred men?"

"A Roman deserter, you say." Philip shifted against his bindings. "I might know something, but these bindings are so painful I cannot think of anything but my poor wrists."

"We're not freeing him," Falco said, snapping his head up. "We'll do the world a favor if his hands rot by sunrise. So he stays tied."

"I agree." Varro narrowed his eyes at Philip. "You're not in a position to make a bargain. If you want those bindings removed, then you'll march doubly fast to our camp tomorrow. Now, I asked a simple question. Did you meet the deserter who showed Galba's position?"

Philip's sly smile faded to a sullen frown. He leaned back as if to ignore the question, but betrayed his fear when he snapped his head toward Falco, who had simply raised his hand to scratch his cheek. Realizing the king feared a blow, Falco raised his fist as if to strike him.

"The gods will curse you for striking a king." His eyes fluttered as if anticipating a slap across the face. But Falco kept his hand hovering.

"Just answer him and we'll not have to learn if the gods are watching."

"I don't know the man," Philip said, turning to Varro. "We have more than one deserter among us. Rome does not treat her sons with dignity, and so they run to me."

"But do you know the name?" Varro shifted closer, now hopeful Philip might share more.

"You are serious? Roman, I am king of the greatest country on earth. My blood is royal. I do not stoop to learn the name of every prisoner in my camp. I do not know Lars Gallio. More than one Roman led us to Galba's camp. For these men, I let my officers dispense with them as they saw fit. Most would have been made slaves. If any were difficult, then they would've been executed. But I'd not make them officers."

"You said you'd make him an officer." Falco fed a handful of dry grass into the fire and used a twig to push it into position.

"He would be sparing my life. That is entirely different than someone who just fled his own companions." Philip straightened up and tried to work sincerity into his reptilian countenance. "That offer remains, Roman. Ignore your dull-witted companion and make the sensible choice. You may serve a lifetime with your own people and never rise to any account. But you would be my youngest and brightest officer."

Varro folded his arms. That Philip lied was certain to him, but Gallio's fate remained unclear.

"I saw Lars Gallio in battle," he said, ignoring Philip's offer. "Is there any chance he would've been allowed to fight against Rome?"

Philip slumped and closed his eyes. "Roman, that is detail far beneath me. Is it possible? Of course it is. Is it likely? Not at all. Not among my pikemen, in any case. He might have found a home with the Illyrians or Cretans. If he did, then you might have actually seen this man."

"I did see him." Varro rubbed his chin, recalling vague and confused memories of Gallio's outline moving among the enemy.

With nothing more to discuss, they settled into the night. Though they had piled grass over the ground, Varro still found it too damp for comfort. Philip protested against his bonds. But Varro did not relent and helped the king settle on his side for the night.

Sleep overtook Varro at some point. He had wanted to arrange a shift with Falco to guard against Philip's tricks. He might walk off and chance the swamp. But exhaustion had claimed him before he could make any plans.

He awakened suddenly, terrified Philip was gone.

Instead, the king was sitting upright again by the guttering fire. Shadows twisted across his sneering face as he looked to Varro.

Falco stood in a wary crouch, hand on the hilt of his sheathed sword and head cocked.

Varro heard nothing as he blinked away the vestiges of sleep. Something had awakened him, but he did not know what. Nothing seemed out of place.

Except he did not hear the frogs anymore.

He got to his knees, then searched the surrounding darkness.

All around them, small globes of orange light bobbed across the swamp. Hundreds of orange points reflected in long streaks into the marsh.

Philip snickered at Varro's sudden realization.

"That's right, Roman. You should have made a bargain with me earlier. That is my army searching for me. It seems you'll have a chance to discover if your friend joined my troops after all."

Varro stood now and watched the circle of torchlights converging on them. He saw no way out of the ring and the orange points grew brighter and larger.

They had little time before they were trapped. Philip laughed.

19

Varro kicked over the fire, sending sparks flying into the black night and Philip flying back in shocked horror. Even Falco jumped at the sudden spray. But the weak fire blinked out, leaving only dull sparks to twist and vanish into the cold darkness. The orange points of light still floating in the blackness were the torchlights of Philip's men searching the marsh for their king.

"Stuff something in his mouth," Varro snapped at Falco. "And tie his legs. We can't let him give us away."

Falco leaped atop the king as if intending to murder him. He crushed his hand over Philip's mouth, and the two wrestled on the muddy ground while Varro scattered the smoldering campfire. Twigs and sticks hissed with steam as they rolled into the marsh water. When he had finished dispersing their campfire, Falco had bound Philip's legs with his own cloak.

"It'll trip him up if he tries to flee," he said. "But it's not going to keep him from kicking us. We should have tied his legs from the start."

"No matter," Varro said. "He can't shout?"

"I stuffed his mouth with muddy cloth. Serves the snake right. He's as trussed as we can make him. So let's go. They've seen our fire and will be here soon enough."

Together they lifted Philip off the ground. He thrashed like a fish at the end of a line, and Varro dropped the king's legs twice. His struggle made it impossible for two of them to carry him.

"We can try to brain him," Falco said. "Like Gallio did to you. Plenty of rocks around."

"That's more likely to kill him. I just got lucky. Also, he is a king, Falco."

"He's not my fucking king."

"I know that," he said, drawing closer. Philip now sat on the ground, arms and legs bound and mouth full of cloth. He glared up, but listened to Varro.

"He's a king, and if we abuse him who knows what the consul and tribunes will say? Maybe Consul Galba wants to make a peace treaty, and as part of that treaty Philip demands our lives. You have such a mind for evil politics, Falco. So I'm surprised you haven't thought this far. We can't think like farm boys anymore. We can't abuse a king. It will never go well for us."

Philip shook against his bonds as he made a muffled, indignant agreement. Even in the darkness, his eyes gleamed with hatred.

"I think he's beyond liking us," Falco said.

"Binding his legs will not work," Varro said. "He'll have to walk. Put your sword at his back."

"You just told him we won't kill him."

Kneeling beside Philip, he began to unwind the cloak tied around his feet.

"Falco will keep his sword to your back and you'll march along with us. I want to take you back alive. But if you are killed, I'm sure Consul Galba can make a treaty with someone else in your camp."

Philip nodded vigorously and Varro assisted him to his feet.

"There is a dark patch in their circle," Varro said. "I don't know what direction it is. But at least we will not be caught that way."

They set off for the blank spot in the tightening circle of torchlight. Some were close enough now that Varro saw the vague outlines of faces illuminated in the globes of light. They redoubled their pace.

If footing was treacherous during daylight, in darkness it was deadly. Varro led the way, with Philip behind and Falco pushing the king along. Having discarded his ruined pilum, he had used a long branch to plumb the water during their daytime journey. In their haste now, he had forgotten it. His foot plunged into water without bottom. The weight of his shield and bronze armor nearly sent him falling into the dark. Yet he regained his balance and tried a new approach.

"At least the Macedonians have to be as careful." Varro regained his balance on the patch of earth, looking back to check the progress of the closing circle. A cluster of torchlights were close behind.

"They'll go slow until they find the camp," Falco said. "Then they'll know we're near and know where we went. It's just like flushing game from the underbrush. We're trapped."

Both Falco and King Philip were faint outlines in the blackness. He was not certain how close they were, nor was he certain what lay two paces ahead of him. Escape in utter blackness seemed impossible.

"We can't run," Varro said. "We'll drown. I almost proved that conclusion with my life."

He stared at the two figures in the darkness. Their bodies melded together to create a humanoid shape that broke the line of bobbing orange globes drawing ever closer. There was one way out alive, and he hated the choice. But he could think of no other.

Reaching a hand out to the black shapes, he found King

Philip's face. He groped about it until his hand brushed onto the balled-up cloth stuck into the king's mouth. He tore it free.

Philip spit violently, groaning with disgust.

"What are you doing?" Falco asked. Though Varro couldn't see him, he knew the exasperated and indignant expression his friend wore. He had seen it enough to never forget it.

"I'm saving our lives."

Once Philip had ceased spitting, he struggled with Falco who still held him close. Whether his sword was at the king's back, Varro couldn't see.

"You filled my mouth with shit," Philip said. "Is this how you treat a king?"

"Here's my offer," Varro said, ignoring the king's indignation. "We will set you free. Just walk back the way you came and you'll join your men. You lead them to your camp and let us find our way through the swamp without fear of pursuit."

The mass of shadow that was Philip and Falco did not move. Neither spoke, and Varro imagined Philip's reptilian face smirking in cold calculation.

"Let me make your decision easier," Varro said. "We'll kill you then throw you into this deep water. Your men will search for days, and if we escape then we Romans will know where to find them. You will die and your successor will likely die."

"You would not kill me."

"Falco will. After all, it's dark and I cannot see what's happening until it's too late." Varro drew a long breath. "Besides, I've reconsidered. Your death could save thousands of lives."

"You think so? Well, my people—ouch!"

The shadows jerked then grew still. Falco growled low.

"Give us a king's oath you'll call off your men and let us go, or I'll finish driving my sword through your back."

"It's not much of a choice," Philip said, laughing nervously. "I swear I will do it. But you must preserve my dignity. Unbind my hands."

"No." Falco's voice was loud enough that Varro feared the Macedonians might hear it.

"Honestly, am I going to fight the two of you in the dark with no weapons? If you let me return to my men with my dignity intact, then I shall lead them away as I've agreed."

"I said no."

The mass of shadow wavered as the two struggled. But Varro grabbed one of them, Falco by the hardness of the arm he latched onto.

"We've no time to argue. We'll undo his binding and set him off. We'll have lead time to escape."

"I don't trust him, Varro."

"You fool," Philip said. "Remove your sword or else finish me now. I'll scream before I die. You'll be captured and tortured to death. So you have to let me go."

"He's delaying for time," Varro said. "That's his real trick. His men are about to find our campsite. Undo his bindings."

Varro knew Philip would call for help once safely away. He would not be brave enough to find his path through the swamp in the darkness but would want his men to guide him. So a good lead was necessary, and Falco's bickering with Philip diminished it with every moment.

"All right, you're free," Falco said with a grunt of disgust. The makeshift bindings plopped into the water.

Philip's shadow broke from Falco's and he moaned with relief as he stretched his arms overhead.

"Excellent. Now, to conclude our agreement, return my dagger."

"I'll kill you first."

"Return the dagger, Falco. We need to run now. Look."

A cluster of torches hovered directly behind them on the

hillock where they had camped. As if to reinforce Varro's warning, voices began calling out into the darkness.

Falco's sword raised, catching an orange flash from the torches. "You scream and I'll run you through."

"Peace," Philip said, raising his hands. "I'm as eager to get away from you as you are to flee. But that dagger is important. Return it."

With a groan, Varro patted around Falco's waist for the dagger while the sword remained poised at Philip. His hands slipped around the cold, golden hilt. He drew it carefully then held it forward.

"Here it is," Varro said. "Take it and remain here until we're away. Then you can scream yourself hoarse. Do I have your word as a king?"

"Of course," Philip said calmly. His shadowy hand reached out beneath Falco's hovering sword.

"Swear it," Varro said, pulling the dagger back.

"I swear I will make no sound to give you away, and once united with my men I'll return to camp. The gods will decide your fates."

"Lower your sword, Falco. We've got to run and pray we don't drown."

"I don't like this," he said. Again his sword gleamed with a point of orange light as he lowered it.

Varro spun the dagger in his hand and Philip grabbed the hilt. He tore it away, no doubt hoping to cut Varro's hand. But he had wisely left his palm open then dropped it the moment the king grasped his dagger.

They stared at each other across the short gap. The King of Macedonia was no longer his prisoner. Varro felt a pang of regret, for in his deepest heart he would have enjoyed being the hero to have captured a king. But surrendering his royal captive was his best strategy for escape.

Behind them Philip's men called his name into the darkness. Had they known how close they were to him, they would be shouting in triumph.

"You have my word, Roman. Why are you staring at me? Flee while you may."

"Thank you, King Philip," Varro said. "We will meet again on the battlefield."

The shadowed outline of the king shrugged.

"Let's go," Falco said. "It's like you're leaving a fucking girlfriend. Gods, Varro."

They both turned to face the cold darkness ahead.

Only Falco screamed in surprise.

Then splashed into the water.

Philip laughed, already retreating toward his own men.

"I'll keep my word, Roman. But I can't help it if you make so much noise someone comes to investigate. Farewell!"

"Falco!"

Varro ignored the king, instead turning toward the splashing and choking of Falco struggling in the water.

"Help." It sounded more like a statement than a plea. And Varro heard the gurgling in Falco's voice. He was slipping beneath the water, bronze armor and shield dragging him to the bottom muck.

"I'm here!"

Varro tramped into the water, hoping it was not so deep that he would drown as well. Their combined weight would probably sink them into the mud so deep it might be a thousand years before their bones rose to the surface again.

Locating Falco by his weak splashing, he sank to his knees in the cold water. It flowed behind the bronze greave on his left leg making it feel as if it would pull away. But with one stride he felt Falco's body bump against his shin. He thrust his arms into the marsh.

His hands slipped around the bronze pectoral covering Falco's chest. He smiled in triumph, hauling up and raising his friend out of the water.

Falco gasped and coughed and threw his arms around Varro's legs.

"I've got you," he said. "Work with me, Falco."

He hauled his friend backward to the lump of firm earth. At first Falco struggled in panic, but once they had climbed back onto solid ground, he regained control of his fear. Soon, the two lay gasping and dripping wet side by side.

"I'll kill him." Falco's voice was ragged and breathless.

"He gave his oath. I can't believe he did that."

"Shows what his oath's worth."

They rested together. Varro lay in a world of darkness, for the sky above and the world around appeared nothing other than black. Yet more terrifying was the clammy, cold wind creeping over him. It would be a mild breeze to someone dry and safe. To him, it was the terrifying clutches of death twining around his soaked body and threatening to sap all his warmth.

The shouts of the Macedonians grew both louder and more excited.

"Sounds like they found Philip," Varro said, struggling to his feet. "They'll be right on us. Let's go."

Falco's hands were like ice in his as Varro hauled him up. They turned toward the blackness. A tight knot twisted in Varro's stomach. They had to get away from this spot. Yet how could they navigate this marsh without splashing into the water?

After only two steps forward, Varro drew them up short. Falco crashed into his shoulder.

"Philip knows we're heading for the dark gap. We can't go that way."

"Where else can we go? They're right behind us and Philip is there too."

Varro looked for the thinnest line of torches, then pointed at it.

"We go back toward them and hide until dawn. Philip thinks we're fleeing into the blackness where none of his men are. So he will direct them toward us. But he won't think we moved back toward his own soldiers."

"That sounds like a reasonable idea," Falco said. "Except they can just catch us in daylight."

Shaking his head then realizing Falco couldn't see the gesture, he grabbed his arm again and started toward the thin line of torches, explaining as he picked his way along the solid ground.

"They'll converge on Philip once he's found. They don't even know to be searching for us right now. Even if they saw us, they might assume we're one of them. In any case, Philip will likely leave someone to search for us during the daylight. He probably wants to get back to being king rather than searching for us in the marsh."

Their path forward proceeded with a controlled run that amounted to a pace little better than a brisk walk. Whenever Varro felt cold water touch his feet, which was nearly every other step, he had to prod ahead. Once within water, they had to slow to keep from splashing or from stepping off into deep water.

At last, they were slipping between the gaps of the search parties. At the same moment, a horn sounded and behind them cheers rose up. Philip had found his men.

The searchers were mere orange and black figures in the night. They carried long spears for each man to prod his own path. To both the left and right, the search teams were comprised of six men. As they closed, Varro and Falco ducked into the grass and kept low.

"Once they've passed us," Varro whispered, "we should be able to find a hillock to hide within until morning. They won't return this way, I'm sure."

So they huddled among the grass and the search party on their left passed, each man pointing ahead and chatting excitedly.

The party on the right was even with them, and closer. They maintained a broader distance between each other, and their speech was low and less excited. The torchbearer held his brand aloft so that the globe of its weak light reached the edges of their line.

Varro watched as they glided past, their feet sucking against the mud as they prodded toward their king. Their expressions were stern, rendered harsher for the stark light flickering above them. The man on the end was olive skinned with short wavy hair. The deep lines of his cheeks filled with shadow as he kept his head down and watched his step. Varro held his breath as he passed.

Falco stifled a sneeze.

Both he and Varro ducked lower into the grass, staring at each other with wide eyes. The olive-skinned man paused, the shadow from his brows drawing together as he peered toward them.

He called out in clipped, inquisitive words that Varro did not understand. The rest of his line slowed, and the next closest enemy also paused. Both men now squinted hard at Varro and Falco as if trying to confirm what they were seeing.

The lead man took a cautious step forward with a spear in both hands. His neck craned as he tried to make out what dwelled at the edge of his light. Yet the torchbearer, while paused as well, did not move closer.

Varro's heart raced as he imagined how best to escape their situation. He had the advantage of surprise. If he could eliminate the torchbearer then the fight would be somewhat evened out. Yet he would likely fall into the marsh and drown in the ensuing chaos. So he could not fight, nor could he run. He and Falco were trapped between enemies and the darkness. Both hunkered down, pressing their shields into the muck to prevent them from betraying their position.

The torchbearer shouted angrily at his two companions, who poised like hunting dogs that had located their prey. Yet neither man moved closer. Instead, they stared directly at Varro and Falco and kept their spears lowered.

Others joined the irritated torchbearer in shouting at the two men. The olive-skinned man at last relented, but argued with the others. The final man stared a moment longer before shaking his head and turning aside. The line of enemies moved on, none of them looking back.

Once their torchlight became only a small globe did Varro and Falco move again.

"Water up my nose made me sneeze," Falco offered in a wet whisper.

"Don't worry for it. The gods preserved us. We just need to pass the night and we'll get out of here by daylight."

Falco nodded, then sneezed twice as hard as before.

20

When dawn arrived as a white strip on the horizon Varro and Falco were already moving from their hiding place. Neither had slept much on the tree-studded hillock they now abandoned. Falco had sneezed through the night and rubbed at his nose constantly. In the twilight Varro could see the dark circles around his eyes and the waxy pallor of his skin.

Varro himself was sore and hungry, but at least did not feel ill. They both still carried their scutum shields, though the iron edges were already tinged with rust. Varro did not even bother to examine his sword, but instead ensured his mother's pugio remained clean. Satisfied they had done all they could to prepare, they now dashed from one mound of earth to another and splashed through shallows when they could not.

Philip, true to his word, had not pursued them. Varro checked over his shoulder for signs of pursuit but found none. Perhaps Philip was not as vindictive as he had seemed. More likely, he did not want to reveal he had ever been taken captive so he could fabricate something more heroic. They had been saved for vanity rather than any sense of honor on Philip's part, at least as far as Varro was concerned.

As they reached the edge of the marsh, signs of battle dotted the area. Soldiers from both sides had perished here. A Roman bronze helmet gleamed clean and bright with its three black feathers upright and unstained. But it sat on the edge of deep water, marking where its owner must have drowned. Farther along, they found an enemy corpse that exploded into a cloud of black flies at their approach.

Despite the grizzly signposts, both he and Falco grew more energized knowing they would soon clear the swamp and regain the road. The smell of rot informed them the road was still a fresh battlefield and nearby. When at last they reached the dry stretch of field edging the road, they chose to remain away from it. Varro saw the black flocks of crows come to feast and their ghastly caws chilled his already cold flesh. He and Falco exchanged glances, both agreeing to keep away from the carnage.

Returning to camp was now assured. Falco sneezed and sniffed, but his voice was bright as he spoke.

"A hot bath, Varro. I'd trade my gold necklace for a hot bath."

"We'll have quite a story to tell when we return. Though who'd believe us? I guess we can tell our children one day."

Falco lowered his head and his cheeks reddened. Varro did not understand the reaction, but he was too distracted to ask after it. For as they followed the road, he strained to see every corpse lying in the grass. If any were about the size of Curio or Cordus he would veer closer, scaring off a crow or else raising a swarm of flies.

Once they arrived within sight of camp, the sun had risen over the eastern horizon. The thick clouds of the prior day had broken apart during the night and warming shafts of pale morning streaked from behind to point the way home. Varro's waterlogged, heavy feet lightened as he approached the eastern gate.

They were not the first or only stragglers to arrive. Nor were they the worst off. Guards at the opened front gate questioned two men, one who had a stump of his right arm wrapped in blood-soaked bandages. His friend supported him, but the two seemed to interact without any great urgency or care. Varro imagined he would be frantic if he had lost his arm from the elbow down.

Their arrival was met with the tired nods from the guards.

"From the foraging party?" one of the two asked, leaning on his pilum.

"Spent a cold night in the marsh," Falco answered.

"It was a hard night on everyone," the guard said. "What was the password from yesterday?"

"Red spear," Varro said.

He was already straining to look beyond the gate at the soldiers gathered beyond. He wanted to find Panthera and Sura waiting for him. He wanted to discover Curio and Cordus had arrived ahead of him. He had a duty to report Otho's death. After spending a night believing he would drown before dawn, he was even looking forward to seeing Optio Tertius again.

The guard at the gate waved them inside. "Go find your officers."

"I never thought I'd say it," Falco said. "But I love the sight of these tents. You won't hear me complain about sleeping in one now."

He sneezed, blowing snot and spittle into a cloud.

"Well, don't sneeze like that in the tent or we'll all feel like we're in a swamp."

Falco laughed, thick and nasal. Together they followed the main road to report to headquarters. Soldiers crisscrossed the parade ground. Varro looked to the hospital and found men lined up at the door where the doctor's assistants tended them. He was glad to avoid a visit this time.

The parade ground by headquarters was full of Macedonian

captives. Varro estimated over a hundred of them sat on the ground, stripped to their basic tunics and surrounded by soldiers in heavy chain coats and long spears, most likely triarii. Nearly as many captured horses were held nearby, their sleek necks shining as they nosed into makeshift troughs set out for them.

"Horses and slaves," Falco said. "A fine sight. I could eat one of those horses myself."

They found Centurion Drusus with others of his peers. He at first did not recognize Varro, who stood with Falco at attention a good distance away. Both were aware of their marsh stink.

"Now here's a sight," Drusus said at last. The furrows on his forehead bent in delight when he finally recognized them. "I was beginning to think I was a centurion without a century."

Both saluted, but Drusus looked to Varro for a report.

He provided a detailed account, excerpting any mention of King Philip. Everyone would know soon enough he had survived his run through the marsh.

"Otho was killed, sir. Died in the cavalry charge that scattered us. He was very brave, sir. I hope that can be noted."

Drusus waved it away. "Of course. Now I wish I could say more about the rest of your contubernium. They might not have had the sense to report in like you two. Find Optio Tertius, as he's been closer to reorganizing the men than me."

The lightened spirt Varro had felt since arriving bled away. He and Falco traced their steps back to their tent row. But upon arrival, their tent was empty.

"Are we really the only ones?" Varro asked. "All the others died?"

"Curio isn't dead," Falco said. "Trouble always finds the way home. The others, I'm not so sure. Panthera gets too panicky and Sura is just like him. Maybe Cordus will catch some of Curio's luck."

Without anyone to greet them, nor any sign of Optio Tertius, they used their time to clean up. The two slaves assigned to their contubernium, captured Illyrians Varro assumed and men without names, brought them water and tubs to clean as best they could. Falco talked at length about a hot bath, which was impossible except for maybe the consul himself. He also sneezed and emptied his nose into the grass throughout.

"Marsh water," he muttered after every expulsion of snot. "I guess I'm not out of the swamp yet, am I?"

Varro offered him wine from his pack, but Falco waved it off and found his own. Varro sat outside the tent, cleaning between and beneath his toes with a wooden pick, and stared at the other soldiers greeting their friends or else sitting in pleasant conversation.

"They seem happy enough," Varro said, scowling. "Someone should remind them a fucking war is on."

Falco, who now lay down just inside the tent, laughed, which devolved into a mucus-laden cough.

"Hard words from you, lily. Can't blame a man for being happy he's alive today. Tomorrow we could all be dead."

"And you call me a philosopher."

"The others will be back. Don't worry for it."

Varro continued to pick mud out of his toenails while Falco drifted off to sleep. Despite having been hungry before escaping to the marsh, he now had no appetite. It seemed wrong to eat and drink while Panthera and Sura might still be lost in the marsh or Cordus and Curio lying dead for crows to eat. He worked on and off at clearing the muck from the creases of his feet, imagining he and Falco as the only survivors of the contubernium. Gallio was the only other one, fighting for the enemy who had wrought all this death on Varro's friends. If the gods should strike anyone dead, it should be Lars Gallio. Yet Varro heard no crack of thunder and received no vision of his former companion being stricken down. Instead he heard Falco snore behind him. At last he tossed the wood pick aside and sat back, staring vacantly at his feet.

As he sat in gloomy silence, a shadow fell over him. He looked up to find Optio Tertius flanked by Curio and Cordus. Varro sprang up and nearly pounced on them.

"You're alive! How did you get back?"

"I could ask the same of you," Optio Tertius said. "Centurion Drusus asked you to report to me. Yet here I am, come to find you two having a nice rest for yourselves."

Falco sneezed from within the tent, betraying his wakefulness. Tertius scowled, even as both Curio and Cordus smiled at the excitement of their reunion.

"Get outside," Tertius commanded. "Enough rest."

Falco slapped the flap open, then staggered out. He stood to a limp attempt at attention, then regarded Curio and Cordus. Varro touched his chest in shock. Falco seemed to have melted during his brief nap. His face and mouth sagged and his breathing was audibly thick with mucus.

"What did I tell you? The little ones always survive."

"Good to see you, too," Curio said. "When we returned from scouting, we found Otho dead and you two gone. We ran ahead and managed to reach camp to deliver a warning."

"We avoided the worst of the fighting," Cordus said, though his enthusiasm drew a frown from the optio.

"It's fortunate you were able to report the ambush, but have a care for those trapped behind you." Tertius now scowled at Falco. "Too bad you're sick. Because there's no rest in sight for you or anyone else. Plenty to do. Prisoners to sort. Casualties need care. Bodies to recover. You two look like prime elephant shit collectors."

"Thank you, sir." Falco saluted.

"Sir, Panthera and Sura were chased into the marsh along with us. Have they returned?"

Tertius did not answer immediately, and that answered Varro's question. Still, the optio lowered his head.

"We're not hopeful for anyone who entered the marsh. It's cold and treacherous, and doubly so at night. I suppose I don't have to tell you. The good news is that King Philip is reported to have fled into it as well. So if the gods are kind, he might have drowned and saved me the trouble of cutting off his head."

"One can hope, sir." Varro looked to his feet, sneaking a glance at Falco who did the same.

True to his word, Optio Tertius did not allow them further rest. By midday Varro regretted not eating when he had the chance. He and Falco were assigned to clean the elephant pit, since a good number of their handlers had joined the forage team and never returned. Yet the elephants did not agree with unfamiliar faces and eventually both he and Falco were assigned other work.

Throughout the day, news trickled into the camp. Philip was reported to have rejoined his men. This brought a strange mixture of regret that their enemy had not perished and excitement for potentially reaching some sort of truce. For the Macedonians had lost a large portion of their cavalry, according to the rumors Varro heard. This led some to speculate the Macedonians would yield to Rome. Having met the vain and treacherous King Philip, he doubted the loss meant much other than an adjustment in tactics while he raised more cavalry. He would need to be thoroughly defeated before he ever agreed to a truce.

Varro and Falco ended their day working guard duty at the western gate. Varro had hoped to take the eastern gate and review the stragglers still arriving. Even cavalrymen had become lost and arrived over the course of the day. Yet he never received word of Panthera or Sura.

"Looks like we've actually got work to do," Falco said, standing before the gate while the deep blue sky yielded to darkness. Varro, who had been looking up at the first stars of the evening, now searched ahead.

A rider approached up the western road. His white horse seemed to glow with the final rays of daylight. He held overhead in his right hand a cluster of olive branches. Varro moaned.

"An emissary from Philip," he said. "Right at the end of our watch."

Falco called for the gates to close and relay the arrival of the emissary before he even arrived. While he appeared alone, a trap was always possible.

"Peace, Romans!" the rider called out in a near-native accent, holding his olive branches overhead. "I come with a message from King Philip to Consul Galba."

He drew up his horse out of range of Varro's light pilum. Weary and hungry, Varro sighed as he challenged the rider.

"Dismount your horse and hold your hands away from your sides. If you are here in peace, you will be treated with respect."

"I am," the rider said, dismounting with ease. He wore a white tunic in the Greek style and carried only a long sword in a sheath suspended from his shoulder. This he unhitched and offered to Varro. "My only weapon, for defense along the roads here. Please keep it and my mount safe for my return."

Varro took the horse and sword. The rider was young, perhaps only in his mid-twenties. He had a firm smile and squinting eyes. A deep scar ran along the base of his chin, marring an otherwise classic profile.

After some back and forth with the officer on watch, the emissary was allowed inside and the gates closed behind him. He and Falco both listened to the exchange with the officer, who questioned the nature of the message.

"It is for your consul to hear," he said. "But it is not a dire secret. Simply, we have lost a great number of cavalrymen on a road you control. We wish for a temporary truce to retrieve their bodies for proper burial. That is all."

The officer nodded, he picked two of his own men, plus Varro and Falco.

"The four of you conduct this visitor to Consul Galba's tent. I'll see his horse and sword are cared for in the meantime."

Varro and Falco were in the rear of the box formed around the emissary, whose stride was confident and brisk. He looked from side to side as they trod down the main road to headquarters, humming with appreciation at everything he saw. Soldiers paused to stare after them, and the emissary smiled patiently to them as he passed. Varro believed the emissary was sent simply to judge their condition after the confusion of battle from the day before.

Their arrival at Galba's tent went poorer than Varro expected. His personal guards berated them for disturbing the consul at this late hour. He was at rest and could not be disturbed for such a trifling message. Therefore, the emissary was to be settled for the night and offered food and wine. Galba would receive him in the morning.

The other two escorts claimed they had to return to their posts soon, so the duty for settling the emissary fell to Varro and Falco.

"This fucking day will never end," Falco muttered through his congestion. "I can't fucking breathe and I want to sleep."

They eventually met with the tesserarius coordinating all the night watches and arranged for a tent and guards. When the emissary was finally settled and Varro believed he was free to return to his tent, the emissary called to them.

"The consul's guards mentioned food and wine? I am quite hungry. Will you bring me something simple? Not too much at this late hour, please."

The mucus in Falco's chest grumbled as he prepared to curse the man. But Varro barred him with his arm.

"I'll take care of it. Go back and rest while you can."

Falco glared at the emissary standing in the opening of his newly erected tent. Then he nodded to Varro. "Steal something for yourself, too."

The two guards now assigned to the emissary laughed at this. He and Falco parted and the emissary closed his tent flap. Varro paused in thought, unsure where he could secure food and wine after dark. He would again return to the tesserarius, as no other officer would be available to direct him. Yet he was also an easily angered officer, and more irritable than ever after the confusion resulting from a battle that could either be deemed a victory or a humiliating defeat. No one seemed to agree if they had carried the day or not, leaving many in a foul mood. So Varro decided to ask the guards who had made the original offer. No need enraging an already angry officer who might be asleep at his desk.

The decision was the correct one. For the guards outside the consul's tent simply nodded and one fetched a slave to help deliver the food.

"Wine, cheese, and bread," said the other guard. "If he expects a feast tonight, he can get fucked. It's better than he deserves."

"Agreed," Varro said, folding his hands over his stomach. He was so hungry now that the pangs had long subsided. Instead he felt lightheaded and unfocused. Perhaps the emissary may only receive wine and cheese. White bread would be a rare treat for Varro, but probably not missed by a royal messenger.

The other soldier returned and pointed him at another tent near the consul's grandiose tent. "The slave will meet you there. You take it over to him."

"Of course!" Varro hoped he didn't seem too excited. His mouth was already salivating.

He found the tent flap open and a dim lamp spilling yellow light into the blue night. Ducking inside, he found the tent full of supplies of every kind, including casks of wine and pots of olive oil. A wood tray was set out on a crate, and white bread and cheese had already been laid out. A small cluster of red grapes shined in the low light, pushed against the cheese. Varro swallowed and his stomach growled at last, anticipating a mouthful of those grapes.

But when the slave emerged from behind the boxes, holding the lamp and a clay decanter of fresh wine, Varro's mouth dried.

It was the slave girl that had stared so hatefully at him.

She smiled at his shock. Her brown hair was cut short, reading her earlobes. Her dark eyes were round and beautiful, surrounded by thick lashes. Strangely, the heavy lashes made Varro think of Tribune Primanus. It all took him back to that day when he stood before Consul Galba.

"Who are you?" he asked. He wanted to grab her by the arm and force her to explain herself. But being Consul Galba's property, any violence to her would be equal to kicking down the consul's tent. So he tried to act uncaring.

The girl laughed, then set the decanter on the wood tray.

"I help carry. Short way."

Her Latin was garbled. Perhaps she had only just learned it in service to the consul. So Varro nodded agreement. She took the lamp in one hand, then braced the tray between her free hand and hip.

He followed her outside. She was slender and tanned, and moved with a boyishness that did no justice to her feminine beauty. She wore a cream-colored stola that was clean and tailored to her. After all, the consul would not have slaves in ragged clothes, particularly one this attractive.

"I help, short time." She spoke to the guards outside the consul's tent. One frowned but waved her on.

"She's the consul's prize," he said to Varro. "Don't put any handprints on her, if you know my meaning."

He led the way with the slave following in silence. She seemed to understand his frustration, smiling wickedly at him whenever he looked back. They delivered the food, which Varro did not get to steal because of the slave girl. Did she know he wanted it? Such an evil woman.

With the emissary settled, he followed the slave girl down the same road, this time with her in the lead. Once they came within sight of the consul's tent, Varro drew a sharp breath.

"Why do you hate me?" He had to ask, since he might never get an opportunity again.

"Ah, do I hate you?" She paused, turning to put her calloused hand to her neck in mock surprise. Her already big eyes widened to shine in the wavering light of the torches set at intervals along the road.

"You could have killed me that day in front of the consul. But why? Do you understand what I am saying?"

The slave smiled, then glanced down the path to where the consul's guards watched them. She interposed herself between them and Varro, so that she showed her back to the guards. Her eyes narrowed and her pretty face wrinkled with a snarl.

Her finger hooked the collar of her stola, then she pulled it down to reveal her chest.

A thick, lumpy scar of dull red had been slashed in a line just over her girlish breasts.

She gritted her teeth and leaned in to whisper.

"You killed my uncle and my brother. Cut me. I hate you."

Varro stepped back and blinked.

This slave had been among the Illyrian bandits that had captured him last summer. He had thought her a boy at the time. She had led him around by a rope leash and seemed eager to torment him even then. He had made the cut that scarred her. In turn, she had smashed him over the back of his head. His hand reflexively touched the spot she had struck. Her smile widened at this.

"You will die." She spoke low with as much threat as she could muster before alarming the guards watching in the distance.

"Be careful of your threats," Varro said. "You're a slave and I am a citizen. I don't care that you belong to the consul."

Either she did not understand or did not feel threatened. For she leaned closer and smiled wider. She stroked her hands along her neck, as if pulling on an invisible necklace.

"Are you missing gold? I took it. My dead brother's necklace. You will never have it. Never!"

21

"I don't know who was her uncle and who was her brother," Varro said. "I killed both of them. That's the truth. And it doesn't matter who was who."

He crouched around the cooking fire. It was the rarest of mornings when Optio Tertius did not have some assignment that needed attention at dawn. The hastati in the neighboring tents also had time to prepare a breakfast, resulting in many cautiously upbeat voices filling the brisk morning air. Varro stirred the pot of boiling wheat as Curio dropped in lard and salt. While he had eaten hard tack before bed to cure his hunger, it was nothing like a hot meal on a cold morning.

Falco, who had ensured Cordus was away on a trifling errand, stood over them with hands on his hips. His shadow fell across them and the cooking fire smoke blurred him.

"And you just let her walk off?"

"The consul's guards were watching. Was I supposed to enter his tent and start searching?"

"Well, at least we know the little whore stole our gold. That took some guts to do, even if she did it while the camp had cleared out. But how did she know we had it?"

"That is my question as well," Varro said. He broke apart the lard Curio dropped into the boiling water, helping it dissolve faster. "It's all too much for me to understand. I'm just happy to be alive today."

"Well, don't be so happy that you give up on getting the necklace back." Falco shifted his weight, then put up his hand to stop the conversation. "Cordus is returning. We'll talk about this later. It's not like we can just grab the consul's slave. Besides, she's not going to get rid of it. So there's time still."

He then doubled over and began coughing.

Once Cordus rejoined them, the conversation shifted to the state of Falco's health. It was not good but he proclaimed he wouldn't die yet so celebrations would have to wait. Curio explained how to improve their breakfast with the simple addition of a sliced onion. Cordus stared into the fire with a blank expression.

No one talked about Panthera or Sura. After two days, they were considered missing and presumed dead. Varro could not prevent wondering how they must have perished. Did they die of thirst or exposure? Had Philip's men captured them or killed them? Did they kill each other? The stress of being lost and hungry in the wilds must have been an unendurable strain. Worse still, what spirits haunted that marsh? Did ghostly hands drag them off safe paths to drown in the cold, dark waters? Did vengeful spirits steal their breaths? Did they follow lights in the night that led them to doom?

He kept imagining Panthera leaping from one earth mound to the next, but slipping. He splashed into the water and sank under the weight of his armor. Gone forever without a sound and nothing to mark his passing. Muck enfolded him, burying him from the memory of all but a few. The imaginary scene raised bumps on Varro's arms.

As they broke down the cooking trestle after breakfast, Optio Tertius arrived with news of a reorganization. Tribune Primanus and his centurions had spent the prior day determining how to complete units and where reinforcements would be placed once these arrived in the spring. For the winter, they would have to function with what they could raise from local allies. No more Romans were coming.

Varro's hands went cold, expecting their contubernium would be broken up. He resisted looking to Falco, who coughed throughout the optio's explanation.

"Don't worry, Varro. You'll be getting four replacements to your contubernium. We'll be reorganizing this morning. So I hope you enjoyed your relaxation, because once we form up we're going on a nice march together. Nothing builds camaraderie like a full-gear march up a mountain."

The four replacements were not recruits. Each came from a contubernium of hastati that had been reduced to one or two members. Varro's century remained under-strength, but many were still at their full sizes. At the end of the organization Tribune Primanus gave a long-winded speech about duty and honor. It was only in the final phrases that he praised those who had died in service to Rome, naming them heroes and calling for the assembled soldiers to cheer for those gone on to the Elysian Fields.

As he cheered with the rest of the soldiers, Varro found tears streaking his cheeks as he remembered the friends he had lost. He stopped the tears by remembering Lars Gallio was alive with the enemy. Even if Tribune Primanus had likely forgotten his threats against the contubernium, Varro would still do his utmost to find Gallio and bring him to justice.

Panthera, Otho, and Sura were owed this much.

As promised, the newly formed contubernium joined the

entire century with Centurion Drusus and Optio Tertius for a full-gear march into the steep hills surrounding the camp. While exhausting, Varro appreciated the view from the top of these hills. Fields of grains spread out on farmland near their camp. These fields were empty now, but it nonetheless reminded Varro of the expanses of golden barley of his own home.

A glimpse was all he could enjoy, as he labored and sweated over rocky, uneven ground. But he now had a full belly and renewed energy. Falco, by contrast, appeared ready to fall apart. Snot ran continuously from his nose and his mouth hung open to aid his breathing. Yet he dared not complain, especially in front of four new soldiers. Varro hid his smile, as Falco clearly wanted to be known as the hardiest and strongest man among the eight of them. While Otho had been physically strong, his simpleness had made him unthreatening. These four new men seemed to know their business as well as, and maybe better than, he and Falco.

The march was marred by the discovery of a dead cavalryman. First his horse was found grazing. Later in the march, they found his body. He had apparently struck his head on a tree limb and fell from his horse. Since he was discovered lying on his back beneath a tree, this was the assumed cause of death. Varro thought it a strange way to die for a cavalryman. But he should not have been in these hills and had likely pursued Macedonians into them. The century paused to recover the horse and to detail men to bury the body.

They returned to camp and received frantic news of the Macedonians' withdrawal. While nothing was certain, it seemed the emissary from the night before had been a distraction. Philip had left campfires burning all night to appear as if his army was still present. But by midmorning scouts reported the Macedonian camp had been abandoned. Philip's emissary had already departed by the time of this discovery. So no one knew why the Macedonians had left or where they had gone.

Centurion Drusus was summoned to an emergency meeting with the tribune shortly after arriving to this news. The century was dismissed to Optio Tertius, who was in the same state of confusion as his men. So everyone was to stand by for further instructions and dismissed to their tents.

The four additions to the contubernium followed the others. Varro felt a strange resistance both within himself and from the new arrivals. No one was eager to make friends. Friends were hard to let go when they died. Yet the system they lived in was designed to force these friendships, or else sort out men who could never work together. They now eyed space in an eight-man tent that probably was best sized for six. They would get to know each other well in short order.

One of the replacements, Septimus Dama, had lips so thin his mouth was no better than a reptilian slit. Varro took an instant dislike to him for the arrogant cast of his face. He now frowned at Cordus.

"Are you even old enough to enlist?"

"I'll be seventeen next year," Cordus said, straightening his back to appear taller. "Just like Varro and Falco."

Dama blinked and searched between them, stopping on Falco. "He's the only one who looks old enough to be in the hastati. You should all be velites, and this one lied about his age to enlist. I've been assigned to take care of the children. Great."

Varro cocked his head and stepped in front of Dama.

"You had best take care of yourself, and needn't worry for us." He felt that old rage trembling through his hands, the kind he felt went he wanted to fight back against Falco's beatings. "As for your assignment, you're not the officer in charge. So there's no one for you to look after, especially children. You're one of us soldiers. Do you understand?"

Dama narrowed his eyes and held Varro's gaze. But he was not going to yield to this newcomer who thought himself superior to everyone else. He stared until Dama laughed and turned aside.

"Touchy little group, I see. Calm yourself, Varro. I was only half-serious."

Varro turned to Cordus, then patted his shoulder. The young man returned a stern expression, trying to look more manly but only emphasizing his youth.

The other three newcomers distanced themselves from Dama. They introduced themselves amicably and promised to look out for one another. All were tired and footsore from their march. They stretched out on the grass before their tent, along with dozens of other similar groups, and took advantage of the opportunity for rest.

Within the hour, Optio Tertius summoned the century to the parade ground to hear an address from the consul. Once again, being in the rear with the hastati and velites made hearing him a chore. The gist was that Philip had fled for some reason and the entire camp would mobilize to find him, save the elephants and a small holding force of triarii. In order to prepare for an extended march, grain would be collected from the neighboring farms. This would begin today.

Varro did not like the idea of robbing farmers of their winter stockpiles. But this was the reality of maintaining an army in the field and he had to accept it. He prayed there would be no violence and the locals would wisely surrender what Galba required of them.

Once they reached the countryside beyond the hills, they extended long trains of men between the farms and camp to move the collected grain. Varro found the newest members of the contubernium were competent and friendly. Even Dama cooperated, though Varro noted the backhanded compliments and subtle complaints voiced as so-called observations. On the whole, no one had time to bicker as they moved from farm to camp and back again all day.

After two days they were prepared to march out in search of the vanished Macedonians.

"Hey, maybe Gallio will betray his new masters and lead us to them," Falco said the morning they assembled for the march out. They were breaking down their tent and loading it onto their pack mule which the contubernium's slaves would lead on the march.

Falco's comment caused Dama to stand up from crouching over his pack, his thin lips opened in surprise.

"You are the ones who had the traitor?"

Varro and the rest of the original contubernium looked to each other as if seeing who would admit it. Varro cleared his throat and nodded.

"I know Gallio is with the Macedonians in one of their auxiliary units. I've seen him during a battle." He looked to Falco, who raised a brow to the claim but otherwise remained silent. "I have sworn to bring him to justice."

"Who cares about that?" Dama said, lacing his fingers over the top of his head. He looked to the three other replacements. "The tribune blames you for his desertion. You're all cowards. Everyone knows this."

The other replacements lowered their eyes, avoiding anyone. But Varro had enough.

In one stride he reached Dama. His uppercut landed under Dama's jaw with a meaty crack, sprawling him across the bundled tent. The two slaves skipped back toward the mule, laughing. But Varro did not stop. He pounced atop the sprawled out Dama and grabbed him by his crotch. He then leaned in to whisper into his ear.

"You ever call me or my brothers a coward again and I'll tear these tiny nuts free of your body."

"I didn't call you a coward." Dama's voice rose as Varro twisted his grip. "Let me go!"

"Next time I won't," he said, releasing his grip on Dama. He then shoved back to his feet, glaring at the snickering slaves who immediately shrank away. He then turned to the others.

"We've all faced the same dangers. We've all fought the same battles. You think we're cowards because one of our number ran off? Don't worry for it. My shield is steady, and the same for the others. Don't judge me or anyone else a coward until you see it with your own eyes."

"I was just saying what the fucking rumors are." Dama now climbed to his feet, keeping his legs wide. "How do you think I feel being lumped in with a group that the tribune hates?"

"I know what I feel," Varro said, pointing at Dama. "I feel proud. And you will as well, if you can become one of us."

Again he found himself staring down Dama, who was now more docile. He returned to fixing his pack and preparing for the march. Optio Tertius arrived just after the scuffle, and everyone jumped back to their own preparations. Only Varro remained still staring after Dama.

"Good morning," the optio said, following Varro's glare. He paused as if understanding the conflict, but simply shrugged. "We're in the vanguard. So get up front and get there now. Stop wasting time with whatever foolishness is going on here. We're on a hunt for Macedonians."

Once Tertius moved on, Varro returned to securing his pack and weapons. He turned his back to everyone, suddenly embarrassed for his outburst. Falco sidestepped toward him until they were able to whisper together.

"You're a changed man, Marcus Varro. If you'd have thrown punches like that when we were kids, I'd have left you alone."

Varro shook his head as he struggled to tie his pack, then

shoved it away with a sigh. "That was not good. I shouldn't have offered violence to mere words."

Falco coughed and cleared his throat before speaking. "Well, if I was feeling better I'd have broken those thin lips of his, along with his yellow teeth. Face it, Varro, violence is all that some people understand. I think he's getting the point to shut up and cooperate. You can't ask a man like him nicely. He's got to have it pounded into his head. Good job, Tribune."

"Don't call me that. You don't see tribunes throwing punches at simple insults."

"Of course not. They hire men to do it for them."

"Well, if anything, this just proves we have to do something to change our reputation. I don't want others talking about us like that. Even if it's baseless, things like that can get out of control. Who knows what will come of it? Reputation is everything."

Falco shrugged. "Wait long enough and anyone who remembers will probably die. It's a war, after all."

But Varro would not wait. He knew what he saw, and if Gallio was out there he would find him.

They assumed their position in the vanguard. The tenth maniple of the tenth century would be among the first to encounter any Macedonians. For once Varro was eager for it. He knew Philip, having just lost a chunk of his cavalry, would not leave his prized pikemen as a rearguard. That would fall to his auxiliaries to cover the escape of his main force, and that meant the possibility of finding Gallio.

Their march out of camp was a glorious display of a consular army going to war. Galba led from the front with a contingent of cavalry guards along with the tribunes of each legion, Primanus being directly in front of Varro's position in the column. He wished to turn and see the long column of soldiers and the attendant baggage train, but he had to keep the brisk pace and couldn't see so far back.

After two days of marching, where they constructed a new camp each night complete with a ditch and stakes, they had arrived at a place called Pluinna. To Varro, it seemed like any other place in Macedonia. It was full of golden grasses, high hills, and mixed forests of dark pines and naked trees. Local people fled at their approach, leaving behind their stores for Galba to pillage. But they did not find signs of Philip here. Varro had no idea how Galba knew where to look. He simply lined up each day and waited for Centurion Drusus to shout an order to march. As a soldier, he had no responsibility to think beyond the current order. Yet he wondered when they might locate Philip.

To his horror, he soon found himself climbing into steep and mountainous terrain where he was no longer marching but climbing. Even without encountering a single Macedonian, they still experienced casualties from rockslides and falls. No one had died but many had broken a leg or ankle. Varro himself had misstepped enough times to wonder when it would be his turn to scream in agony at a broken ankle bone.

On the morning of the fourth day as the long column picked its way through the narrow passes, Varro heard something unusual. At first he thought it was Falco wheezing beside him. The congestion in his chest sounded like a fly buzzing in his throat. In looking at him, Falco's mouth hung open and he rubbed at his nose with hands white with dust. But he made no sound.

He heard the whizzing sound again, this time followed by a wooden plink.

As he stepped forward, he saw an arrow shaft lying in his path. It sat atop two small rocks, its black feathers fluttering in the chill breeze. He had the nonsensical thought that someone had placed it there on purpose, as it looked so fresh and new. Since he had to keep pace with the climb into this pass, he had no time to consider it.

Until he realized what he heard zipping past him had been arrows.

It was ranging fire from a hidden force, and a volley was certain to follow.

"Falco, get your shield up."

"What?"

But in the next moment, Centurion Drusus shouted the same order. The pass filled with the warm thrum of snapping bowstrings and black arrows crowded the sky.

22

Varro plunged into shadow as he raised his shield in time. The steep and rocky incline vanished behind the massive wooden shield that enveloped him. Within the space of a breath, the first volley of arrows skittered across it. He felt the impacts vibrate through the wood and heard the iron heads scoring its face. But he crouched low, clutching his light pilum to his body and tucking his head into his shoulders.

The plink of iron on rock and wood flowed like a wave across the vanguard. Varro heard it rolling behind him along with the muffled curses of fellow soldiers huddled under their shields. Falco coughed behind his, but made no other sound. Like all other Romans soldiers, he remained silent now that they had contacted the Macedonians. Down the slope some men screamed in pain as an arrow still found a mark.

Braced against the brown rocks and clumps of weeds, Varro's shield sat like an immobile wall between himself and danger. Yet a second volley followed on the first, with the same result. One arrow struck the iron top of his shield and shattered with a crack, showering him in bright splinters and sending the broken shaft spinning into the cold sunlight.

"Forward!" Centurion Drusus shouted the order. "Shields up!"

"Like he has to tell us," Falco muttered from Varro's right.

They pulled up their shields, progressing up the hard slope. But Varro's feet slipped on the scree and even his hobnails struggled to find purchase. The line drew together instinctively, and even though Varro was encased behind his shield he still tucked his head down and pointed the top of his bronze helmet at the enemy. It was like he marched into a rainstorm.

A third volley hissed down the slope, and again clattered across the shields. From Varro's left, Curio shouted in surprise as an arrow skimmed across his foot, drawing a dark line of blood across the top. He hopped and hissed, but gritted his teeth and continued to keep pace with the slow climb. Varro blinked at the amazing shot. As completely covered as they were, he could not believe an arrow could reach anyone's foot.

They crawled higher still with the centurions of the vanguard leading the way forward. Centurion Drusus led Varro's line and so his shouts were thunderous even sheltering behind a shield.

"Don't lag. Keep the line straight. We close the distance then we'll cut them to bits. Stay with me, boys!"

Varro was blind beyond Falco and Curio. He felt the weight of men behind him and heard their grunts of effort to follow along the slippery path. Yet he could only focus on the step ahead. As he climbed, his shield thumped against a hard rock, forcing him to separate from Curio and push into Falco as he skirted around it.

He kept his shield ready and pressed against his helmet. Despite the chill air, sweat rolled down the sides of his face. His breathing was ragged. He heard Falco wheezing through his congestion next to him. At any moment he expected another volley of arrows to arc down on them. Yet he progressed steadily ahead, flowing around and over bushes and boulders on the climb. Their enemy had gone silent.

This piqued Varro's interest. Rarely had he time to think in battle, at least the few battles he had fought in his young career. Why hadn't the enemy attacked in arcing volleys, and instead shot straight down the slope? Why only three quick volleys and nothing more? It seemed to Varro that the Macedonians—more likely their Cretan archers—had only wanted to kick the dog so that it would turn and chase them.

But experienced soldiers like Centurion Drusus and Tribune Primanus would know better than he would. If they ordered a climb into the enemy position, then it must be correct. They knew war better than Varro. Yet with each step forward where the archers did not fire Varro suspected something far worse awaited them.

At last he chanced peeking from behind his shield. Ahead of him Centurion Drusus and his signifier carrying their century standard led the path forward. They both crouched behind shields, though the signifier had a harder time with the long pole of the standard to manage. Varro was less than a half-dozen paces behind, and could line up with them when the battle began in earnest. Beyond them, he stared up into dark shadows cast by massive rocks and jutting outcrops. With only a glance, he could not immediately spot the enemy position. He wondered if Centurion Drusus knew where they hid, or if he was simply following other centurions in the line.

He peeked again, hoping to see something that indicated they were headed for an enemy. Still all that showed along the rugged slope were open stretches of brownish rock and the stubborn bushes that survived among them. Plentiful cover meant scores of archers could be waiting unseen.

"We're almost there," Drusus shouted. "Get your—"

A tremendous rocky scraping like the entire mountain was

sliding apart interrupted the command.

The ground shook with intense violence, raising dust over Varro's feet. Then in the next instant a wave of dirt and rocks washed into his sandals.

Lowering his shield, he looked up to a wall of earth and rocks crashing down at him. He screamed then snapped the shield back in place.

Falco dragged him by the strap of his bronze pectoral and they both dodged into the cover of a boulder half sunk into the earth. He crashed against it and others piled up behind him. Curio and Cordus both leapt atop him, as did others. Varro's face pushed up against the cold, hard rock and his mouth filled with the bitter dust turning the air dirty gray.

Screams were lost behind the shuddering crashes of boulders tumbling past. A wave of earth slewed through the spot where Varro had just stood.

As swiftly as the landslide had released, it stopped. The brown waves of earth lapped and trickled like real water, and an errant stone rolled down the top of it to make one last flip before settling in place. Moans and shouts rose up in the blinding dust. Varro's sight could not penetrate it.

One man in their dog pile against the boulder was screaming in agony. Varro had to wait for Curio and Cordus to peel off him before he could stand up to see what had happened. One soldier had accidentally impaled his thigh on a light pilum. The dozen hastati who had landed on this side of the landslide stood dumbfounded around the man, who gripped his leg and writhed in the dirt. The bloody pilum point jutted from the front of his leg and was bent so that it could not be extracted without a doctor's aid.

Varro shoved his way to the man, who was not of his contubernium but one he knew nonetheless. He pulled off his pack and began removing a bandage.

"Someone break off the shaft," he said. "It's going to cause more damage otherwise."

Two worked on this while Varro tried to tie off the leg above the wound. Falco held the soldier down so he did not fight out of reflex. But his screams were brilliant and sharp as they echoed off the surrounding boulders. These kinds of screams echoed all around in the distance.

"Form up!"

Centurion Drusus waded out of the dust, his signifier with him. Both were like brown ghosts, only their eyes and mouths free of dirt.

Varro completed the tie. His hands were slick with blood, and he wiped them on the soldier's tunic. It seemed disrespectful, but after all, it was already ruined.

Drusus paused at the sight of the injured man, then shook his head.

"A fine trap they set for us," he said. "Walked right into it and now we're cut in half. Fuck!"

Varro stood with Falco's help. His mouth was gritty and his eyes watered from the dust, but he recovered his pila and shield. The impaled soldier had a folded cloth clenched between his teeth, and he had stopped screaming. But despite the tourniquet, blood leaked in fat drips from the horrid wound. Varro doubted he would survive.

Centurion Drusus clapped his hands. "All right, I said to form up. We don't know where the enemies are but they're in the front. So don't show your backsides to them."

They had landed in a safe but impassible space. The boulder they sheltered behind was one of dozens that studded a slope that led to a vertical wall of cracked, gray stone. This was too high to scale without climbing gear and led only to another wall farther back. It seemed unlikely that all but a few enemies could hide there. Yet even a dozen bowmen could pick them off standing in the open.

They reassembled into what passed for a loose organization. Varro was at least glad the centurion had landed on their side of the divided line. He wondered what might have befallen Optio Tertius at the rear of the century. Dust still billowed in the air, rolling in curling patterns that caught the sunlight. They stood silent and watching, centurion as well. For once it had settled enough to see through, they could all assess their situation.

Varro saw another group of soldiers on the far side of the tongue of earth that had released on them. He could not guess at the casualties, but spotted points of bronze among the dirt and rocks. Whether those were lost helmets or the exposed portions of corpses, Varro did not know.

Drusus called to his counterpart across the divide. Yet far down the slope the consul and tribunes had been out of danger. In the end, Drusus received his orders from the tribune via Optio Tertius, who came jogging up the slope. His face was clean and bright.

"Glad to see you survived, sir." He saluted, then glanced at Varro and the other survivors. "Tribune Primanus has ordered us to withdraw and regroup."

"Of course," Drusus said. He rubbed dust out of his eyes and mumbled. Varro was close enough to catch it. "Galba's good sense, I'm sure. Primanus would order a charge."

A smile flashed across Optio Tertius's face. "Sir, the rest of the century was out of the way. The trap only caught the front ranks."

"They sprang it too early," Drusus said. "Good planning ruined by nerves. Fortunate for us. All right, men, I want an ordered withdrawal. Carry the wounded. We'll be back for revenge."

They scaled back down the slope, which was harder than climbing it. The loose ground shifted under Varro's sandals and slid him toward the man in front. The two bearing their impaled companion both fell, causing the wounded man to scream again.

Yet at length they regrouped with the rest of the century at the base of the slope.

Galba, his tribunes, and mounted guards sat atop their horses and observed the reorganization. Behind them the legions stretched out like a gleaming, golden river to vanish behind the outcroppings and turns in the narrow pass. Varro shook his head at the size of the force reduced to the strength of only a few centuries due to the mountainous terrain. He wondered how few enemies had delayed so many.

For it was only a delay. Already Centurion Drusus leaned into a circle of other officers, junior centurion, and both optios of the tenth maniple. As they spoke, all glanced up the slope and pointed out different approaches.

"Looks like the tenth hastati is going to lead the way," Curio said. He patted dust off his white tunic, now stained brown with dirt.

"I bet you wish you were back with the velites," Falco said. But Curio shook his head. One of the three black feathers of his helmet broke and hung at an angle.

"Pay is better as a hastatus."

So they kicked the ground and stared up at the mound of fresh earth. Varro wondered if he was going to walk over men buried alive.

"Shouldn't we try to dig out anyone buried?" He looked to Falco, but he just stared wide-eyed ahead and shrugged. Varro watched the officers returning to their men and used his final moments to speak before Drusus led them back. "Thanks for pulling me out of the way. I just froze up and hid behind my shield."

"It might work against a man," Falco said. "But it certainly won't against boulders. Anyway, you'd do the same for me. You did, actually, back in the marsh. We're even now, I expect."

Varro smiled. "Even for now."

Typical of Roman military tactics, Centurion Drusus led them once more up the same slope they had just been pushed off. Varro did not doubt the senior officers would throw more men at any barrier encountered. It seemed how the army solved all its challenges. So he thumped up the same path with the same heavy pack on his back and shield on his arm. Yet this time, no arrows flew down the slope.

They reached the soft earth and loose boulders. As he had feared, Varro and the rest of the century clambered onto the pile of earth. It was soft but gritty and made for better footing than the first time up the slope.

"Testudo!" Centurion Drusus shouted the order, and Optio Tertius repeated it at the rear of their line.

As Varro's feet sank into the ground, he placed his shield to the front and lined it up with Falco and Curio. Behind him, Cordus raised his shield over his head as part of a massive, mobile block of shields. With Centurion Drusus at the center of the front line, they continued their ascent.

A face showed through the dirt underfoot. Varro screamed as he nearly stepped on it. Only the victim's eyes and nose were visible. His mouth had filled with dirt. Varro wondered if he was still alive but just pinned in place. He jostled against Falco, who cursed him for a fool. But he would not step on a fellow soldier's corpse.

"There are men under foot, sir," Varro said across Falco's back to the centurion.

"Of course there are. So we're going to get them revenge, Varro. Keep moving."

Holding the testudo formation while navigating a steep and rocky slope challenged even the best of the men. Light flashed into the shadows of the formation as soldiers slipped or else lagged. But thus far no enemy appeared. Varro guessed the holding force had either fled after springing their trap or were conserving their arrows for better shots.

"We're almost there," Drusus shouted, his voice rocky like the earth underfoot.

Peering through the narrow gap between shields, Varro could not determine what Drusus referred to. It seemed they were approaching a low rock face in the mountains.

Then something heavy thudded atop their formation. A man screamed in surprise behind them.

Another heavy thud followed, and soon dozens of thuds filled the crowded and dark space under the shields. Varro's own shield, held forward, encountered nothing. But Cordus cursed when something struck his shield and fell through a gap to skim Varro's shoulder. It was a rock as big as his own head.

The enemies dropped rocks on them as they neared the top of the slope. Varro felt their presence from the falling stones, but still saw no actual enemy.

Until Drusus ordered them to wheel right.

A prepared position came into view. A light rock wall had been built up and reinforced with sharpened stakes. It led up into an outcropping where the enemy had a view of the slope and now likely dropped rocks from. This was the continuation of the pass, and it was fully blockaded.

"Ten strides, boys!" Centurion Drusus had a smile in his voice. "Hold together ten strides and we'll have some payback."

The testudo formation charged the blockade. A score of archers popped out of hiding, and shot directly at them. A shaft slammed into Varro's shield, sticking into the multilayered wood. He heard it vibrating and was glad it had not found a gap.

The surprise volley only galvanized the front lines, and Varro found himself charging alongside the others. The archers knew their chances for a second shot, and instead took up spears to set against the charge.

Centurion Drusus pointed his gladius forward. "Use your swords. Kill every last one of them!"

The formation opened and Varro found himself screaming his war cry and charging ahead with Falco to his right and Curio on his left. His pila remained clutched in hand, but he drew his gladius. He reached the rock barricade, and enemies with round shields extended their spears to ward off the attackers.

But Varro trusted to his scutum. He reached the barricade, angling himself into the curve of the shield as he did. The spear thrust failed to find any way around it. Also by the nature of the barricade itself, the spearman could not thrust at his feet. He was completely protected.

The enemy was not. The instant the spear struck his shield Varro slammed it forward then stepped into a punch with his sword. This too deflected off the enemy shield. Yet now he was at the barricade, pushing against it to test the sturdiness of the blockade. He wasn't strong enough to knock the rocks over, and the wood spikes made it too risky to leap. But if he remained in place and forced the enemy to attack him, he would be safe while the others reinforced his position.

The narrow frontage with no depth due to the stone wall behind the enemy led to their withdrawal. They fought only long enough to allow their companions to file out of the chokepoint and into the surrounding terrain. Varro did not kill a single man in the short fight. His sword had only cut an exposed forearm, and then not terribly. The defenders fought simply to delay, and at their first advantage they fled rather than press the attack.

"Over these barricades," Drusus shouted. "Bring me prisoners. Hurry, you laggards!"

Varro and Falco both wrestled the stakes out of their settings. Curio and Cordus along with the rest of the contubernium aided them. Once these stakes were tossed aside, leaping the low wall was simple enough.

Varro was the first in and immediately felt exposed running into the narrow pass with his head ducked behind his shield. High rocks around him still afforded hiding places for enemies, and he expected a stone to be dropped on his head. But he did not delay, instead sweeping forward with his shield in pursuit of the fleeing defenders.

With his shield held forward like a plow, Varro threaded the short path and stumbled out into the wider pass. Scores of enemies scurried over the rocks to melt away in every direction. The main holding force had likely fled after springing their rockslide trap. These were the archers and spearmen left to delay pursuit.

An arrow struck a rock at Varro's knee height. Instead of shattering, it skipped up and struck him square between the eyes on the rim of his helmet. This knocked it over his eyes, blinding him momentarily as he fumbled backward in shock.

Varro pushed his helmet up with a muttered curse. Falco came to his side, shield forward, and Curio joined also as the first out of the narrow passage. He looked back to the fleeing enemy.

And he saw him.

"Lars Gallio!"

Varro pointed with his sword at a figure that had just mounted a high rock and prepared to leap behind its protective bulk. But the figure paused at the name.

Falco and Curio both dropped their shields and followed his pointing sword.

"Gallio, surrender!" Varro stepped forward, dropping all thought of protecting himself from further bowshot.

The figure was Lars Gallio. He knew that profile, and the man who paused turned slowly to his name.

"By the gods, it's him!" Falco said. He raised his sword overhead. "Get the fuck back here, you fucking traitor! I'll cut your balls off. I swear it! You fucking pig-loving shit!"

But Gallio shook his head, then jumped behind the boulder and vanished.

23

Varro shoveled away another spadeful of brown earth and rocks. He was one of the few of the maniple remaining at work. But one soldier was still unaccounted for and he volunteered to continue to dig. Another task force was removing the barriers ahead on the pass. Philip had apparently done far more than initially realized to narrow this choke point to something impossible to a full army. He had not squandered his lead. Many soldiers said they were fortunate the choke point could not hold more than a small enemy force, otherwise they might never make it through alive. As Varro dug, he wondered if the five men buried in this landslide would have agreed.

His spade crunched into the earth, and he forced it in with his heel. Sweat rolled down his face from beneath his helmet. At least he had been allowed to set aside his pack and shield. Digging with a bronze pectoral and greave was challenging enough. Falco dug beside him, as did the rest of the contubernium.

"So that was the traitor," Dama said as he levered away a large rock. "You're certain it's him?"

"Of course we're fucking certain." Falco stabbed his shovel into the dirt. "Can you ask a different question? You repeat the same shit over and over. It's driving me mad."

"I just want to be sure," Dama said, unperturbed. He continued to dig. "If you catch him, then your reputations will be improved."

"You?" Falco grabbed his shovel and began working again. "We is more like it. We are all in this together. So we will bring that piece of shit to justice."

"We'll catch him," Varro said. "Don't worry for it."

He glanced at Curio, who dug with single-minded purpose. He had been Gallio's closest friend. While Falco still wondered if Curio had planned to desert with him, Varro did not. He could have run off at any time, particularly during Philip's ambush. But the short man's mood had gone cold and silent after discovering Gallio among the enemy. Varro couldn't blame him. He felt the same ice in his own blood.

"I don't think the last man is under here," Cordus said. He set his shovel aside and wiped his brow.

Then someone called out, one of the new men, Gaius Senna. He had removed his helmet to reveal his balding head, and now stared down at his feet. The others joined him, and when Varro entered the semicircle around Senna's discovery, he saw the back of a man's head and shoulder.

"Let's get him out," he said, his voice tired. "He's the last one."

"Luck only got five of us," Falco said. "They really set the trap off too early."

The final corpse extracted from the landslide had a blue cast to his skin. Varro hoped he had not suffocated, and instead had broken his neck. The body was already rigid and hard to drag from beneath the stones that had pinned him. Eventually hauling him out, they set him beside the four other corpses.

Such efforts would not have been made in other circumstances. But with a full consular army stuck on a blocked road with nothing to do, Galba had to ensure everyone was busy. Only so while teams of men cleared the path forward, the rest were set to work scouting or foraging. The tenth hastati, having been the ones to take the defended position, were exempted from work in recognition of their efforts. But Varro wanted to work off his frustrations at finding Gallio with the enemy.

Now that his anger had burned off, he accepted water from the contubernium slaves who had been brought up from the rear to serve them. He and the others retired from the grizzly efforts of body recovery and now went to sit along a shaded rock wall with the rest of the maniple. Falco groaned and wheezed as he settled beside him. The others dropped in wherever they found space.

The cold stone against his back was hard and rough, as was the ground beneath him. But Varro's feet and hands throbbed with relief. He set his helmet aside, brushing his hands over the tall black feathers as he did. Then he stretched out his legs and waited.

Optio Tertius rose from his seat among the men and approached Varro. He had a grim smile.

"That was good work. You led the way up and into that pass. Varro, Falco, you two were first in. Didn't hesitate at all. Very commendable."

"Thank you, sir." Varro thought he should stand. But Falco hadn't and Tertius did not demand it.

"You saw Gallio?" Tertius checked over his shoulder as if his question were a great secret.

Falco coughed, wet and phlegmy. "Word gets around fast. Doesn't it, sir?"

"Not too fast. Well, even if you saw him once, you won't see him again."

Varro shifted against the stone wall and squinted up at Tertius.

Light and shadow cut him perfectly in half, with his upper body in the yellow sunlight.

"Why do you say that, sir? Did they find his corpse?"

"Maybe the gods struck him dead," Falco said. "Jumped off that rock and broke his stupid head."

Tertius frowned and looked away. "There are thousands of enemies somewhere ahead of us. Finding a specific one is impossible. I don't want any of you doing something foolish."

"Afraid we'll get hurt?" Falco elbowed Varro as if bringing him into a joke. "I think it's Gallio who's going to get the worst of it, sir."

"No, I mean your rash action might endanger the rest of the century." Tertius folded his arms and shifted his weight so he moved fully into shadow. "Don't go running off or do something without orders. I want Gallio brought to justice too. But he's just one man and there's a whole army here. Don't think the actions of a few soldiers can't change the course of a battle. You two run off and do something foolish then everyone here might pay the price."

"Yes, sir." Varro spoke the words and lowered his head. But he would do anything to have revenge against Gallio. He was certain the gods revealed him twice as a promise of revenge. His hand shifted to the pugio at his left hip, the gift from his mother and blessed at the temple of Mars.

Seemingly satisfied, Tertius nodded and returned to resting with the others. The tenth hastati remained quiet or else whispered amongst themselves. Like Varro, they probably feared if they were too lively, officers would decide they had energy for other work.

Falco leaned closer and whispered. "If I see Gallio, I'm going to slit his throat and nothing is going to stop me. Really, we're not going to botch the whole war because we stepped out of line to grab him. Tertius is just trying to frighten us into obedience."

"We'll get him. I'm going to drag him before Tribune Primanus myself. Then he'll be judged for his actions and we'll be cleared with the tribune."

First snorting then spitting to the side, Falco grumbled. "Maybe. I think he's decided to hate us for whatever reason. Makes no fucking sense, but what does?"

"Nothing makes sense," Varro agreed. "But Primanus chose us for his legion. Why should he hate us?"

"He picked a lot of men that day. Doesn't mean he thought much about any of us. Anyway, we've got to catch Gallio first. So until then, I guess we better enjoy this rest."

Efforts to clear the pass consumed the remainder of the day. When it was declared suitable for the cavalry to pass, the sun was nearly to the horizon. So a team had been sent to scout a camp location, and the army setup there for the night. The work-exemption did not extend past the clearing of the blockade. So Varro and the others dug perimeter ditches in the hard, rocky earth and pounded in sharpened stakes. By the time they had set up their tents and ate their final meal of the day, he was begging for rest. Even with seven other men, and one who snored heavily, Varro collapsed into blessed sleep.

The next day they broke camp and resumed the march through the pass. They proceeded with greater caution now that the enemy was known to plant ambushes, and paused to receive scouting reports. Throughout, Varro concentrated on his goal of finding Gallio. He had fled ahead of them and hid somewhere along this mountain pass. Every stride took him closer to the moment he would have justice for Gallio's crime.

They encountered nothing the entire day and had to camp once more. Many wondered how an army as large as Philip's could vanish into the mountains. But the following day, the column halted along the mountain road leading into a pass at a place called Eordaea. Varro heard this name repeated dozens of times as the rumor for the stoppage spread among the troops.

Philip's army had established another blockade along the road, this time something far more formidable.

The definition of formidable seemed to mean different things with each new rumor reaching Varro, strangely from behind his position in the column. Some said he had constructed a fortress defended with war machines and thousands of archers. Others said he had collapsed the pass behind him. As each rumor floated up, speculation among the idle troops rose and the manner of defense grew more outlandish. At last Centurion Drusus, along with his peers in other centuries, shouted them into silence.

Varro shared a shrug with Falco and both leaned on their shields to await the next order.

At last, they resumed a march ahead with no clarification offered for the delay. The officers did not need to explain things to their soldiers, and Varro was confident he would learn soon enough the truth of the rumors.

By early afternoon they arrived at Philip's blockade, this time halting beyond bow range. Being in the vanguard afforded Varro a clear view of the defenses in their path. The consul and his leading troops blocked some of this view. The rumor closest to the truth had been the collapsed pass. Indeed, a large section of rock wall on the left side had been broken off into the path to tighten the approach. The pass itself narrowed to another choke point that had also filled with stone, though this was more purposeful and evidently constructed. It augmented already large boulders in place along the pass and was reinforced with gravel ramparts. Finally, wooden barriers of sharpened stakes had been prepared and set across the path along with a wide ditch deep enough to delay men or horses.

At the top of the wall, easily the height of four men standing on each other's shoulders, Varro saw nothing but the dull blue sky and thin clouds. Yet he was certain archers would fill that space the instant they approached. He looked to the edges of the pass, having recently learned a hard lesson about enemies hiding there. He saw many places for concealment, but no enemies were in sight.

A dozen curses formed in Varro's mind. This was truly Philip's best effort to use the terrain against them. The days they had spent collecting grain, Philip had spent rushing ahead to construct blockades. While he was no tactician, Varro saw the glaring error in Galba's calculations. Some had speculated he should have pursued Philip's forces after their debacle at the marsh. Many felt the war could have ended that night. Varro had taken Galba's side in the argument, but now as he looked at this wall he realized the consul had wasted time. They would not have needed grain rations for an extended time in the field if they had pursued Philip even with just a light, harrying force. Breaking through this plug in the pass seemed an impossible task.

Centurion Drusus ordered his forces into position. The tenth maniple of hastati shifted to the right flank as another maniple of hastati moved into the center and right. But to Varro's relief, the flanks were ordered to hold in place. The main unit in the center was to form a testudo and begin the approach.

Varro decided he did not like watching a battle. He would rather be in the midst of it, unknowing of the broader circumstances and only interested in fighting the enemy to his front. But here he saw the testudo of bright shields in a prefect square trundling slowly toward the barriers. His stomach tightened in anticipation. He recalled the men who had led a battering ram to a town wall and how fire had poured down on them. He did not want another similar memory bringing him nightmares.

The testudo reached the first barriers and could not find a way around them that maintained formation. Despite thousands of men and horses filling the pass, there was nothing but eerie silence so that the centurion's shouted orders echoed back to them. They began destroying the barriers.

Varro closed his eyes the moment he heard the bowstrings release. The snap and hum filled the space of the pass and the thump and plink of shafts striking shields followed. Some screamed, shrill and distant. But the centurion bellowed more orders. While the words were indistinct, Varro could guess the order to stand firm and keep shields up.

At last he opened his eyes. As expected, the wall in the road had filled with archers and more still popped out of hiding places along both sides. Arrows like black streaks streamed at the hapless testudo from all sides. But they stubbornly remained in place over the barrier. Some of the soldiers must be working on dismantling it while their companions protected them.

Tribune Primanus, who now stood at the middle of their line rather than the rear which would put him too far back, ordered the maniple to retreat as arrow after arrow fell around soldiers in the open. Without hesitation, the testudo seemed to rise higher then swiftly withdraw out of bow range. The arrows stopped the moment the Romans backed away.

It had been a display to instruct Consul Galba on the manner of his army's destruction should he choose to assault.

Never to be dismayed by the possibility of his army's destruction, Galba leaned from his horse to pass his orders to Tribune Primanus, which then flowed out to the centurions. Varro and the others were already readying their shields when Centurion Drusus shouted the command.

"Testudo! We're going to swarm those barricades and take them down. Hurry now."

Once more, Varro raise his shield so the edges touched Falco's and Curio's and a shield from behind touched his. It felt like retreating into a house with tiny slits for windows. Centurion Drusus held his place at the center of the maniple and ordered them forward.

No one spoke in the shadowed silence. Varro marched

forward, knowing he would be safe enough in this formation. But with so many arrows shot, some would thread the gaps and find flesh. He just prayed it would not be his own.

His feet now cracked the carpet of arrows that scattered on the ground. Perhaps this was a plan to waste Philip's arrows. Varro did not like being the target for them, but if that meant the depletion of their ammunition, the end result would be worth it to the overall effort.

Being on the right flank, now joined with two other maniples in this narrow pass, Varro's group had to angle up a small slope to reach the first barricades. He couldn't see beyond the front gap, nor could he look up.

"Move past the barrier," Centurion Drusus shouted. "Cover the middle while they break it down."

So Varro encountered the first barrier, a trestle construction of heavy logs and sharpened stakes lashed together with thick ropes. He shuffled around and past it, already looking ahead to the next one. He expected the clank of arrowheads on shields, but nothing happened.

"Halt! Get to work on that barrier." The centurion was out of Varro's sight, but his order was as clear as if he stood beside him.

The Macedonians at last acted. The blood-chilling hum of released bowstrings proceeded the scream and scrape of arrows on the shields. Some men cursed while Drusus shouted encouragement, which Optio Tertius echoed from the rear. Varro stood with his shield in place, cold sweat running from beneath his helmet.

The sharp pings of arrowheads striking iron bosses or else snapping on rocks grated on him. Ahead he saw arrows and broken shafts falling into the dirt, catching between rocks, even sticking into the next barrier. It seemed the Macedonian auxiliaries had an endless supply of them.

"Work faster," Drusus shouted. "Don't have to make it pretty. Just flatten the thing and move on."

Varro heard swords hacking into wood and men grunting with the effort to pull down the barriers. He glanced to Falco, whose eyes were lost to the shadow of his heavy brows. But his mouth hung open and he panted. No doubt, he too worried for an arrow to slip between the gap and strike him. Yet this testudo was tighter than many Varro remembered. It seemed the barrage of arrows would never end, but then he heard a shout from behind.

"It's down, sir."

"All right, next one. Forward!"

They relocated to the next barrier. Varro could not see the progress of the center and left. His world was reduced to a slit between his shield and the one overhead. Being at the edge of the formation was generally more dangerous, but Varro was glad he did not need to hold his scutum overhead for so long. He might not have the strength for it.

As he settled around the next barrier, he realized the arrows had stopped. He wondered if the enemy had spent all their ammunition in an undisciplined, desperate volley.

But he heard something unusual.

Something full and wooden thumped to his right coming from the slope.

Then he heard a crack and a whoosh of air.

And men screaming.

Optio Tertius shouted from behind.

"Fire attack!"

24

Heat flashed through the testudo and men on the right edge of the formation screamed in terror. Bright orange light filled the darkness under the shields. Falco leaped back toward Varro, leaving a gap in the testudo.

Now the arrows fell again, this time into gaps the panicked soldiers created trying to escape the fire.

"Hold the formation!" Drusus shouted. "Retreat!"

Fighting primal terror of fire, Varro began to back up. The rear of the testudo was open until it set down as they were now. A reversal meant Varro had to walk backward and pray he did not trip. Generally, the formation was not useful for retreating.

But now with fire licking at their flank and arrows clattering into the gaps, the men jostled and screamed. Varro collided with Cordus behind him, who either hadn't moved or was frozen in place.

"Keep formation!" Drusus shouted again. "If you break it, I'll kill you myself."

Varro's heart pounded so fast he could not catch his breath. The brilliance of the fire had vanished and he did not smell burned flesh. But he expected more fire would follow, and if the retreat did not get underway they would all be roasted alive.

"Move, Cordus." Varro shoved his back against him, and this time Cordus yielded.

The testudo, harried by arrows seeking gaps in their broken discipline, began a swift march in reverse. Varro had no practice at this and knew he would trip. If he fell, he would be left behind and likely skewered with arrows.

"We're going to die," Falco said as he backed up.

But somehow the formation withdrew and Varro did not trip. His feet rolled over stones, arrows, and even the discarded stakes of the first barrier. But he remained in place. He could see smoke and the tips of orange flames rising from behind some rocks.

At last, they had retreated enough that the arrows ceased and Drusus ordered them to turn out of formation.

"Return in good order, but hurry! The consul is watching you."

So it was that three maniples of hastati returned to the line in little better than a terrified run. Despite their defeat, the rest of the soldiers lined behind them cheered. Drusus and Tertius both ordered and shoved men into place. They sorted any injured, which for all the screaming Varro thought the entire maniple had been destroyed. Yet no one had been burned and none of the arrow wounds were better than gouges. The fire had missed its mark and body-length scutum shields remained effective even if not locked together.

Falco blinked in disbelief then stared at Varro, who broke into a relived smile.

"We're not dead."

"How did we even get out of that?"

"Nothing makes sense, remember?"

Now Falco laughed. The rest of the contubernium added to it. Curio scrubbed his face with his free hand, shaking his head as if he too could not believe it. Dama nearly cried with joy. Their officers let them enjoy the moment of release, but soon Tertius shouted them all back into silence.

"Stand ready. We're not done here."

Varro agreed they were not close to done here. Only four of the barriers were destroyed. Around these he counted the white tunics of less than a dozen men on the ground. One called out for help, his voice small and desperate in the distance. As horrific as that soldier's fate was, Varro was relieved they had not suffered more. As they awaited further orders, those who held their shields aloft in the testudo now pried out arrows from them. The black-fledged arrows were as thick as boar bristles on some.

While the Consul and his tribunes conferred, Varro stood ready knowing Optio Tertius would be ensuring none of them stepped out of formation. But as he studied the rocky walls and slopes flanking them, Varro realized there must be paths up or around this blockade. It was not a man-made fortress, and therefore would by nature have gaps. Philip could not have blocked all of them, nor even have had time to discover all of them.

Surely the consul and his tribunes would realize the same and investigate the possibilities. After all, that was the task of scouting forces, probably velites assigned to such a role.

Yet as the officers conferred and Varro stood waiting for the next order, he began to doubt the wisdom of his leaders. Of course, he did not know better than these august men. But they seemed more intent on traditional battle and earning glory in an ordered battle line. This looked like a wall to knock down to them. It probably was. But taking it from the front was pure folly. Someone had to get around the Macedonians and either divide their attention or crush them in a vice.

At last Centurion Drusus was summoned along with others. Varro strained to watch as much as he dared, but when he turned too far, Tertius shouted at him.

"Up front there. Face the enemy. There's nothing to see behind you!"

So he waited, and Falco mumbled something about being sick and miserable.

At last, Drusus returned. He stood before the maniple with his junior centurion.

"We're going to scout the pass for a way around. So hold this position until we learn more."

As the rest of the maniple seemed to relax at this news, a burn erupted in Varro's stomach. This was his chance to capture Gallio.

"Sir, I volunteer for this task."

Drusus paused and searched the line for him, then shook his head.

"I wasn't asking for volunteers."

"Sir," Varro now stepped forward. "I volunteer. This is important to me, sir. I think I can find a way in, and find a traitor at the same time."

Drusus stepped up to him, his creased forehead glistening with sweat. Varro was certain he was about to strike him for stepping out of line. But instead the centurion grunted with a nod.

"All right, a little glory for the tenth hastati wouldn't be a bad thing. Find a path around this mess and you'll be a hero." Drusus smiled and raised his eyes to the others behind Varro. "I'm glad you volunteered for it. But the rest of your contubernium probably won't be as pleased. All of you go with Varro. A lone man might not make it back with news."

"I'm going to kill you, lily." Falco then coughed and spit phlegm to the side. "If a climb into the hills doesn't kill me first. I can't even breathe."

The rest of the contubernium said nothing, though Dama glared at him. Varro looked to each man in the contubernium, pausing at Curio who returned his stare. Tight, hateful lines pulled his mouth into a frown. But he said nothing and patted the hilt of his gladius. The others simply looked to him as if he would lead them. He supposed he had taken the responsibility upon himself.

"I'm going with you." Optio Tertius appeared from the rear of the formation. "As I said before, I don't want you running off into trouble."

Varro experienced a strange mixture of relief and irritation at the optio's assuming command. He looked to Centurion Drusus in a vague hope he would prevent Tertius from leaving his station. But he simply waved him on.

"Besides," Tertius said. "If Gallio is in this pass, then I also have a personal stake in bringing him to justice."

"Of course, sir. I was thinking we could try that path." Varro pointed to a gap in the boulders that seemed to lead up into the surrounding mountains.

"Do you have experience with this?" Tertius asked. When Varro shook his head, the optio laughed. "Well, there's another reason you want me along. I come from a mountain village. I'll let you take the point, of course, but rely on me for instruction. That path is as good as any place to start."

Their initial climb into the hills proved fruitless, and they doubled back to their starting position. Varro's hands and feet were already white with dust from climbing over and around rocks. Optio Tertius scrambled up to a high rock to better see the land before him. Varro and the others leaned on their shields while he cupped his hands over his eyes and surveyed a way forward.

With a new direction chosen, they once more climbed into the mountainous terrain. Falco reminded Varro at every rock to climb or ledge to scale that he was deathly ill.

"Stop complaining," Varro said as he waited at the top of another ledge for the others to reach the position. Optio Tertius remained at the bottom, giving a boost to the others to reach the ledge.

"We're not going to find Gallio hiding on one of these ledges," Falco said. "We're not even going to find the Macedonians climbing around out here. If I fall and die, I swear it, Varro, I'll haunt you forever."

"Well, if you die at least I'll have an hour of peace before your ghost finds me. Otherwise, I think you'll never shut up."

The optio at last joined them on the ridge. They then threaded along this narrow path with full packs and shields weighing them down. But then Varro spotted a wide, rock-strewn trail ahead.

"Sir, this looks like it could work," he said. It was a wide path that snaked up into the mountain and appeared to lead back to the main pass. Tertius pursed his lips and considered.

"First let's see if it leads back to where the others can access it, then we'll follow it up."

The path was wide and easy to follow compared to the struggle they had just endured. At the base, it was concealed by heavy rocks and a narrow squeeze. Tertius judged it could be widened and that enough men could feed through to send a formidable contingent this way.

"Now to see if the Macedonian's have discovered the same path," he said.

They again formed up and retraced the path to where they first joined it then climbed beyond. The path grew steeper and tighter, but was still wide enough to allow three men across to pass at once. Rocks and outcroppings created blind corners. But thus far they had no sign of an enemy. Varro noticed how the others began to speak more excitedly about finding the way through. Now Dama was no longer angry, but imagining out loud the glory he would have at finding a way around the Macedonians.

"I'll be a hero," he said. "The consul will praise me for this."

"We'll be heroes," Falco said. "You may have noticed several others with you on this expedition."

Dama simply laughed.

"All right, let's stop imagining thanksgiving feasts being held for us back in Rome," Tertius said. "We can see less and less of the path ahead and we're getting closer to the Macedonian position. I want to get onto that outcrop over there and have a look."

He set his shield against the rock, then hooked hand and foot into cracks Varro could not see. Tertius climbed up to the wide, flat-topped rock with light and springy steps that made it seem easy. Yet he wore a chain shirt and bronze greaves.

Varro and the others all gathered to the opposite wall of rock to watch. They sheltered from the midday sun in the shadow of an outcrop. Though the mountain air was cold, all of them gleamed with the sweat of their efforts. They set down their shields and watched Tertius clinging to the rock like a metal spider.

"You've got to respect that kind of strength," Falco said.

"Optio Hercules." Varro's joke set the others to laughing.

Tertius mounted the top, then lay flat to rest. He drew a sharp breath.

"What are you laughing at? Do you want to alert the enemy?"

They fell silent, but the positive mood remained. It seemed no one guarded this pass and it could be the bypass everyone sought. Now Tertius gathered himself up, his chain and greaves scraping over the flat rock. He rested on his knees and cupped his eyes again to look ahead.

"By the gods, this leads clear through," he said. "You can see the bottom from—"

A sharp snap and twang burst over Varro's head from the outcrop.

Optio Tertius cried out then collapsed with a thump.

"What happened?" Falco stood forward from the shadows, straining to see above.

Varro did the same, but Tertius had fallen flat and beyond sight. He cried out in pain.

"Sir, what happened?" He waited for an answer, but he only heard Tertius moaning.

"He's been shot," Curio said, then pointed overhead. "Someone above us. You heard the bowstring?"

"Shot?" Dama said. "We're right under the enemy?"

Another arrow hissed down from above. Varro heard the snap of chain and another agonized scream from Tertius. His leg jerked into view, then fell.

"They're going to kill him," Varro said. "We've got to stop that archer."

"Well, how many are up there?" Dama asked. He looked to the others. "They can't see us down the path and the optio said it's clear. We should go report this."

Varro blinked in amazement. "You're saying we abandon our optio?"

"I'm saying we found the way forward and should report it before it's sealed off."

"You disgust me." Varro spit at his feet then turned to the others. "We round this corner, shields up. Use your pila if you can then close on them. There can't be many up there. I'll lead the way. You all better be behind me."

"I'm behind you," Falco said.

Varro glanced up at the rock as Tertius groaned. A third shot shattered beside him.

With shield forward, Varro rounded the corner and scrambled up the sharp slope. He held to the wall and crouched low. A bank of stones had been set across the path. Deftly stepping across it, his hobnailed sandals crunched into the dirt as he rushed ahead. He looked over his left shoulder as the top of the outcrop came into view. Dark heads moved there, but did not seem to face him.

The natural wall lowered the closer he approached the top. With a last check behind him, he found Falco and Curio close behind and the shadows of the others following.

A foreign voice called out as Varro appeared over the top. Five enemy archers watched this pass. They seemed to be straining to see beyond the limits of their perch, but whirled on Varro, bows ready.

He released his light pilum, which landed plumb in the gut of one archer. He did not have the space for another cast. Instead, he bounded ahead.

The enemy had spears set against the ledge of their station. Some reached for these. But Varro sprinted across the gap then slammed his shield into the nearest man. The enemy flattened against the wall with a curse. He drove his gladius into the enemy's open side, feeling it glide into the flesh and drag across the bone. Ripping it out with a howl, he whirled on the next man. He had traded bow for spear, but Falco now careened into him, smashing him hard enough to send him headlong over the edge.

The battle ended with sudden violence. All the enemy lay dead without ever having struck a blow. Dark blood pooled against a low, makeshift wall of stacked stones. They had evidently not been here long enough to build a real defense.

Varro looked across to where Optio Tertius moaned and rolled on the flat rock, a streak of bright blood like the edge of a cloak beneath him. When he mounted that rock, he had stepped into clear view of the archers. Yet the pass they had climbed was hidden from sight. Still, for anyone to make further progress he would have to pass this choke point which when blockaded would be as impassible as the main path.

Then he saw a shadow running along the tops of rocks opposite of their position. The man crouched low, carrying a round shield and spear. Varro realized it was an enemy heading for Optio Tertius.

In an instant, he saw the path and understood. The archers here had limited arrows. They did not want to waste these on finishing the optio. So one had gone to follow a path of raised rocks that were now visible from this vantage. He was near enough to Tertius that he could not be stopped before reaching him.

Varro knew the enemy was beyond the range of a pilum. They had no javelins.

"Optio Tertius, look out!" He leaned across the barrier and shouted. He repeated as the enemy jumped across to another stone closer. This time, Tertius looked up. Varro pointed at the approaching danger.

This seemed to calm him, but he was doubled over as he tried to draw his gladius. Wounded and on the ground against a spearman, the optio stood no chance.

Varro snatched an enemy bow, then pulled an arrow from a small quiver set beside it.

His first shot spun away with a limp snap of the bow.

"What are you doing?" Falco asked, then stopped. "The optio. Varro, you don't know what you're doing. You'll hit him."

The enemy now leaped onto the rock with the optio. He glanced across the distance, likely expecting his friends but instead seeing Varro and the others. He ducked back when he spotted the bow trained on him. Yet as Varro fumbled his second shot, this time bouncing it off the top of the optio's rock, the enemy spearman turned back to Tertius.

The optio shoved back, gladius forward and left arm across his stomach.

Varro fished out the last arrow in this quiver. He set it to the bowstring, now understanding the strength and calm needed to shoot with any precision. Taking a deep breath and holding it, he drew the arrow to his cheek and aimed.

Great Apollo, he thought, lend me a silver arrow and bring down my enemy.

He released and knew it was a true shot. The hiss was clear and the snap of the string against his forearm stung.

The enemy fell back with a scream, reaching for his leg.

Optio Tertius, wounded as he was, now scrambled to his feet and jumped on his would-be killer. His gladius flashed then he collided with the enemy, both collapsing into a dark pile. A shrill scream echoed across the gap, but Tertius pushed up from his defeated foe to collapse on his back. Varro saw the optio's gladius sticking up from the prone corpse.

"We've got reach him," Varro said. "Follow me. I see the way."

Without waiting for the others, he dropped the enemy bow and threaded his path along the rocks his enemy had followed. Despite the weight of his pack and shield, he sped unerringly from rock to rock. His hobnails clacked underfoot as he landed on the flat rock where the enemy lay dead in a dark puddle of blood. His neck arched back as if he were straining to look at Varro, but his dead eyes stared into nothing. Skipping past the corpse, he knelt beside Optio Tertius.

"That was a good shot," he said through clenched teeth. "Too bad the enemy also had a few good ones."

His hand pressed to his right side where a black-fledged arrow protruded between his fingers and leaked blood. A second arrow had shattered in his left forearm, the bloody bronze head protruding out the opposite side.

"Sir, we've got to bind these wounds." Varro set his shield aside and slung off his pack, searching for bandages.

"Don't worry for the arm," he said. "The arrow is plugging the wound. It's my gut. I'm getting cold already."

Varro did not know what to do for the optio. He forced Tertius's hand aside to reveal the broken chain links and the scarlet blood bubbling up between them. He could not reach the actual wound through the chain mesh. He looked to Tertius, who returned a grim smile.

"You have to cut the chain shirt to reach it, and then you'll have to push the shaft out the other side. I'd rather a doctor do it, but I don't know if I'll live to see one."

"You'll live," Varro said, removing the bandages from his pack. "If you have the strength to complain, then you'll make it."

"Complain?" But Tertius looked away as Varro pulled at the chain shirt to widen the break. He only snapped one more weak link, but it was enough to slip in the balled-up cloth bandage. Varro's fingers shined with bright blood as he guided his optio's hand back atop the wound.

"Put pressure on it, sir. We'll get you back to the lines."

At last the others arrived, and Varro organized the optio's rescue. Curio hung off the edge of the rock then dropped back into the pass. He handed up Tertius's shield. Falco and Cordus lifted him onto it then carried him back down the way they had come. It was a slow process, stopping to rebalance after passing him across the short gaps. Fortunately none were significant and they reached the floor of the hidden pass.

"Thank you, Varro." Tertius was now ashen and sweaty. Black circles ringed his eyes, which struggled to remain open as he lay atop his shield stretcher. "You saved my life, at least for a short time."

"You'll survive, sir. You're too ill-tempered to do us the favor of dying. I fear I'll still have to endure your vine cane."

Tertius puffed a weak laugh. "You'll get the cane for speaking to an officer like that."

"Dama, take Falco's position on the shield." Varro pointed to the other two new men. "One of you take over for Cordus, and the other lead the path back to the lines. Report to Centurion Drusus at once, and get the optio to the doctor."

Tertius stared blankly as Varro issued orders. Only a quick blink indicated he was still alive. Dama accepted the edge of the shield from Falco, but he frowned.

"And the rest of you aren't coming?"

"No," Varro said. "We're going to bring back Gallio."

25

"It's too expensive to leave behind." Cordus was the last to remove his bronze helmet, but clutched it to his chest. Varro, Falco, and Curio had already set theirs alongside their bronze pectorals and greaves. Their scutum shields and pila leaned against the low rock wall where the blood of four dead Cretan archers now attracted flies.

"If we stroll in with full gear, they'll know us for Romans at a glance." Varro adjusted the new helmet on his head. He then drew the gray wool cloak around himself. The archers hadn't worn these but the weather was cold enough to justify their use. Besides, he needed to hide his gladius and pugio and their harness.

"Just do it," Falco said. "Your life is worth more than whatever it'll cost to buy new gear. Plus, you can get a loan if you need it. I'm sure someone would be happy to make you a slave for a handful of coins."

Cordus cringed and turned aside as if someone would snatch his helmet.

"Enough of this," Varro said. "We've no time to waste. Cordus, stay here and guard our gear. We'll be back. And if we don't come back, then you're welcome to everything since we'll all be dead."

"Don't say that," Cordus said. "Why do you have to do this?"

Varro straightened up before the young soldier.

"The honor of our contubernium depends upon it. And I owe Gallio for nearly killing me to run away. Not to mention Panthera, Sura, and Otho who are all dead by the very enemy he joined. They must be avenged. Do you need more reason than that?"

"But you could die."

"I will die, eventually. But I'm not going to live in fear of that day."

Curio pulled the gray cloak around his shoulders and frowned.

"Gallio was my friend, and he betrayed me. No one does that and gets away with it."

Falco now folded his arms.

"Well, I've got to make sure these two don't get themselves killed. Look, guard my gear but don't touch my pack. If you touch my pack, I'll know it. Then I'll pull out your eyes, cut off your fingers, and hang you upside down from this ledge. You don't want that, right? So just stay with our gear. If we don't come back, then don't listen to Varro. Take our gear back to the line. We might have had to return by another way and not really died. And even if I'm dead, don't touch my pack. I'll haunt you."

Disguised now as Cretan archers, Varro and the others took up the round wooden shields of their enemies. They slung bows over their shoulders and carried spears. These did not seem made for throwing, but Varro guessed he might still use one as a pilum. Only Triarii used spears, and Varro had many years ahead before he trained in its use. The Cretan shield seemed flimsy and weak, but it was better than the horror of fighting with nothing in his left hand.

They followed the pass toward the rear of the enemy line. Varro had a thin plan that had at least convinced Curio and Falco.

He hoped to keep their heads down and search for Gallio. Once they found him, they would lure him out for capture. Varro found rope among the supplies the Cretans had gathered at their post. They had been preparing to build barriers judging from the collected wood. Now that rope would bind a traitor.

He had still not solved how to remove Gallio back for judgement. His hope was to remain in hiding until the Romans attacked, then rejoin them once the pass was captured.

Despite the vagueness of the plan, he was confident. His great-grandfather had told him that Fortuna favored daring men but spurned the overcautious and hesitant. Varro was not sure if this plan was bold or foolish. But he knew Gallio was among these Cretan auxiliaries holding the pass. He had to exhaust every chance to bring him back to face justice or he would never sleep a peaceful night.

The hidden pass exited far behind the Cretan blockade. Once Consul Galba led his men to this place, he could form up tight ranks and march directly into the rear of the Cretans and crush them against their own barricade. While this heartened Varro, he still faced the same challenge of picking Gallio out of more than a thousand men. They kept to the shadows as they followed the pass in, letting Curio lead them. His size allowed him to squeeze into smaller hiding spots than either Varro or Falco could. When he judged the way forward safe, he would wave Varro and Falco ahead. Soon, they had arrived at the rear of the Cretan encampment.

They crouched in the shadows of jumbled boulders. The cool air did not relieve the sweat trickling down Varro's temples. His feet and hands were as cold as if he stood in a bitter winter wind. But both Curio and Falco seemed to look to him for leadership, and so he clamped down on his fears and studied their approach.

Rows of gray tents filled the pass. These appeared empty of

occupants. With Consul Galba to the front, everyone but slaves should be standing ready to confront a breakthrough.

"We should be able to use these tents for cover," Varro said. "We need to get closer so we can locate Gallio."

Falco grumbled, the phlegm in his chest making a thick, wet noise.

"That's not much of a plan, lily. You've not thought of anything better?"

Ignoring the jibe, he shook his head and strained to glimpse anything beyond the tents. He heard men shouting to each other, the scrape of rock and metal, but he saw nothing but a scattering of shadows as enemies moved at the fore of the tents.

"I've got nothing better," he said at last. "But here's what I think. Gallio has as much skill with a bow as I do. So he won't be up on the walls facing our men. And since he only arrived here just ahead of us, I expect they stuck him in the infantry rather than send him to guard another approach like the one we just destroyed."

"I thought you did fine with a bow," Falco said. "But I'm not sure your guess is right. He's probably guarding another way in. They used him in a delaying force once, so why not again?"

"Because that delaying force was meant to be thrown away," Varro said. "Gallio and the others were probably ordered to fight to the last. But I'm sure when they fled here these Cretans were glad enough to have them. Think about it. Philip is gone. You're just a mercenary. If you had to hold this pass against the world's greatest army, would you waste even one person? You'd plug him into the line."

Falco snorted and coughed.

"I think you're right," Curio said. He had remained silent and searching ahead while Varro and Falco had debated. Now he pulled himself from his hiding spot and moved toward the tents. "I'll find us a path through. Just keep behind but stay in sight."

Curio ducked low, holding spear and shield close to his sides as he rushed to the edge of the tents. Varro and Falco both crouched low and followed. If there were men inside, Curio had found a path free of them. They seemed to lack any organization and their haphazard arrangement kept the enemy out of sight. They hopped from tent to tent, soon reaching the front edge.

They pressed to a tent wall and leaned forward to look out on the rear of the barricaded pass.

As expected, makeshift ladders reached to the top of the wall where platforms had been built. It seemed nothing supported these, but Varro noted scores of archers sitting on them out of sight from the Romans. More ladders climbed into dark crevasses at either side indicating where the flanking archers had taken their positions.

Of immediate interest was the pass floor. More rubble had been strewn across the rear of the main blockade, which would hinder the proper formation of battle lines in the event Consul Galba broke through. Varro smiled at this, knowing the attack would come from the undefended rear along a clear path. A dozen yards ahead of Varro's hiding spot ranks of spearmen stood in loose formation facing the barrier. These would engage any breaching force that made it through. They spoke among themselves in quiet voices, but none seemed alert for danger. Many squatted on the ground. Varro spotted an officer shouting at one such soldier, and surprisingly the soldier was slow to rise. In Varro's army, that small gesture of rebellion would earn a flogging. These Cretan mercenaries were lax.

"Now all we have to do is walk through about two hundred spearmen and check for Gallio." Falco shook his head. "We should go back before we've gone too far."

"We're close," Varro said. "He's with these spearmen somewhere. Just be patient."

Falco again snorted and spit, seemingly his answer to every disagreement.

When they could not find Gallio in the rear ranks, Curio wove another path through the confusion of tents. They then studied from the right flank, again finding nothing. Varro's feet had grown cold enough to burn. Cretans had glanced toward him at least four times, but had either not seen him or not cared to investigate. He wondered how long before an officer noted him and tried to issue commands.

They repeated their search on the left flank and again did not spot Gallio.

"We can't find him," Falco said. They sheltered in the shadows of a gray, billowing tent. The noon sun cast sharp shadows around them as they all stared at the block of Cretan spearmen. "If he's there, then he's in the center and we'll never get him out."

Varro stared at the block of enemies lingering in the pass with their round shields painted with strange symbols or fearsome beasts. No matter how relaxed they appeared, every Cretan glanced up at the pass wall as if expecting it to burst open and pour thousands of Roman troops on them.

Gallio, if he was even here, remained out of sight.

"I suppose you're right." Varro said. "Maybe if we wait in hiding we'll find him when Consul Galba surprises them from the rear."

"It's probably safer to withdraw," Curio said. "I want to get Gallio as bad as you, but our luck is done."

"We're so close," he said. "He's practically in our hands."

"But out of our sight," Falco said. "Let's go. We can guide Consul Galba the final distance. Maybe we'll find Gallio among the dead after we've cleaned up this pass."

Falco snorted once more, the mucus of his lingering cold seemingly endless.

In the same instant, Varro saw Gallio.

He was not with the spearmen. He was on the left flank closer to the blocked pass. He carried a spear but no shield. Like the others, he stared at the blockaded pass in a posture of dejection. His spear hung low against his lap, and it seemed he was supervising three slaves loading rocks into a wagon. Yet he paid them no attention, no doubt wondering when his former allies would break through that pass and bring him death. He wore no armor except for the single bronze greave on his left leg. His white tunic was stained brown.

Before he could point Gallio out to the others, Falco's snort devolved into a cough.

Though he tried to stifle it, Falco's coughing only worsened.

A voice called out to them, and Varro, staring at Falco red-faced and choking on his own spit, realized their luck had vanished. One of the Cretans shouted at them.

He looked back to Gallio, who was too distant to notice, then turned to the Cretan spearman shouting at them. He was a thin man with a wispy brown beard. He seemed one of the officers and a few men around him looked on with mild interest as he shouted to Varro and the others, waving them back in line.

"What do we do?" Curio grabbed Falco and pulled him aside as if his coughing could be hidden.

"Get down." Varro yanked Falco to the ground behind the tent. He stared up, cheeks flushed. His voice was strained and whispering.

"What's that for?"

"Keep coughing. Draw your pugio."

Varro turned back to the officer, whose orders grew more insistent. But Varro had seen the defiance among the men and gambled on it. He instead shook his head at the officer, and pointed to Falco lying just out of sight. He feigned urgency and gestured as if asking for help.

The officer rolled his eyes then grabbed another spearman before heading over.

Varro and Curio both pulled back behind the tent.

"They're coming. Let's make it quick."

"Are you mad?" Falco asked, his voice now returning. "They'll be missed."

"There's nothing else to do." Varro spoke just as the officer arrived with his subordinate.

The Cretan officer glared at Varro while the other narrowed his eyes at them. The officer spoke in sharp and irritated phrases, then looked to Falco coughing on the ground between Curio and Varro. The other man raised a hesitant finger to point at Varro, as if he were realizing they were disguised. Indeed, they all wore the heavy wool cloaks that no one else did.

Falco kicked out and tripped the officer. Varro, who had moved his hand to his pugio beneath the cloak, now drew it and plunged it into the officer's ribs. With his other hand, he clamped it over the Cretan's mouth to silence the shocked scream. The stab was not instantly fatal, and the Cretan shoved against him as he struggled, sending both back to crash among the tents.

Now the officer locked his cold and strong hand over Varro's pugio. They squirmed on the ground and Varro lost his grip on the officer's mouth.

He roared in pain and defiance the moment he was freed.

Varro head-butted the officer, stunning him into silence and loosening his grip. The heavy thump on Varro's head reminded him he still suffered the dizzying effects from Gallio's wound. It was enough of a delay to waste the short advantage. He tore away the pugio but the officer was still on him. His blood flowed out onto Varro's stolen cloak.

At last, Falco hauled the officer aside and Curio ran him through his back with his gladius. Yet the officer's dying howl echoed through the pass.

"A fine fucking idea," Falco said. He was splashed with blood over his legs and the other Cretan lay dead at his feet. "Run!"

They fled back into the confusion of the tents. Shouts rose up immediately behind them.

"I found Gallio," Varro shouted as loud as he dared while threading the haphazard tents.

But neither Falco nor Curio replied, and instead leapt though the maze to get as distant from the killing as they could. At last they arrived on the opposite side of the tent camp. Behind, shouts and confusion rippled through the spearmen.

They all huffed, out of breath. Falco coughed again, but they were out of sight from any enemy while hidden behind the rearmost tent.

"All right, we've got to get out of here," Falco managed through his coughing. "What was that about?"

"What were we supposed to do?" Varro asked, feeling his face heat up. "I didn't want to kill them, but we'd be exposed and captured."

"We should've run," Falco said. "They'd have given up after a bit, but now we've killed their friends."

Varro realized this was true. He had miscalculated and now the spearmen were all turning to face the commotion of two murders.

Curio leaned on his knees and lowered his head. "We can get away if we flee now."

"I found Gallio just before Falco gave us away."

"I couldn't fucking help it!"

"It's impossible now," Curio said. "They're searching for us. We'll never get Gallio."

"I'm not giving up," Varro said. "The two of you go on. I'll bring Gallio back."

Both Falco and Curio looked to each other. But Varro was already inching forward out of hiding. He sloughed off his cloak, which was now too bloody to be of use. This exposed his gladius and pugio and the distinctive harness used to wear them.

The spearmen were in chaos now, with Cretans breaking into search groups. Gallio was still posted across the camp but again out of sight. Varro realized, however, with all the attention focused at the rear that he could cut across the front. His shield would block his gladius from easy view while he approached Gallio. The rope hung from his belt, unusual but not something to cast suspicion on him. Once he overcame his former friend, he would bind him up and wait for Galba to arrive.

"We're leaving," Falco said. "This is madness, lily. You're asking for death."

He looked back to Falco and Curio. The shouts of the searching Cretans drew closer. There was no time to argue.

His own honor, the honor of his friends, and the lives of Panthera, Sura, and Otho all demanded he continue.

"I will find a way. I cannot allow Gallio to escape again."

He did not wait for their answers, but picked up spear and shield then ducked out of hiding to seek Gallio.

26

With a bizarre sense of confidence, Varro strode out in front of the distracted block of spearmen now milling about their tents. Glancing to his right, the archers on the high platforms sat dangling their legs. If they looked anywhere, it was over the wall toward the Romans on the opposite side. Varro kept his shield toward the spearmen, blocking the view of his harness and weapons. The lack of any armor made him feel both vulnerable and mobile. If he had to run, he felt as if he could leap over the barrier to return to his century on the far side.

While the spearmen shouted and scratched their heads, Varro straightened his back and continued his brisk walk across their front. There seemed no overall command on the ground, at least none obvious to him. He did not understand how the armies of Crete organized themselves. A large number of spearmen at the rear had broken off to search among the tents. Those in the front ranks observed but did not join the search. No one issued any orders, though Varro would not understand an order if he heard one.

Ahead, Gallio stood at the same spot at the edge of the pass. His spear remained low in his hands and his back curved in a posture of defeat. A dark beard had formed along his chin. Now he stared toward the commotion, but still seemed disinterested. The three slaves he supervised continued their work. One stood in a wooden cart laden with rocks while his two companions used wooden poles to lever stones from the edges of the pass. With Gallio preoccupied, the slaves seemed to have slowed and the one in the cart sat down out of sight.

Varro heard the hobnailed sandals of Falco and Curio scraping the ground behind him. While both had hesitated, in the end they followed him into what was indeed a mad plan. But madness had wrapped his mind, and he embraced it. With each step forward, Gallio came closer to justice. Nothing exceeded the importance of achieving this end.

As he closed the final distance, he sought a suitable hiding spot. The edges of the pass offered dozens of shadowed ledges and high boulders where they could hide Gallio until the consul arrived.

Heart pounding and breath short, Varro now stepped before Gallio who still stared after the commotion in the distance. When Varro's shadow fell across him, he at last looked up.

Varro smiled and leveled his spear to Gallio's gut.

"Put down your spear and don't scream," Varro said. "Or I'll pin you to the wagon."

Gallio's face turned white and his eyes bulged. But two other shadows fell over him, Falco and Curio, and their spearpoints joined Varro's.

"Hello, Gallio," Falco said with a bright smile. "We've been looking for you."

"Order the slaves away," Varro said.

"I don't speak their language."

The voice was only a shadow of Gallio's, weak and thin and

trembling with fear.

"Then just leave with us," Curio said. "They won't care where you went."

It took a jab of Curio, but Gallio surrendered his spear by placing it against the cart. He blinked as if trying to wash away the scene before his eyes. The slaves continued to drag out their work, and if they noticed the hostility none of them reacted.

With Gallio disarmed, Varro and the others put up their spears so as not to draw attention.

"Where are you taking me?" Gallio blinked and sweat beaded on his forehead.

"Up into the pass, out of sight." Varro pointed ahead. "We'll bind you then take you back for judgement."

"Take me back?" Gallio smiled while his manic blinking continued.

"Stop wasting time," Falco said. "Get moving."

Curio led the way into the jumbled rocks of the pass wall. Gallio followed with Varro and Falco behind. They climbed a narrow path that required them to scale over rocks and stretch to reach a ledge. Curio mounted the ledge then pointed his spear at Gallio.

"You climb next, then the others. We'll be safe and hidden up here."

Gallio grunted and blinked as was his manner under stress. Varro remembered how often he and the others had teased him for this habit, and how often they had laughed together. Now he forced a spear against Gallio's back to reinforce Curio's instructions. With some effort, all had climbed onto a boulder then reached the shaded ledge above. They could hold the position out of sight until Galba routed the Cretans.

"Put your hands behind your back," Varro said as he unhitched the rope from his belt. He fed out a length to tie Gallio's wrists, then cut the rest to tie his legs. He would take no chances.

Gallio began to sob as Varro wrapped his wrists. He lowered his head and turned it aside as Falco bound his feet. Curio kept his spear lowered, his face tight and cheeks flushed. They struggled with their footing on the narrow ledge, their feet shifting and crunching on the bare rock as they worked. Soon, Gallio was tied and forced to sit down in the shade of the rock face at their back. Bound as he was, he would not be able to stand again without help.

Tears streamed down his cheeks and he would not look to anyone.

Falco tapped his spear butt to the rock and sneered at Gallio.

"Stop crying. You did this to yourself."

But Gallio only grunted and sobbed harder.

"You almost killed me," Varro said, squatting down to Gallio's level. "My head is still not right. You tricked me into removing my helmet so you could slam a rock over my skull."

"I didn't want to kill you."

Falco coughed then laughed. "But it was a price you were willing to pay for your own selfishness. You knew we could've all been executed for letting you escape. But you didn't care. Ran straight into the enemy's arms. How have you enjoyed being a traitor? Finding Philip a better friend to you?"

Gallio at last looked up, his reddened eyes flashing with hate.

"At least he gave me a chance to live. More than I can say for what Rome offers her own citizens. You just get eaten up and your bones tossed away. What's happening to your farms while you're here? What are you fighting for? When you get back, will there be a farm to return to? What will Rome do you for you if it's not? Nothing! If Rome doesn't kill you before you get back, you'll get nothing for all you've suffered."

Gallio's voice rose steadily, and his shouts now echoed off the surrounding rocks. Varro hushed him to silence, and Curio put a spearhead under his neck.

"Don't try to bring help," he said. "No one can get here fast enough to save your worthless life."

Swallowing hard, Gallio shrank back from the bronze spearhead under his chin.

"We've found a pass around this blockade," Varro said. "I expect the consul will send a force immediately before it is cut off as well. Just sit still and we'll lead you out of here after the Cretans are routed."

They then sat in silence, crouched in shadows behind large rocks. Varro began to gather fist-sized stones in case he should need them. Falco noted this and aided in stockpiling rocks. Only Curio remained glaring at Gallio, spear poised to run him through. His expression had not changed nor had the flush left his cheeks.

"Even if you clear the pass, you'll not catch Philip." Gallio shifted against the wall, his voice weak and sniffling. "He's gone north. There's another enemy to face, and he's left you only his mercenaries."

"And that's what you call a chance to live?" Falco stacked one more stone atop his pile. The ledge was now cleared of large stones. "Leaving you behind to die while he flees? A real noble character."

"Would you have tried to kill me if we met in battle?" Varro patted the grit from his hands, then took up his spear. "You were at that pass. What would you have done if we came face to face?"

Gallio stared at him, then frowned and turned aside.

"You're my enemy now," Varro said. "I have made a vow not to murder or act in violence if I can avoid it. But you've sorely tested me. You led Philip to our camp so that he could surprise us. You took arms against your former friends. Maybe you even killed men you trained with. I don't know what you did in battle, and don't want to know. If we had met, I'd have tried to kill you."

Gallio blinked and sniffled, but did not answer. Varro

continued.

"I'm glad you're tied up. Because I would never kill a helpless man, no matter how much he repulses me. But when you are judged and subjected to the fustuarium, I will strike you five times across the head. One time each for Panthera, Sura, and Otho. One time for the blow you gave me. And one time for betraying Rome. I pray you live to feel each hit."

Tears ran down Gallio's cheeks, mingling with the dust clinging to his skin.

"I won't be so kind," Falco said. "I'll just smash your legs until they're as mushy as overcooked puls. That's for running, you traitor."

Curio did not say anything, remaining grim and silent with his spear leveled.

Varro shook his head then looked between the boulders to check on the Cretan spearmen.

He found Gallio's slaves pointing up the narrow path. Spearmen with round shields crowded behind them.

"They've found us." His calm announcement surprised himself. His hands and feet were no longer cold. His voice did not waver. Their hiding spot had been revealed and now the Cretans would attempt to dig them out. The ledge was hidden from view and surrounded by steep rocks that allowed no purchase. The only mount up was the via the boulder they had used.

Unfortunately, it was also the only way off the ledge. Jumping into the surrounding boulders would trap them between their narrow confines.

"Good thing we've gathered rocks," Falco said with equal calmness. "They've dropped enough of them on our heads. It'll be a pleasure to spill their brains."

Curio said nothing, but now leaned forward to view the approaching enemy.

"They're coming?" Gallio asked, pushing back against the wall.

"We're trapped up here."

"So we are," Varro said. "But we've spear and shield to hold them back, and our gladius and pugio for when they come close. We'll sell our lives at great cost."

"Happy your friends have come to the rescue?" Falco kicked dirt as Gallio, then gathered his shield and spear.

"I can help," he said. "Untie me and I'll fight with you. It's all over for me. Either way, I'm dead. Just let me fight one more time with you."

Falco laughed. "Lily, if you get soft then I'll tie you up alongside him."

"We're not releasing you," Varro said. He did not spare a glance to Gallio, but now readied his shield and picked a heavy stone. The Cretans were out of sight as they climbed into the rocks, but their shouts preceded them.

"There's nowhere to run," Gallio said, kicking the dirt back at Falco with his bound feet. "You can't hold off forever up here. We're all dead. Don't let me die like this. I'm a soldier."

"You were a soldier," Varro said, weighing the heft of the cold, gritty stone in his palm. "But you ran away from that honor."

The first Cretan gained the path about three spear-lengths distant, though sharply angled down from Varro. He let the enemy climb higher, hoping to lure out another before attacking. He glanced to Falco and Curio who cocked their arms as if to cast their pila, instead clutching heavy rocks.

Once another followed behind, they cast their stones.

The lead man cried out as a rock thumped his shoulder and another slammed against his face, knocking him flat. The man behind avoided the stone, but slid back around the blind corner in the path.

They hurled more stones on the prone man, who staggered to his feet before scrabbling out of sight.

"They'll return with shields up," Varro said. "Falco, help me with this larger rock."

Three of the rocks they gathered were too heavy to cast alone. Varro was uncertain how many enemies faced them, but they had a hundred reinforcements to call upon. He was fighting an attritional battle that could only end one way.

He and Falco readied their stone while the Cretans regrouped. Curio readied another cast.

Then they heard Cretan horns followed by thunderous Roman war cries.

Galba's force had arrived.

"We're saved," Falco said, his shoulders slumping. "I thought we'd die up here."

He began to lower the stone, but Varro did not shift.

"What's happening?" Gallio asked. "Is that the consul?"

Varro hissed him to silence. The near-distance was full of screaming and shouting men. He expected to hear their attackers fleeing. But he heard nothing.

The Cretans burst back into narrow path. Their round shields held high over their head in an imitation of a testudo formation.

"Heave away!" Varro shouted as he and Falco swung their rock down the path. It slammed into the lead man, splitting his shield and driving him back.

But the man behind him held his shield forward and stepped over him.

"We can throw one more." Falco reached for another heavy rock while Curio pitched stone after stone into the pass. Varro heard them thudding hard against wood or else thumping against flesh. The Cretans called out curses.

"I can help," Gallio shouted. "Let me free and I'll fight with you. I swear it!"

A second heavy rock flew out of Varro's and Falco's hands. This crashed into the new lead with equally devastating results. The rock struck the rim of the shield, pushing it back as if it were a door, then slammed into the Cretan's face. He crumpled, blocking the passage while Curio pelted the clot of spearmen struggling to reach them.

"Determined lot," Falco said. He reached for the final, large stone. "This is it."

"I'm out of rocks," Curio announced with a cold, measured voice. "It's spears now."

Varro and Falco heaved a final rock over the side, shocked to find the Cretans now filling the path and attempting to mount the boulder to their ledge. The final rock landed among the raised shields, but thudded through them to crash on the ground. The shields relocked as the first man mounted the boulder.

"Free me!" Gallio was frantic now. "I will fight for you!"

Varro and Falco grabbed their spears and shields while Curio covered them. Varro turned back in time to thrust his spear out at the first attacker to mount the rock and shove him off.

A cry went up from the Cretans. There had to be a dozen of them, Varro guessed, though the tight quarters exaggerated their size. To him it seemed every spearman now pressed into the path.

They kept the Cretans off the boulder with their spears. Since the distance forced them to stretch, their blows lacked real power. One Cretan gained a foothold and grabbed Varro's spear. His overreach and one-handed grip made it easy for the enemy to disarm him. With a quick twist, Varro lost his spear.

"Cut me free! I'll fight!"

Varro barely heard Gallio's pleading. He instead drew his gladius and set his shield against the ledge to keep the spearmen from mounting it. There was no space for the enemy on the ledge. But if enough of them mounted the boulder their spears could overwhelm Varro and the others, especially now with Varro armed only with a close-quarters weapon.

"Forget the ledge," Varro said. "Cover me on the boulder."

"What?"

Falco's voice vanished behind him as he leaped into the enemy below. His hobnailed soles smashed into a spearman's face, sprawling him into the surrounding rocks and out of the fight. Varro landed hard on the boulder, but again the hobnails gripped the stone and stabilized him. Though not the mighty scutum he was used to, Varro still punched with his stolen round shield and dislodged the second attacker to tumble back atop his friends. The final enemy fended off Falco's and Curio's spears, leaving him exposed to Varro's gladius. He stabbed the man through his side, who cried out in agony before slumping to the boulder top.

The initial assault shocked the Cretan spearmen, but enough still filled the short path and Varro could not see how many were around the blind corner. He only knew that to remain atop the boulder was to invite enemy spears to cut away his legs.

With a mad howl, uncaring of what came next and a hot pulse of rage driving him, he jumped off the boulder at the Cretans.

Both feet crushed one of the fallen enemies lying at the base. He screamed and Varro fell back against the boulder. He held his shield forward and a spear skidded across it. A second spear narrowly missed his face to scrape the rock behind him.

He shoved forward with his shield and let the terrible power of his gladius stab into the tight press of enemies. Their spears were of no use now, but Varro was in his element. His stabs returned blood and screams, and as he shoved forward, the enemy slid down the path.

When he reached the blind corner, he discovered the Cretans fleeing into the pass. Glancing over the surrounding boulders, the golden gleam of feathered bronze helmets pressed methodically closer to the blockaded pass.

He smiled then laughed. The pass was captured, he realized. While Philip may have escaped, he had lost his mercenaries.

Then he heard a scream from behind, up on the ledge where had left Falco and Curio.

27

He bounded back up the path, leaping the dead or dying Cretans crumpled in a gory pile at the foot of the boulder leading to the ledge. He heard Falco's shouting, but could not determine what he said. He saw the back of his head and shoulders, and his hands flailed around as he shouted.

Unlike the first time, Varro needed no help to mount the boulder then pull himself onto the ledge. His heart raced and filled his body with all the strength needed to regain the ledge on his own.

Falco and Curio stood to either side of Gallio, who sat with hands and feet bound in the shadow of the rock wall. His eyes were wide, reddened, and full of tears. They flashed wider at Varro's appearance on the ledge. Blood dripped from his mouth.

A spear pierced him through his stomach, just beneath the breastbone. Bright blood flowed in a stream, staining his tunic red before pooling at his tied legs. His eyes blinked hard and fast, as if he strained to focus.

"I'm sorry about your head." Gallio's voice was weak and wet with the blood leaking from his mouth. "I'm sorry for everything."

Gallio's blinking stopped and his eyes unfocused.

"Why did you fucking kill him?" Falco screamed the question, flinging his shield in anger to smash into the corner of the ledge.

Curio stared at Gallio.

"He deserved it. Besides, no need to bring him back alive. It's all the same."

Varro knelt beside Gallio's corpse. The dead were always unsettling to see, but it was far worse when it was a former friend. Ignoring the spear in his body, Gallio looked as if he were only daydreaming. But he would never again awaken. Varro stroked his former friend's eyes closed.

"We were supposed to take him before Tribune Primanus," Falco continued. His hobnailed sandals clacked against the stone as he paced in the confines of the ledge. "Now how can we prove we killed him? The tribune will just say the Cretans finished him off. Fuck, Curio! You ruined everything."

Curio stared with a strange mixture of anger and exhaustion. The short man's dirt-whitened hands hung at his side, flexed as if he wanted to grab something. Varro wondered at his motivation. Curio had been Gallio's best friend, and perhaps was sparing him the humiliation of a trial and execution. Varro did not agree with that reason, but could understand it. Or was Curio afraid Gallio might reveal something incriminating?

He shook his head and stood up. That line of thinking was for Falco and not him. Curio had delivered Gallio to his ultimate fate. Though not as fulfilling as an actual trial, Varro was satisfied he had seen justice done.

"The tribune will have to call all of us liars before all the men," Varro said. "I doubt he would do so. Don't worry for it."

Falco snorted and spit, glaring at Curio.

"Who's up there?"

The Roman voice echoed up the path, shaking Varro from his thoughts. He called back, and within moments a small group of principes climbed into the path. They paused at the dead bodies surrounding the boulder, nodding appreciatively. The lead man, broad-shouldered and with a deep voice suitable for an officer, smiled up at them.

"A fine stand you boys made. But the enemy is routed." He prodded one of the Cretans, who gave a weak moan. He stabbed the prone man through his chest, eliciting a final groan from the enemy, then looked back up. "You can come down now. Any casualties up there?"

"One," Varro said. "We can get him down ourselves."

The principes leader waved his bloodied gladius at him, then he and his companions filed out of the pass.

They worked together to carry down Gallio's corpse. They left him tied and with Curio's stolen spear impaled. While Varro did not think it necessary, leaving him in this posture calmed Falco's fears that the tribune would not recognize their achievement.

The pass was nothing like Varro had left it. The tents were all trampled down. The block of Cretan spearmen had vanished. The archers above had surrendered or else fled. Already a cluster of at least a hundred enemies were surrounded by guards. Corpses lay beneath the afternoon sun, tunics flapping in the light breeze to reveal bloodless flesh. Crows already circled in the blue sky, awaiting their feast.

They drew stares as they carried Gallio's bound body toward the main Roman lines. This was not all of Galba's force, but Tribune Primanus had led his legion to this victory. Varro made for the standard proudly raised over the Roman center. Before reaching him, they found Centurion Drusus and the tenth hastati. Drusus was slick with sweat and blood, his cheeks flush and his face dark. His lip curled when he recognized what Varro and Falco held between them.

"Tertius said you were going to get him. I can't believe it. You really hunted him down."

"Optio Tertius will survive, sir?"

Drusus continued to study Gallio's corpse, but offered a grim smile.

"Provided the doctor can remove that arrow, I expect Optio Tertius will live. But he'll be on his back a while."

Varro nodded. He struggled with the weight of Gallio's corpse with the addition of the spear. The trail of blood had at least trickled off now to fat drips that puddled under him as Drusus reviewed their capture.

"Let's take him to the tribune," Drusus said. "I'll be interested to see his face."

"I as well," Varro said.

The rest of the contubernium joined them as they crossed the battlefield toward the tribune's standard. Dama caught up to them, looking into Gallio's dead face.

"This is the traitor? We really did it? We caught him."

"Something like that," Varro said.

"I don't remember seeing you around when we were running for our lives," Falco said. "Think about how you describe this capture or I'll offer you some advice that'll leave you with broken teeth."

"No fighting in the ranks," Drusus said. But his step was light and the dark cloud of battle had left him as they closed on the tribune's location.

Cordus also trailed along with the other new men.

"I have all your gear," he said. "And I didn't touch your pack, Falco."

"Good man! I never doubted you."

They arrived before the tribune, who sat on his brown horse and admired the results of his efforts. His attendants and selected guards surrounded him, but parted for Centurion Drusus who led their small contingent.

"Sir, I bring excellent news." Centurion Drusus stood at attention. Varro would have done as well, but he held Gallio's sagging corpse with Falco.

Primanus's heavily lashed eyes fluttered as if awaking from a dream. "What is that, Centurion? We've already captured the pass."

"Sir, I'll let these men explain."

Varro and Falco stepped forward, placing Gallio's impaled corpse before the tribune's horse. Varro then stepped back to stand at attention.

"This is the corpse of Lars Gallio, sir. He was the traitor who deserted from our contubernium. As I have promised, sir, here is his corpse. We chased him into this camp, captured him, and have returned him to you."

Primanus stared without expression. At last he leaned from his horse and raised his brow to the corpse set before him.

"I thought you were going to bring him alive for judgement? He's tied up, but he's been speared. Why?"

"We killed him, sir." Varro could not think of a lie he would remember later. "He said some things that went too far, and emotions were too strained. We killed him for a traitor. But you did allow us to bring back Gallio's head, sir."

"Don't presume I need reminding." Primanus's eyes flashed with anger as he leaned back on his horse. He stroked its neck as if to apologize for his outburst. He sniffed and nodded to Varro. "It is good to have this justice done. Do not bury him, but throw his corpse among the pile of enemy dead he was so eager to join. Let him rot and be forgotten."

"Yes, sir," Varro said. It seemed his audience was at its end as the tribune now began to turn his horse aside. But for justice to be fully completed he needed the tribune to say more.

"Sir, I request that you rescind your conditions against our contubernium. We have fulfilled our agreement as made before Consul Galba."

Primanus's eyes flashed as he looked over his shoulder at Varro.

"Yes, no need to invoke the consul, young Varro. I am not cowed by titles. But I will grant your request." He turned his horse back then addressed Centurion Drusus. "These men are to be commended for their honor and bravery. Whatever conditions I have previously set to them are fulfilled. As long as they obey military rule and the commands of their officers, they are to be lauded as heroes. For finding the pass and ensuring the way forward was cleared of enemies, award these men an extra month's pay."

"Yes, sir!" Centurion Drusus saluted and smiled at Varro. For once, the centurion seemed genuinely pleased with him.

The tribune departed toward the captives, moving at a slow and regal pace. Yet the moment he was gone, Drusus clapped Varro on the back and the rest of the contubernium drew together in cheers.

"Now that was well done!" Drusus said.

"Is the extra pay for all of us?" Dama asked.

"Of course, you helped find the pass."

Now assured of glory and coin, Dama cheered along with the rest of them.

Though Falco slapped his back and even Curio began to smile, Varro felt oddly cold. Gallio's corpse was underfoot. No matter how he had grown to hate the man, it seemed terribly wrong to celebrate over his dead body. He was once a friend and a brother in arms.

"What's that look for?" Falco finally asked.

"I'm just exhausted. Let's remove Gallio's body. I can't stand to look at it any longer."

The sentiment cooled Falco and Curio, as well as Cordus to some degree. Dama and the other three new soldiers had no feeling for Gallio other than disgust. But even Dama seemed to understand the need for some decorum. Varro and Falco resumed bearing the corpse to the pile of enemy dead being unceremoniouslydumped to one side of the pass, conspicuously placed close to the mercenary captives who now sat disarmed and unarmored in an ever-widening circle of taunting guards.

Together they heaved Gallio's corpse onto the pile. His body flopped and rolled, the spear catching on another corpse so that he stuck up as if someone beneath had run him through. As a final insult, the wind caught his tunic and blew it over to expose his backside.

Falco snorted. "The gods speak. Rot in shame, traitor."

He spit at the edge of the pile, already rank with the smell of blood and death. Some of the braver crows hopped triumphantly atop the pile, flying away with shrieks whenever a corpse landed too near.

So they returned to Centurion Drusus. Despite all their efforts and trials, he offered them no respite. However, before being assigned duties they were first allowed to plunder the camp for anything of value. While the rest of the contubernium found renewed energy with the promise of uncovering the pay coffers of the Cretan officers, Varro knew the tribune had already put a claim on that pile of coins. Anything else he might find would not equal a rest. While the others raced off seeking treasure, Varro sat on a rock at the edge of the battlefield.

Centurion Drusus approached him, wiping inexplicably fresh blood from his hands on his already stained tunic.

"You'd rather sit than get rich? I had you all wrong, Varro."

"Sir, these men seem poorer than us. I'm sure there's something to find. But I need the rest more than a few coins in my palm."

Drusus chuckled, then put his hands on his hips and scanned the battlefield.

"How old are you, Varro?"

"I turned eighteen over the summer, sir. Worst birthday I ever had."

Again he laughed, but now rubbed the back of his neck.

"That's rather young. But I suppose I can just make this a provisional thing for now. There's no one else in the century suitable."

"Sir?" Varro felt his hands chill as he guessed the centurion's intent.

"Well, Tertius might live but how long before he's fit to serve again? Maybe never. Let's face it, Varro, you've got the balls for the job. You know what's right and what to do. You don't need ten years' experience. You just have to look death in the face a few times. That shows the men from the boys in a hurry."

Varro blinked. He stood up, cocking his head. Drusus gave him a bright smile, then clapped his shoulder.

"Enjoy your rest, Optio Varro."

28

Consul Galba's fury at discovering Philip's successful retreat had been like a violent thunderstorm during an earthquake. Varro and everyone else in the army felt his anger through forced marches and relentless pursuit of a foe long gone. For though he had secured the pass at Eordaea with minimal casualties and destroyed Philip's Cretan and Illyrian mercenaries, Galba had allowed Philip's escape. The consul vented his rage on the surrounding countryside.

With not even a day to absorb the reality of his new position, Varro had to become an optio of the tenth century of the tenth maniple of hastati. He had to encourage men to burn countryside people out of their homes and kill any who resisted. His first act as an optio was to spray Consul Galba's rage all over the innocent people who made their homes close to his self-proclaimed defeat. The promise of extra pay and the honor of a promotion within his first year in the army faded behind this horrible reality.

Fortunately, they were soon attacking fortified towns that had better defenses and felt less like slaughter to Varro. Yet standing at the rear and alternately threatening men or praising them was strangely boring to Varro. He wanted to be up in the line with Falco and Curio at his sides, hacking and cutting into stubborn enemies and earning his pay. All he had to do was to ensure Drusus's orders were followed. He never felt in any danger, though these towns offered little resistance. In fact, one surrendered without a fight.

The long weeks of rampage and conquest finally sated Galba's anger. He had marched the army back to Apollonia, near the spot of the original camp they had settled upon arriving here last spring. He had left a garrison behind with the intention of conducting periodic raids for supplies and to keep Philip from reinforcing this area again.

Gallio's desertion and death now seemed like a strange dream. There had been so much frenetic action in between—killing, marching, burning, and besieging—that those events seemed a lifetime ago. Indeed, once arriving in Apollonia, now with the Illyrians fully committed as allies to Rome, Varro fell right into constructing the winter camp. He never rested, nor did anyone else.

So busy had he been, the day of assembly caught Varro by surprise. Consul Galba had not yet handed out the awards and recognitions due the many soldiers who had acted with great bravery during the capture of the Eordaea Pass and the sieges that followed. He assembled with his century in the parade ground with the rest of the legion present. It was a crisp but clear day and surprisingly warm. Though Varro felt a chill being separated from Falco and the others to stand beside Centurion Drusus at the front of the century.

After many long speeches by both consul and tribunes, at last, the tribunes made their awards for bravery in battle. Each man received a short description of his actions and then officers formally recognized his achievement. All awards were made as bonus pay.

Varro clapped and cheered as required. He bowed his head dutifully when posthumous honors were bestowed. But his mind was elsewhere. Did he really belong as an officer? He was nowhere comfortable having the centurion and his other junior officers for tent mates. Didn't they all know he was a not really one of them? He wished he could be with his old contubernium, even if half of them were new.

After what had seemed an entire day, the consul at last ended the ceremony with the awarding of the coveted Civic Crown. There was no higher award to be given a regular solider and Varro was interested to learn who would earn it.

To his surprise, two of Galba's slaves assisted Optio Tertius onto the stage where the consul and tribunes stood. He smiled down to Varro in the front row.

"He looks good," Drusus said. "Maybe you won't be optio much longer."

Varro blinked in astonishment.

Galba called for silence and Optio Tertius spoke. The weakness in his voice betrayed his hale appearance and emphasized why the two slaves had to continue holding him up.

"I am here to give witness to the brave acts of Marcus Varro, who saved my life through quick action at the Eordaea Pass. Would he have not shot an arrow into the enemy seeking my life, I should be dead today. As his officer at that time, I recognize his courage and leadership. For this, I am grateful and indebted to him."

Consul Galba reached out his hand and received the crown of woven oak leaves from another assistant.

"Marcus Varro," he said, searching the crowd. "Come forward."

Varro's hands went cold. He looked to Drusus, who beamed at him. "But I didn't kill the enemy. Tertius did it himself."

"Shut up and receive your award. You earned it."

Mounting the short steps to reach Galba and Tertius, Varro felt as if he were dreaming. The entire consular army stretched out to his left like a sparkling lake of gold. He wanted to find Falco among them, but the consul led him between himself and Tribune Primanus who now joined them. He extended the crown, commanding Varro's attention to the simple wreathe of oak leaves.

"For saving the life of a fellow citizen from an enemy of the Republic in the enemy's own territory, I bestow upon you this Civic Crown and all the rights and privileges attendant to it."

The crown of plain oak leaves settled lightly on Varro's head. Galba smiled as did Tribune Primanus. Whether these were genuine or not, Varro simply blinked and stammered.

"Thank you, sir."

The august award drew stronger applause and cheers. He enjoyed these a moment, before one of the consul's attendants gestured he should exit the stage. Optio Tertius followed him with the two slaves holding him up. They shared a brief smile that became a wince of pain for Tertius. The optio clearly had a much longer recuperation ahead than he tried to make it seem.

Varro wore his crown to return to his century, which offered the wildest and strongest cheers for one of their own. Centurion Drusus slapped his back and pulled him into line. He was so astonished at that he had forgotten how to behave.

With closing remarks completed, mostly about holding down for the winter and then delivering a final blow to Macedonia in the spring, they were dismissed. Unlike previous assemblies, Varro had to ensure his century followed procedure and maintained order in their return to the barracks. It had been much simpler to just stand around awaiting orders with Falco and the others. He held Tertius's vine cane, given to him with some advice about the position. But it sat strangely in his hands and thus far he had not whipped anyone with it.

As they filed out of the parade ground, Varro remained behind the century as if on march or going to battle. He watched Tertius being placed upon a stretcher for slaves to return him to the hospital. He regretted that the optio had to drag himself here so just so he could wear a crown of leaves.

Yet as he slowly followed his century between the clean white tents surrounding the parade ground, he caught the hateful glare of Galba's beautiful Illyrian slave girl. She stood with both hands clutched across her chest, her knuckles white and her face tight with fury.

Feeling the heady touch of wearing a crown that allowed him to sit among the senators at any games and require them to stand to greet him, he stepped out of line to confront her.

"Your hair is growing longer," he said with a smile. "It looks pretty."

She snarled at him, glaring at his crown. "Stupid leaves are nothing. I promise revenge. My brother and uncle will rest, and you will die."

"You've mentioned that," he said, leaning closer. "But I'm not worried. Try your best, little girl. You are a slave and I am a citizen. It doesn't matter if the consul likes to fling you around his bed sometimes. Eventually you'll be among his trash, like all old toys that get used up."

The slave's beautiful eyes welled with tears. She likely did not understand a word, but understood his haughty attitude. He left her steaming in her hatred to see his century to their barracks.

Indeed, nothing could bring him any fear this day. The crown on his head rested easier with every soldier who saluted or cheered him as he passed. At least for this one day, he could wear it without feeling like a pompous fool. Tomorrow, he would have to store it among his prized belongings and get back to the work of learning his new role.

As night fell on a joyous day, Varro found it hard to walk the barrack rows and shout at men to get to their bunks or their posts. Yet he had Optios Latro and Tertius for models, and he simply imitated what he thought they would say. Still, he was in too good a mood and his shouting was met with a cheerful "Yes, sir" from the hastati under his command.

Without realizing it, he came to what should have been his own barracks. Being winter quarters, these were once again simply constructed wooden buildings. The white smoke and bitter scent of the extinguished cooking fire rose up at his feet. The men were already inside. Since Varro was now ostensibly on equal terms with the tesserarius and sharing information, he knew none of them had duties this night. They were preparing for sleep. Regret seeped into Varro's chest as he imagined the cramped and dark room. He could hear Falco shifting on the bunk above him, yawning before falling asleep.

As if summoned by this memory, Falco stepped out of the barracks.

He drew up in surprise, his heavy brows raising with delight. Varro noted how he shifted to the crown on his head, and this suddenly changed Falco's demeanor.

"Congratulations, sir. A well-deserved honor, if I may say so."

Varro blinked at him. Of course, calling him sir and treating him like an officer came naturally on the march and the battlefield. No one had time to overthink things. But now Falco's formality felt terrible. As the sun set and torches fluttered to life along the main roads, it seemed they should set aside ranks and become friends again.

"Thank you," he said.

They faced each other, neither knowing what to say. Varro realized that while most other soldiers had retired for the night, some still looked on. He had his duty.

"Is there a reason you are out here?" He straightened his back and toyed with his vine cane like Tertius would do.

"Yes, sir. I have a reason. I was going to find you. Do you have a moment, sir? This won't take long."

Varro looked around, then nodded. Falco smiled, but it was the kind of smile he used to give Varro just before punching him in the face while pinning him down. He didn't like it.

"Thank you, sir. I think we'd best discuss this in private."

They went behind the barracks, claiming the shadows where they had so often met for their secret discussions. The moment they entered the darkness, Falco whirled on him.

"The Civic Crown! By the gods, lily! You are Fortuna's favorite." He grabbed both of Varro's shoulders and shook him. "And an officer, too. I told you this was going to happen. You should listen to me."

"Thanks," he said again, steadying the crown on his head. "I was surprised at this."

"No surprises," Falco said. "You're a real leader. Optio is only where it starts for you. Just lean on me to keep the men in shape."

"No, I've got to earn the men's respect myself. But I'd appreciate if you do keep the contubernium in line. You lead them now."

"Well, that's not what Dama thinks." Falco gestured at the crown.

Varro lifted it off his head and let Falco hold it.

"Senators will stand in your presence," he said, his voice soft and eyes wide in the shadow. "Everyone will know you're a hero."

"You should have one as well," Varro said. "And the others as well. It's not just for me."

Falco twisted the crown to view it from different angles. "Well, everyone says modesty is a good thing. But you overdo it. Anyway, you deserve a good break, Varro. I'm proud of you."

He felt heat on his cheeks and shrugged.

"A year ago I wanted to kill you."

Falco laughed. "Back then you'd have broken your wrist trying to fight back. Now, I wouldn't raise a hand to you. Not after you jumped into those Cretan spearmen back in the pass. That was madness, but you killed them. You're a killer now, Varro, and a hero of Rome."

"It's a shame those two things must be so deeply linked." Varro accepted the crown and replaced it on his head. "Now, I might be an optio but that doesn't mean I can wander around all night. So why did you seek me?"

Falco fell strangely quiet. He glanced about as if checking they were alone.

"I saw Galba's slave waiting for you. You went to her. What did she say?"

"You noticed?"

"Well, you didn't make much effort to hide what you were doing. Yes, I was watching my optio for any instructions. Come on, lily, what did she say?"

Varro waved off the question. "She wants to avenge her family and kill me. Nothing new."

Falco seemed to digest this, then checked around again.

"She still has our necklace. I mean to get it back."

"It's not worth the risk," Varro said. "She's Galba's property. I may have earned some of his goodwill, but I'm not willing to test how far it goes."

"Listen to me," Falco said, drawing nearer. "Gold is gold. Is there enough of it for anyone? You know, I hated Gallio, but he wasn't wrong about one thing. What are we going to have when this is all over? That crown on your head means senators will stand to greet you. But will they pay for your farm? Will they feed you? No. So that gold is needed and not something you can just forget because you had a nice day. Think of your mother and sister. Think of my mother. Do you believe Old Man Pius can carry them for whole the six years we're in for? We have to get that gold back just to buy our farms out of the debt they'll be in when we're done here."

Varro lowered his head and nodded, his face hot with shame.

"You're right," he said. "Even an optio's pay isn't going to be enough."

"Of course I'm right." Falco coughed and snorted. "Damn that marsh. Why didn't you get sick?"

"Fortuna's favored?"

They both smiled and Falco rubbed the back of his neck.

"Well, Curio might have an idea of how to get the necklace back. It won't hurt that you're an optio now. Gives us a little space to get things done. But anyway, that's still not why I've asked you out here."

Varro folded his arms. "The darkness gathers. Let's have it out before we're both missed."

"Well, you remember catching King Philip."

"I seem to recall it."

"Well, I've not been honest about everything that happened during that time. Not dishonest either. Just I haven't told you everything, and I realize I should before I get killed in battle or something."

Varro unfolded his arms and tilted his head. "What do you mean?"

"Remember how Philip kept complaining that he couldn't feel his hands? Well, when I was wrestling him around the marsh, I swept my hands over his. You know, searching for rings. He's a king after all."

Falco held out two fat golden rings, one studded with small red gems and the other with a single sparkling blue stone. Even in this low light both gleamed.

"One from each hand," Falco said. "He obviously didn't feel a thing, and being slick with mud they just slipped off. I'm sure he was madder than a rabid boar when he finally realized he'd lost these. So he can have his dagger back. I think we got the better prizes."

Varro leaned over the gold rings, astonished at the wealth sitting in Falco's palm.

"You weren't going to tell me?"

"I'm telling you now, right?" Falco jumped the rings in his palm, the gemstones catching the low light. "I don't want others cutting into what is ours. Curio grabbed a third of our necklace. He's not getting in on this. These are just for us. Take them. Now that you're an optio you can hide them better than me. I've been keeping them in my pack. It's a start on what we need to take back home with us."

The two heavy rings that once adorned a king's fingers dropped into Varro's palm. He and Falco stared over them in admiring silence.

"I don't dare say we're rich," Varro said. "Lest I curse us."

"Then I'll say it. We're rich, Optio Varro."

HISTORICAL NOTES

The opening phases of the Second Macedonian War are roughly as presented in this book. Consul Galba oversaw this phase of the war from winter 200 BC until spring 199 BC. Initially unable to locate each other, Philip was led by Roman deserters to Galba's camp. He erected a fortified position on a hill within one mile of the Romans. Perhaps stunned by the sudden appearance of Philip's army, Galba had no response for two days.

By the third day, Galba sent his cavalry and a screening force of velites into the field. Philip entrusted his nobleman, Athenagoras, to lead Cretan and Illyrian mercenaries along with a small force of cavalry into the field. However, the Roman forces defied expectations and fought with enough ferocity to drive Athenagoras from the field in defeat.

A series of failed skirmishes ensued, including a backup plan consisting of hidden peltasts set between the two camps. If the Macedonian forces were losing the battle, they were to lead the Romans toward the peltasts for an ambush attack. Yet the Romans uncovered this force before the ambush and drove the Macedonians once again from the field. A later attempt by Galba to draw out Philip for decisive battle ended with him hiding in his camp. Galba's war elephants even reached his walls but Philip declined battle.

Eventually Galba realized he could not remain in such proximity to his enemy and relocated eight miles away. Philip did not hinder their move to a new camp. He also did not harass them as they foraged, all in an attempt to lull the Romans into believing he was afraid of battle. But Philip merely allowed the Romans to become overconfident. Once a large foraging force was sent into a nearby woods, he cut them off and attacked.

The initial reports by fleeing Romans filtering into Galba's camp were confused. He sent out the cavalry, but they chased shadows until Philip's real location was determined. In the meantime, Philip destroyed the Roman foragers, but eventually lost control of his men who attempted to pursue the Romans that fled.

During this battle, Philip would have been captured or slain were it not for the heroic actions of one of his own cavalrymen. Being thrown from his horse, he narrowly escaped trampling. The Romans were bearing down on him, and a defeat was at hand. A cavalryman offered his own horse to Philip and died while the king mounted the horse to flee into the nearby marsh. He eventually emerged out the other side to arrive at his camp, alive but beaten. The Romans had claimed two hundred Macedonian cavalry dead and another hundred captured. At least eighty horses were added to the Roman stables.

Galba has been criticized for not pursuing the Macedonians back to their camp and finishing them off. Without their king, and their cavalry destroyed along with a portion of their mercenaries, it seemed Rome could end the war that night. Yet Galba rightly believed to pursue Philip would be to commit the same error that had cost Philip his battle. The entire Macedonian infantry maintained Philip's camp and would have put up a strong fight against a haphazard force of Romans.

Worse news came to Philip that night. Dardians had invaded Macedonia from the north and he needed to answer this immediate threat. He split his forces and fled, sending one force north while he went south. To buy time he sent an emissary to Galba, who refused to meet him at the late hour. The next morning under a false pretense of burying their dead, the emissary negotiated a temporary truce. Shortly after his departure, reports arrived of the Macedonian escape. They had left campfires burning all night to make it seem as if they were still in their tents. But they had gone and Galba did not know where.

Galba spent the first two days after this news gathering grain to prepare for an extended march. He led his entire army out in pursuit, but could not catch the Macedonians. At last he found them at a mountain pass in Eordaea. They had established all manner of blockades and walls on a narrow, difficult road. They could not bring their phalanxes to bear, and only Cretan archers had much use. But they could not defeat Roman shields. They resorted to rocks hurled down on the Romans, who assumed testudo formations and pressed ahead. Some Romans found a detour to help open the road. The Cretan defenders were subsequently dislodged from the pass.

After capturing the pass at Eordaea, Galba destroyed the surrounding countryside. He then destroyed Elimeia to the south, followed the Haliacmon River to Orestis and destroyed it as well. He began an assault on the town of Celetrum, but the terrified townsfolk surrendered without a fight. At last he went to Pelium and captured it. There he left a strong garrison to conduct raids into Macedonia. At last, Galba returned to his base in Apollonia and ended hostilities for the season.

This history brings us to the point in time where Varro and Falco are just completing their first year of enlistment. Most property-owning citizens eligible for military service completed a six-year continuous posting and then joined campaigns as needed until fulfilling his sixteen years of required service. The financial strains on farm owners as depicted in this story were a true concern and planted seeds of discontent that would eventually contribute to the fall of the Roman Republic many decades hence. Yet the roots of that eventual fall started here, as Rome evolved from a city-state to an empire.

Varro and Falco are two small figures amid this great canvas of history. Their own stories leave much ahead as they push on into what will eventually lead to Rome's conquering of the Hellenistic world.

ALSO BY JERRY AUTIERI

Ulfrik Ormsson's Saga

Historical adventure stories set in 9th Century Europe and brimming with heroic combat. Witness the birth of a unified Norway, travel to the remote Faeroe Islands, then follow the Vikings on a siege of Paris and beyond. Walk in the footsteps of the Vikings and witness history through the eyes of Ulfrik Ormsson.

Fate's Needle

Islands in the Fog

Banners of the Northmen

Shield of Lies

The Storm God's Gift

Return of the Ravens

Sword Brothers

Descendants Saga

The grandchildren of Ulfrik Ormsson continue tales of Norse battle and glory. They may have come from greatness, but they must make their own way in the brutal world of the 10th Century.

Descendants of the Wolf

Odin's Ravens

Revenge of the Wolves

Blood Price

Viking Bones

Valor of the Norsemen

Norse Vengeance

Bear and Raven

Red Oath

Fate's End

Grimwold and Lethos Trilogy

A sword and sorcery fantasy trilogy with a decidedly Norse flavor.

Deadman's Tide

Children of Urdis

Age of Blood

NEWSLETTER

If you would like to know when my next book is released, please sign up for my new release newsletter. You can do this at my website:
http://jerryautieri.wordpress.com/

If you have enjoyed this book and would like to show your support for my writing, consider leaving a review where you purchased this book or on Goodreads, LibraryThing, and other reader sites. I need help from readers like you to get the word out about my books. If you have a moment, please share your thoughts with other readers. I appreciate it!

Copyright © 2021 by Jerry Autieri

All rights reserved.

No part of this book may be reproduced in any form or by any electronic or mechanical means, including information storage and retrieval systems, without written permission from the author, except for the use of brief quotations in a book review.

Gladius Photo 72551947 © Vitalii Gaydukov | Dreamstime.com